Buffy the Vampire Slayer™

The Script Book:
Season Two, Volume One

Buffy the Vampire Slayer™

The Script Book:
Season Two, Volume One

POCKET PULSE

New York   London   Toronto   Sydney   Singapore

For information regarding special discounts for bulk
purchases, please contact Simon & Schuster Special Sales
at 1-800-456-6798 or siness@simonandschuster.com

An *Original* Publication of POCKET BOOKS

 POCKET PULSE, published by
Pocket Books, a division of Simon & Schuster, Inc.
1230 Avenue of the Americas, New York, NY 10020

™ and © 1997, 2001 by Twentieth Century Fox Film
Corporation. All rights reserved.

ISBN: 0-7434-1014-9

First Pocket Pulse trade paperback printing August 2001

10 9 8 7 6 5 4 3 2 1

POCKET PULSE and colophon are registered trademarks of
Simon & Schuster, Inc.

Printed in the U.S.A.

Contents

BUFFY THE VAMPIRE SLAYER

"When She Was Bad"

Written and Directed By

Joss Whedon

SHOOTING SCRIPT

June 30, 1997
July 7, 1997 (Blue Pages)
July 8, 1997 (Pink Pages)
July 14, 1997 (Yellow Pages)

BUFFY THE VAMPIRE SLAYER

"When She Was Bad"

CAST LIST

BUFFY SUMMERS............................. Sarah Michelle Gellar
XANDER HARRIS............................. Nicholas Brendon
RUPERT GILES.............................. Anthony S. Head
WILLOW ROSENBERG.......................... Alyson Hannigan
CORDELIA CHASE............................ Charisma Carpenter
ANGEL..................................... David Boreanaz

JOYCE..................................... Kristine Sutherland
HANK...................................... Dean Butler
JENNY CALENDAR............................ Robia La Morte
MR. SNYDER................................ *Armin Shimerman
ANOINTED ONE.............................. Andrew J. Ferchland
ABSALOM................................... Brent Jennings
TARA (GIRL VAMPIRE)....................... Tamara Braun
VAMPIRE BOB...............................
VAMPIRE JANE..............................
VAMPIRE WALT..............................

THE BAND.................................. Cibo Matto

BUFFY THE VAMPIRE SLAYER

"When She Was Bad"

SET LIST

INTERIORS

SUNNYDALE HIGH SCHOOL
    HALL
    LIBRARY
    SCHOOL LOUNGE
    CLASS ROOM

BUFFY'S BEDROOM

THE BRONZE

THE FACTORY
    FACTORY CELLAR

JOYCE'S CAR

EXTERIORS

SUNNYDALE HIGH SCHOOL
    *QUAD
    *PALM COURT

THE BRONZE
    ALLEY BY THE BRONZE

GRAVEYARD
    STREET BY GRAVEYARD

THE FACTORY

BUFFY THE VAMPIRE SLAYER

"When She Was Bad"

TEASER

1 ANGLE: A HEADSTONE   1

   It's night. We hold on the stone a moment, then the camera
   tracks to the side, passing other stones in the

2 EXT. GRAVEYARD\STREET - NIGHT   2

   CAMERA comes to a stone wall at the edge of the cemetery,
   passes over that to see the street. Two figures in the near
   distance.

   XANDER and WILLOW are walking home, eating ice cream cones.

                    WILLOW
          Okay, hold on...

                    XANDER
          It's your turn.

                    WILLOW
          Okay, Um.. "In the few hours that we
          had together, we loved a lifetimes
          worth."

                    XANDER
          Terminator.

                    WILLOW
          Good. Right.

                    XANDER
          Okay. Let's see...
                    (Charlton Heston)
          "It's a madhouse! A m--

                    WILLOW
          Planet of the Apes.

                    XANDER
          Can I finish, please?

                    WILLOW
          Sorry. Go ahead.

                    XANDER
          "Madhouse!"

   She waits a beat to make sure he's done, then

                                                          CONTINUED

2 CONTINUED: 2

                        WILLOW
          <u>Planet of the Apes.</u>   Good.   Me now.
          Um...

                        XANDER
          Well?

                        WILLOW
          I'm thinking. Okay. "Use the force,
          Luke."

He looks at her.

                        XANDER
          Do I really have to dignify that with
          a guess?

                        WILLOW
          I didn't think of anything. It's a
          dumb game anyway.

                        XANDER
          You got something better to do? We
          played rock-paper-scissors long
          enough, okay? My hand cramped up.

                        WILLOW
          Well, sure, if you're ALWAYS
          scissors, of course your tendons are
          gonna stretch --

                        XANDER
                   (interrupting)
          You know, I gotta say, this has
          really been the most boring summer
          ever.

                        WILLOW
          Yeah, but on the plus side, no
          monsters or stuff.

She sits on the stone wall. He leans on it next to her,
looking off towards the graveyard.

                        XANDER
          I know, but I'm so restless! I'm
          actually glad school is starting
          again.

                        WILLOW
          Yeah, and that has nothing to do with
          a certain girl that we both know that
          is a vampire slayer?

                                              CONTINUED

2 CONTINUED: (2)   2

                         XANDER
          Please. I'm so over her.
                    (REAL casual)
          Did she, uh, say when she was getting
          back, about which I don't care?

                         WILLOW
          I haven't heard from her. I mean, I
          got a couple of postcards after she
          went to L.A. and then, like, nothing.

                         XANDER
          Yeah, I never heard... well, she's
          probably having fun with her dad.

                         WILLOW
          And you don't care.

                         XANDER
          Okay, so maybe there's some interest.
          I'm a man, I have certain desires,
          certain needs...

                         WILLOW
          I don't wanna know.

                         XANDER
          Don't you?

The playful intimacy here is becoming ever so slightly less
playful. He's kind of close to her, smiling at her.

                         XANDER (cont'd)
          I got a movie for you.

He dabs his cone at her, leaving ice cream on her nose. She
stares at him wryly.

                         WILLOW
          Xander...

                         XANDER
          Come on.
                    (dabs again)
          You're Amish, you won't fight back
          because you're Amish, I mock you with
          my ice cream cone, Amish Guy...

                         WILLOW
          Witness. My nose is cold.

                         XANDER
          Let me get that --

                                                       CONTINUED

2 CONTINUED: (3)   2

He makes as if to lick it. She starts back, laughs.

                    WILLOW
          Xander!

                    XANDER
          What can I say? It makes your nose
          look tasty.

He daubs it with a napkin (he has the only one or she would).
And then, yeah, they're pretty close, her arm on his
shoulder, looking at each other, then less looking than
gazing...

3 CLOSE UP: THEIR FACES   3

Come pretty close, right into the awkward almost-kiss-zone.
A moment, and they stop, their heads separating.

There is a vampire right between them. Leering, ravenous,
and practically in the kiss zone himself.

He's on the other side of the wall from them, the dirt and
the tux hanging on him speaking of a fresh rising. The kids
see him and start back -- Willow clumsily jumping from the
wall -- he easily vaults it, coming swaggeringly at them.

                    XANDER
               (stepping in front of
               her)
          Willow, go!

                    WILLOW
          Xander --

The vampire jumps him. He steps back and slugs it -- but it
isn't phased, grabbing his neck and pulling him in for the
kill.

Willow desperately searches about for some kind of weapon,
finally grabbing the vampire's arm, trying to wrench him off
Xander --

A HAND clamps down on the vampire's shoulder. Pulls back and
spins him around, straight into the path of a lightning fist.

The punch is followed by a roundhouse kick -- and another.
The vampire finally gets time enough to lunge at the
figure -- who easily FLIPS him onto the ground, turning to
the others.

                    BUFFY
          Hi guys.

                                                        CONTINUED

3 CONTINUED: 3

The vampire rears up behind her and without looking back she
SLAMS her foot into his chest, sending him flying back --

4 ANGLE: A TREE   4

with a broken branch sticking out of it. The vampire slams
backwards right onto it, exploding into dust the moment he's
impaled.

BUFFY doesn't even look back.

                    BUFFY
          Miss me?

               END OF TEASER

ACT ONE

5 EXT. SAME - GRAVEYARD - MOMENTS LATER - NIGHT   5

Xander and Willow hug Buffy, excited to see her. Xander
perhaps slightly more so.

                    WILLOW
          Buffy!

                    BUFFY
          Hey, Will.

                    XANDER
          Man, your timing really doesn't suck.

                    WILLOW
          When did you get back?

                    BUFFY
          Just now. Dad drove me down. And I
          knew you losers would be getting into
          some kind of trouble.

                    WILLOW
          I think we had the upper hand. In a
          subtle way.

                    BUFFY
          Does either of you even have a cross?
          Very sloppy...

                    XANDER
          Well, it's been a slow summer. That
          was the first vampire we've seen
          since you killed the Master.

                    BUFFY
          It's like they knew I was coming back.

                    XANDER
          What about you? How was your summer?
          Did you slay anything?

They are walking again, Xander keeping close to Buffy.
Willow tries to keep up.

                    BUFFY
          Strictly R&R. Hung out, partied...
          shopping was also a major theme.

                                                CONTINUED

5 CONTINUED: 5

                           XANDER
              Well, you haven't lost your touch.
              That vampire --

                           BUFFY
              I did kind of wail on him, didn't I?

                           XANDER
              I really like your hair.

                           BUFFY
              So, how did you guys fare? Did you
              have any fun without me?

              XANDER   WILLOW
    No.   Yes.

                           XANDER
              Summer was a little yawnworthy. Our
              biggest excitement was burying the
              Master.

There is a subtle hardening in Buffy's face whenever they
mention that name. Neither friend notices.

                           WILLOW
              That's right, you missed it! Right
              out by that tree.

She points to

6 ANGLE: A TREE   6

deep in the graveyard.

                           WILLOW
              Giles buried the bones and we poured
              holy water and chanted and we got to
              wear robes!

                           XANDER
              Very intense. You shoulda been.

                           WILLOW
              Have you seen Giles?

Buffy is staring at the tree Willow pointed at. She answers
crossly:

                           BUFFY
              Why would I call Giles? I'll see him
              at school.

CONTINUED

6 CONTINUED: 6

                    XANDER
          Man, I'm really glad you're back.

                    BUFFY
          Yeah.
                    (unconvincingly, as
                    she looks at the
                    tree)
          Me too.

                                        CUT TO:

7 INT. BUFFY'S BEDROOM - NIGHT   7

     HANK and JOYCE SUMMERS are unpacking Buffy's things. Hank
     brings in a large suitcase as Joyce puts clothes away.

                    JOYCE
          More clothes?

                    HANK
                    (guiltily)
          Uh, do shoes count as clothes?

                    JOYCE
                    (re: large suitcase)
          That's shoes? How much shopping did
          you let her do?

                    HANK
          Oh, I'm spoiling her. Did I forget
          to mention that?

                    JOYCE
          What you forgot is that I'm gonna
          have to deal with another year of
          "Daddy would let me buy that."

                    HANK
          I just thought I'd save you from the
          big back-to-school clothes nightmare.

                    JOYCE
          My nightmares about Buffy and school
          have nothing to do with clothes. Did
          she manage to stay out of trouble in
          L.A.?

                    HANK
          She did, yeah. She was, you know...
          great.

                                        CONTINUED

7 CONTINUED: 7

There isn't much GREAT! in his "great".   Joyce stops
unpacking.

                    JOYCE
          But.

                    HANK
          She was just... I don't know.
          Distant. Not brooding, or sulking,
          just... there was no connection. All
          on the surface. The more time we
          spent together, the more I felt like
          she was nowhere to be seen.

                    JOYCE
          Hence the shoes.

                    HANK
          I may have been overcompensating a
          little. It was strange. At least
          when she was burning stuff down I
          knew what to say. As for example,
          "don't burn stuff down". But now...

                    JOYCE
          Welcome to my world. I haven't been
          able to get through to her for so
          long... I'll just be happy if she
          makes it through the school year.

                                        CUT TO:

8 EXT. QUAD - DAY   8   *

First day. Kids run to and fro, greeting each other, looking
for classes.

CORDELIA walks along with a couple of Cordettes. As usual,
all the talking is done by

                    CORDELIA
          It was a nightmare. A nightmare.
          They **promised** me we were going to St.
          Croix and then at the last minute,
          they just **decide** we're gonna visit
          Tuscany instead. Art. Buildings.
          Totally beachless for a month and a
          half. No one has suffered as I have
          suffered. Of course I think that
          kind of adversity builds character.
                    (more)

                                                  CONTINUED

8 CONTINUED: 8

                    CORDELIA (cont'd)
          But then I thought, well I already
          have a lot of character, I mean it is
          possible to have too much character,
          isn't it?

They move out of frame and we pick up MR. SNYDER walking
along with GILES, watching the students around them.

                    MR. SNYDER
          The first day back. It always gets
          me.

                    GILES
          Yes.

                    MR. SNYDER
          I mean, it's incredible. One day the
          campus is completely bare, empty...
          the next, children are everywhere.
          Like locusts. Crawling around,
          mindlessly bent on feeding and
          mating, destroying everything in
          sight in their relentless, pointless
          desire to exist.

                    GILES
          I do love these pep talks. Have you
          ever considered, given your
          abhorrence of children, that school
          principal is perhaps not your true
          vocation?

                    MR. SNYDER
          Someone's gotta keep an eye on 'em.
          They're just a bunch of hormonal
          timebombs. Why, every time a pretty
          girl walks by, every boy turns into
          a jibbering fool.

                    GILES
          Ms. Calendar!

JENNY CALENDAR is passing. She stops, happy to see Giles.
Snyder doesn't even see her -- he's watching the kids.

                    JENNY
          Mr. Giles.

                    GILES
                 (jibbering fool)
          Well, uh, dyeh, nnnn, hello.

                                                    CONTINUED

> MR. SNYDER
> I've seen the way these kids gaze at
> each other, all moony --

Giles and Jenny gaze at each other, all moony.

> JENNY
> It's good to see you.

> GILES
> Yes.

> MR. SNYDER
> You think they're thinking about
> learning?

> GILES
> Are you heading towards the faculty
> room?

> JENNY
> That sounds like fun.

> MR. SNYDER
> I try to talk sense to 'em, tell 'em
> about the really important things in
> life. Responsibility, discipline,
> punctuality... I might as well be
> talking to myself.

Which, in fact, he is -- the other two have gone.

                                        CUT TO:

9   INT. SCHOOL HALL - MORNING   9

Giles and Ms. Calendar are walking together.

> GILES
> And how was your summer?

> JENNY
> Extreme. I did Burning Man in Black
> Rock. It's such a great festival --
> you should have been there. There
> were drum rituals, naked mud-dances,
> raves, mobile sculptures, you would
> have just... hated it with a fiery
> passion.

CONTINUED

9 CONTINUED: 9

                         GILES
              Yes, I can't imagine finding any
              redeeming -- naked?

                         JENNY
              You probably spent all summer with
              your nose in a book.

                         GILES
              I suppose you'd consider that
              terribly dull.

                         JENNY
                    (flirtatiously)
              Depends on the book.

Xander, Willow and Buffy approach.

                         WILLOW
              Giles!

                         XANDER
              Hey, G-man! What's up!

                         GILES
              Nice to see you and don't ever call
              me that.

                         JENNY
              Hey, kids.

                         GILES
                    (to Buffy)
              How are you?

                         BUFFY
              Alive and kicking.

                         WILLOW
              Buffy killed a vampire last night!

A few surrounding students react to that.

                         BUFFY
              Uh, I think you can get a little more
              volume if you speak from the
              diaphragm.

                         WILLOW
              Sorry.

CONTINUED

9 CONTINUED: (2)   9

                    JENNY
          We got vampires? I thought the
          Hellmouth was closed.

                    GILES
          Closed, not gone. The mystical
          energy it emits is still concentrated
          in this area.

                    XANDER
          Which means we're still the undead's
          favorite party town.

                    GILES
               (to Buffy)
          This vampire -- could you tell where
          he might be from?

                    BUFFY
          Local talent. Fresh. He was still
          wearing his funeral ensemble.

                    GILES
          Which means there are other vampires
          about, and they're already killing.
          I should have been on top of that.
          I wonder if they're here for some
          particular purpose...

                    BUFFY
          You're the Watcher. I just work here.

                    GILES
          Well, I'll have to consult my books.

                    XANDER
               (looking at his watch)
          Eight minutes and thirty three
          seconds.
               (to Willow)
          Pay up.

Xander looks at the others as Willow digs a dollar out of her
pocket.

                    XANDER (cont'd)
          I called ten minutes before you had
          to consult your books about something.

                    WILLOW
          We better get to class.

The three kids start off.

                                        CONTINUED

9 CONTINUED: (3)   9

                        GILES
            Buffy.
                  (she stops, turns)
            I realize you've only just returned,
            but when you're ready, I think we
            should start your training again.

                        BUFFY
            I'm ready. I'll see you after school.

                        GILES
            Well, I understand if you need a few
            days to --

                        BUFFY
            I'm ready.

                                        CUT TO:

10 INT. LIBRARY - AFTERNOON   10

    TRAINING MONTAGE -- We see various quick pops of Buffy in
    action. She's in great shape, moves with grace and power.

    -- Buffy doing a series of highkicks at a retreating Giles.

    -- Buffy doing an aerial flip.

    -- Buffy throwing a stake into a man-shaped target. Nothing
    but heart.

    -- Buffy punching a wooden post.

    This last she does with increasing intensity, her fists
    flying at the beat-up post, her face rapt with concentration.
    As we go CLOSE ON her face, we see a flash -- so quick it's
    near subliminal - of

11 THE MASTER   11

    leering at the camera.

12 INT. LIBRARY - AFTERNOON   12

    She continues to rain blows on the post, Giles watching her
    with a small blossom of concern in his eyes.

                        GILES
            Buffy... I think that's enough...
            Buffy!

                                        CONTINUED

12 CONTINUED: 12

At this last she jerks back from the post and with all her
might KICKS it, easily snapping it in half. Looks at Giles,
breathing heavily, a trickle of sweat on her forehead.

                    GILES (cont'd)
          Safe to say, you've stayed in shape.

                    BUFFY
          Well, I'm ready for anything those
          vampires want to throw at me.

                                        CUT TO:

13 INT. THE FACTORY - NIGHT   13

It's a dark brick building, old machines and rusted hooks and
chains making up its decor. A group of vampires, including
TARA (girl vampire) stands on the balconies and rafters,
listening to someone on the floor below.

ABSALOM is long -- long in the face, the body, the fingers.
His face, like those around him, is vampiric. He is too old
and powerful to bother assuming a human visage. He moves
with grace and authority, and speaks with same.

                    ABSALOM
          We have been put down, my kinsmen.
          We have lost our way, and we have
          lost the night. But despair is for
          the living. Where they are weak, we
          will be strong. Where they weep, we
          rejoice. Where they bleed, we drink.
          Within these three days a new hope
          shall rise. We put our faith in
          him...

He looks over at someone.

It is the ANOINTED ONE, standing quietly in front of the
factory's huge furnace. The flames behind frame his dark
visage.

                    ABSALOM (cont'd)
          And he will show us the way.

The Anointed One almost smiles.

                                        BLACK OUT.

                    END OF ACT ONE

ACT TWO

14 INT. SCHOOL LOUNGE - DAY   14

Buffy sits on a couch by the coffee table, lost in thought.
After a spell, Xander and Willow join her, sitting opposite
each other, Xander next to Buffy.

                    XANDER
          Buffy. Buffy!

Buffy snaps out of it as they sit.

                    BUFFY
          Fine! I'm fine!

                    XANDER
                (huh?)
          Good. It's good that you're fine.

                    WILLOW
          What were you thinking about?

                    BUFFY
          Nothing.

                    XANDER
          Come on, you can tell us! We're your
          bosom friends. The friends of your
          bosom.

                    WILLOW
          Xander...

                    BUFFY
          I wasn't thinking anything. Really.
          Did I have think-face? 'Cause there
          was nothing going on.

Xander and Willow both have bag lunches, which they start
digging through.

                    WILLOW
          What'd you do last night?

                    BUFFY
          Slept.

Xander holds up a breakfast bar, Willow an apple. With
unspoken accord, they toss them to each other.

CONTINUED

                         BUFFY (cont'd)
               Had weird dreams. I can't really
               remember them, I just know they were
               all over the place.

                         XANDER
               Dreams are meaningful.

                         WILLOW
               They sure are. The other night I
               dreamt that Xander --
                         (stops herself)
               Uh, it wasn't Xander. In fact, it
               wasn't me. It was a friend's dream,
               and they don't remember it.

                         BUFFY
                         (smiling)
               I'll bet they don't.

Giles approaches. Buffy rises to meet him.

                         BUFFY (cont'd)
               What's the buzz? You look worried.

                         GILES
               This vampire activity -- I think I
               know what they're up to.

                         BUFFY
               Well, don't stress. We'll deal.

                         GILES
               I hope it's that simple.

                         BUFFY
               It is not to sweat. Trust me.

                         GILES
               I don't know. I mean, I killed you
               once. It shouldn't be too difficult
               to do it again.

                         BUFFY
                         (it stops her)
               What?

He PUNCHES her, sends her sprawling onto the coffee table.
Before she can even move he's on her, grabbing her throat.
She tries to fight him off, eyes widening, but he's too
strong.

15 ANGLE: XANDER AND WILLOW   15

Are paying no attention to what's happening next to them.

No one is. Students mill about, laugh, talk -- while Giles
chokes the life out of a weakening Buffy.

She claws at his face, but only succeeds in PULLING IT OFF,
to reveal beneath it the FACE OF THE MASTER.

                                        SMASH CUT TO:

16 INT. BUFFY'S BEDROOM - NIGHT   16

Buffy awakes with a start, gasping and sweating. She is
completely freaked, sitting up and running her hands through
her hair. She looks around the dark room.

17 ANGLE: FROM OUTSIDE HER WINDOW   17

She looks small and vulnerable in the frame. Starts to
settle back down -- a **figure suddenly appears** near camera,
right outside the window.

Buffy hears a noise, looks out there. She stares, but she
doesn't scream.

                    BUFFY
          Hello.

ANGEL is crouched outside the window.

                    ANGEL
          Mind if I come in?

                    BUFFY
                (noncommittally)
          Be my guest.

He steps gracefully in, standing near her bed.

                    ANGEL
          How are you?

                    BUFFY
          Peachy.

There is a moment of uncomfortable silence; she's not making
this easy.

                    BUFFY (cont'd)
          So, is this a social call? It's kind
          of late. Or, it is for me. For you
          this is, what, lunch hour?

                                        CONTINUED

17 CONTINUED: 17

                        ANGEL
                  (bridling slightly)
            It's not a social call.

                        BUFFY
            And that means grave danger. Gosh,
            it's so good to be home.

                        ANGEL
            I'm sorry. I wish I had better news.

                        BUFFY
            Let me guess. Some of your cousins
            have come for a family barbecue, and
            we're all on the menu.

                        ANGEL
            The Anointed One. He's been
            gathering forces somewhere in town.
            I'm not sure why.

                        BUFFY
            I guess I'll find out soon enough.

                        ANGEL
            You don't sound too concerned.

                        BUFFY
            I can handle myself. I could use a
            little action, anyway.

                        ANGEL
            Don't underestimate the Anointed One
            just because he looks like a child.
            He has power over the rest of them.
            Its source is deep, and old. They'll
            do anything for him.

                        BUFFY
            Is that it? Is that everything?
            'Cause you woke me up from a really
            nice dream.

                        ANGEL
            Sorry. I'll go.

He heads for the window. Stands facing it as Buffy hunkers
down in bed, facing away from him.

                        ANGEL (cont'd)
                  (quietly)
            I missed you.

                                              CONTINUED

17 CONTINUED: (2)   17

She can't reply, but the hardness in her face melts away.
After a couple of beats she turns, her true emotions about to
spill out --

                    BUFFY
          I missed --

But he's gone. She stares at the window, unhappy.

                                        DISSOLVE TO:

18 INT. SCHOOL HALL - DAY   18

Buffy is with Willow and Xander. She betrays none of her
vulnerability with them.

                    WILLOW
          Angel came by? Wow. Was there, I
          mean, was it having to do with
          kissing?

                    BUFFY
          Willow, grow up. Not everything is
          about kissing.

                    XANDER
          Yeah! Some stuff is about groping.
               (to Buffy, worried)
          It wasn't about groping...?

                    BUFFY
               (to both of them)
          Hello, Hormones on Parade... it was
          pure shop talk. You know, vampires?
          Ring a bell? Pointy teeth, they walk
          by night...

                    WILLOW
          What'd he say?

                    BUFFY
               (shrugs)
          Something's up. Nothing I can't
          handle.

                    XANDER
          Oh! Hey! Did you guys know? Cibo   *
          Matto ["cheebo motto"] is gonna be at   *
          The Bronze tonight.   *

                    WILLOW
          Cibo Matto? They're playing?   *

                                        CONTINUED

18 CONTINUED: 18

                         XANDER
          No, Willow, they'll be clog-dancing.

                         WILLOW
                    (excited)
          Cibo Matto can clog-dance? -- Oh.   *
          Sarcasm. Right.

                         XANDER
                    (to Buffy)
          We should attend, no? If you're not
          busy with fighting or anything.

                         BUFFY
          Sounds like fun.

Cordelia arrives, cute jock in tow.

                         CORDELIA
                    (witheringly)
          Oh, look. It's the Three Musketeers.

Brief confusion crosses the faces of our heros.

                         BUFFY
          Was that an insult?

                         XANDER
          Kinda lacked punch.

                         WILLOW
          The Three Musketeers were cool.

                         CORDELIA
                    (considering)
          I see your point...

                         XANDER
          I would have gone with "Stooges".

                         CORDELIA
          Well, I just meant you all hang out
          together. So, did you guys fight
          demons all summer?

Panic from the three.

                         WILLOW
          Yes! Our own personal demons!

                         XANDER
          Such as lust... and, uh... thrift.

                                                       CONTINUED

> BUFFY
> (re: the other two)
> I think I would have to go with
> "Stooges" also.

> CORDELIA
> What are you guys talking about? I'm
> talking about big squiggly demons
> that come from the ground. Remember,
> on prom night, with all the vampires?

> BUFFY
> Cordelia. Your mouth is open. Sound
> is coming from it. This is never
> good.

They draw her away from the jock, who's not really paying
attention anyway.

> XANDER
> You see, we can't mention that stuff
> in front of other people. Buffy
> being the Slayer and all.

> WILLOW
> You haven't been talking about our
> little adventure all summer, have you?

> CORDELIA
> Are you nuts? You think I would tell
> anyone that I spent the evening with
> you guys? Besides, it was all so
> creepy. That Master guy, screaming...

Once again, nobody notices the effect the name has on Buffy.

> CORDELIA (cont'd)
> I don't even like to think about it.
> Your secret is safe with me.

> BUFFY
> That works out great. You don't tell
> anyone that I'm the Slayer, and I
> won't tell anyone that you're a moron.

She leaves, leaving Cordy a little hurt and the others a
little nonplussed.

> XANDER
> See, now that was a good insult.

> WILLOW
> A little TOO good...

CONTINUED

18 CONTINUED: (3)   18

                         CORDELIA
               What's up with her?

                         WILLOW
               I don't know.

                                             CUT TO:

19 EXT. THE BRONZE - NIGHT   19

     Kids (and young adults) pour in. A big sign advertises CIBO   *
     MATTO.   *

                                             CUT TO:

20 INT. THE BRONZE - CONTINUOUS - NIGHT   20

     Cibo Matto is just finishing a song. Xander and Willow sit   *
     and watch. She has a little ice cream sundae, he has a soda.

                         WILLOW
               I just think something's up, is all.

                         XANDER
               Willow, you're paranoid.

                         WILLOW
               Buffy's never acted like this before.
               Ever since she got back, she's
               different.

                         XANDER
               Buffy's always been different.

                         WILLOW
               She's never been mean.

                         XANDER
                    (cranes to look for
                     her)
               Any sign of her? She said she was
               coming.

                         WILLOW
               No... The band's cool though.

                         XANDER
                    (distracted)
               Yeah. Cool.

                                             CONTINUED

20 CONTINUED: 20

Willow looks a little glum that he's not paying attention.
After a moment, she takes a little spoonful of ice cream and
dabs it on the end of her nose. Waits for Xander to look at
her.

When he does...

                        XANDER (cont'd)
            Got something on your nose.

He turns back to the door and she wipes her nose, dejected.

                                        CUT TO:

21 EXT. THE GRAVEYARD - NIGHT   21

We see the tree Willow pointed out. TILT DOWN to see the
earth -- the grave of the Master, to be precise. It has a
series of little crosses all around it, but no headstone.

A spade is stuck in the earth. Another, and a third. They
all begin digging up the grave.

22 ANGLE: ABSALOM AND THE ANOINTED ONE   22

Watch as the three vampires dig. More vampires around them.
The Anointed One looks at Absalom, who turns to the vampire
standing nearest.

                        ABSALOM
            Dig. All of you. We have to hurry.

The vampires move to the grave and begin digging with their
hands. A couple of their hands begin to smoke.

                        VAMPIRE 2
            Aagh!
                  (turns to Absalom)
            The ground is consecrated! It burns!

                        ANOINTED ONE
            Dig.

The vampire obeys, grimacing from the pain. Finally they dig
up:

23 ANGLE: A SKULL   23   *

Which they uncover further.

                                        CONTINUED

23 CONTINUED: 23

The Anointed One looks on, impassive.

                                        CUT TO:

24 INT. THE BRONZE - NIGHT   24

Buffy enters. Sees Xander and Willow, and starts crossing to
them. As she makes her way through the crowd, Angel appears
before her. It takes her just a second to throw up her
defenses.

                    BUFFY
          Oh. Hi again.

                    ANGEL
          Hi.

                    BUFFY
          Is there danger at The Bronze?
          Should I beware?

                    ANGEL
          I can't help thinking I've done
          something to make you angry. That
          bothers me more than I'd like.

                    BUFFY
          I'm not angry. I have no idea where
          that comes from.

                    ANGEL
          What are you afraid of? Me? Us?

                    BUFFY
          Uh, could you contemplate getting
          over yourself? There's no "us". I'm
          sorry if I was supposed to spend the
          summer mooning over you, but I
          didn't. I moved on. To the living.

She leaves, heads for Xander and Willow. Passes Cordelia,
who appears to have overheard the exchange.

                    WILLOW
          What's wrong with Angel?

                    BUFFY
          Beats me.

The band starts playing. Buffy looks over at Angel, still
hovering about in the back. She grabs Xander's hand.

                                        CONTINUED

24 CONTINUED: 24

                         BUFFY (cont'd)
                  Let's dance.

                         XANDER
                  Uh, uh...

     But she's leading him on the floor. They start to dance.

25 ANGLE: BUFFY DANCING   25

     Buffy's moves are a little too close, a little too hot. It's
     pure bad girl, and Xander doesn't know whether to be
     suspicious, aroused, or panicked.

26 ANGLE: WILLOW   26

     Looking on, unhappy.

27 ANGLE: ANGEL   27

     Unhappy.

     Hell, even Xander is looking a little upset. Buffy smiles at
     him.

                         BUFFY
                  Xander, did I ever thank you for
                  saving my life?

                         XANDER
                  No.

     She brings her body up against his -- is she gonna kiss
     him? -- then whispers in his ear:

                         BUFFY
                  Don't you wish I would?

     And with that, she leaves. Leaves the floor, leaves The
     Bronze, leaves a wake of unhappiness behind her.

                                            CUT TO:

28 EXT. THE BRONZE - CONTINUOUS   28

     She is about twenty feet out when she hears her name.

                         CORDELIA
                  Buffy.

     She stops, turns as Cordelia steps out of The Bronze towards
     her.

                                            CONTINUED

                    CORDELIA (cont'd)
You're really campaigning for bitch
of the year, aren't you?

                    BUFFY
As defending champion, are you
nervous?

                    CORDELIA
I can hold my own.
          (stepping forward)
We've never been close, Buffy, which
is nice, 'cause I don't like you very
much. But you have, on occasion,
saved the world and all that stuff,
so I'm gonna do you a favor.

                    BUFFY
Joyous me.

                    CORDELIA
Your friends can't do it, 'cause they
like you. And they're sort of afraid
of you.

                    BUFFY
What's the favor?

                    CORDELIA
I'm going to give you some advice.
Get over it.

                    BUFFY
Excuse me?

                    CORDELIA
Whatever's causing the Joan Collins
'tude, deal with it, embrace the
pain, spank your inner moppet but **get
over it,** 'cause pretty soon you won't
even have the loser friends you've
got now.

                    BUFFY
I'd say it's about time for you to
mind your own business.

                    CORDELIA
It's long past. Nighty night.

Buffy turns and leaves. Cordelia watches her go. As she
does, we see two vampires emerge from the shadows behind her,
moving slowly toward her.

                                        CONTINUED

28 CONTINUED: (2)   28

                        CORDELIA (cont'd)
                    (calls out)
          I'll just go see if Angel feels like
          dancing.

     Getting no response, she turns to go - and they grab her.
     Hand over her mouth, they drag her off.

29 ANGLE: BUFFY   29

     Walking away, oblivious.

                                        BLACK OUT.

              END OF ACT TWO

ACT THREE

30 INT. FACTORY CELLAR - NIGHT   30

    Cordelia is brought in by a pair of vampires. They bring her
    down the steps and push her into the dark -- near **pitch**
    dark -- room. Go back up and shut the door on her.

    Cordelia is terrified. She looks back at the door, at the
    black room. Takes a step forward, her eyes slowly adjusting.
    Takes another step and

31 ANGLE: A HAND   31

    appears in frame just as Cordelia's foot nudges it.

    She jumps back, then looks down at the figure on the floor.
    Kneels, pulling the figure onto her lap, seeing that it is

32 JENNY CALENDAR   32

    who groans, unconscious. Her face bloody and bruised.

                        CORDELIA
              Ms. Calendar? Oh God...

    She looks around at the dark, up at the stairs. In a very
    small voice she says:

                        CORDELIA (cont'd)
              What do they want?

                                           CUT TO:

33 EXT. GRAVEYARD - NIGHT   33

    Buffy enters the graveyard from the street. She is lost in
    thought, wandering seemingly aimlessly. She sees

34 ANGLE: THE TREE   34

    That Willow said the Master was buried under. Heads toward
    it.

    As she nears it she slows down. Her expression changes -- or
    rather sets, like concrete. She stops.

35 ANGLE: THE MASTER'S GRAVE   35

    Is empty.

                                           CONTINUED

35 CONTINUED: 35

Buffy tries very hard to stay controlled. She takes but one
faltering step back -- and the Master is right beside her.

She spins. No one's there. But she's closer to the edge
than ever. She looks back at the grave, shaking, whispering
to herself:

                              BUFFY
                    He's dead, he's dead.... he's dead...

                                        DISSOLVE TO:

36 INT. JOYCE'S CAR - MORNING   36

Buffy is in the passenger seat, silent and sullen. Joyce
looks at her.

                              JOYCE
                    How are your new classes?

                              BUFFY
                         (not looking at her)
                    Good.

                              JOYCE
                    Good.

More nothing. Finally:

                              JOYCE (cont'd)
                    Is there the slightest chance that if
                    I asked you what was wrong, you'd
                    tell me?

That actually gets Buffy to look at Joyce, though she says
nothing.

                              JOYCE (cont'd)
                    Of course not. That would take all
                    the fun out of guessing.

                              WILLOW (V.O.)
                    She's possessed!

                                        CUT TO:

37 INT. SCHOOL LOUNGE - DAY   37

Willow and Xander are talking to Giles.

                                        CONTINUED

37 CONTINUED: 37

                         GILES
          Possessed?

                         WILLOW
          It's the only explanation that makes
          any sense. You should have seen her
          last night. That wasn't Buffy.

                         XANDER
          Are we overlooking the idea that she
          may just be very attracted to me?
                    (off Willow's look)
          She's possessed.

                         GILES
          Possessed by what?

                         WILLOW
                    (excitedly)
          A possessing thing!

                         GILES
          Well, that narrows it down.

                         XANDER
          You're the expert. Maybe when the
          Master killed her, some mystical bad
          guy transference thing happened.

                         WILLOW
          That's what it was.
                    (aside, to Xander)
          Why else would she be acting like
          such a B. I. T. C. H.?

                         GILES
          Willow, we're all a little old to be
          spelling things out.

                         XANDER
                    (working it out)
          A bitkha?

                         GILES
          I suggest the explanation for her
          behavior may be somewhat more mundane.

Second bell RINGS, most kids filtering off towards classes.

                         GILES (cont'd)
          She may simply have what you
          Americans refer to as "issues".
                    (more)

                                              CONTINUED

> GILES (cont'd)
> Her experience with the Master must
> have been extremely traumatic. She
> was, for at least a few minutes,
> legally dead. I don't think she's
> dealt with it on a conscious level.
> It's too painful. She's convinced
> herself that she's invulnerable for
> the very reason that she feels --

Xander notices Buffy coming up behind Giles and hastily
interrupts:

> XANDER
> That's a very interesting point about
> trout! That you made just now.

> GILES
>   (confused)
> Trout?
>   (sees Buffy)
> Trout! Yes! The trout... is a fish.
> Good morning! Did you sleep well?

> BUFFY
> Like a rock. The Master's gone.

> GILES
> I'm sorry?

> BUFFY
> The Master. I went by his grave last
> night and they have a vacancy.

> GILES
> Good god.

> WILLOW
> What would somebody want with Master
> bones?

> XANDER
> Trophy? Horrible conversation piece?

> BUFFY
> They're gonna bring him back.

A moment. Buffy stares at Giles.

> BUFFY (cont'd)
> They're gonna bring the Master back
> to life and I seem to recall you
> telling me he was history.

CONTINUED

                         GILES
         Buffy, I've never heard of a
         revivification ritual being
         successful --

                         BUFFY
         But you've heard of them. Thanks for
         the warning.

                         WILLOW
         Buffy, Giles did bury him in
         hallowed --

                         BUFFY
         This is Slayer stuff, okay? Can we
         have less from the civilians, please?

                         XANDER
                 (truly pissed)
         Okay, that's just about --

Snyder appears beside them, preempting Xander's tirade with:

                         MR. SNYDER
         I believe that some of us have
         classes.
                 (to Giles)
         And some of us have jobs.

                         GILES
                 (to the kids)
         I'll see you all in the library after
         school. And we can finish our
         discussion.

                         WILLOW
         About trout.

The kids disperse, Buffy giving Giles one final look.

                         MR. SNYDER
         There's some things I can just **smell.**
         It's like sixth sense.

                         GILES
         No, actually, that would be one of
         the five.

                         MR. SNYDER
         The Summers girl? I smell trouble.
         I smell expulsion. And just the
         faintest aroma of jail.

                                              CONTINUED

37 CONTINUED: (4)   37

                        GILES
            Well, before you throw away the key,
            perhaps you'd consider giving her the
            benefit of the doubt. She may
            surprise you.

Snyder looks him over for a beat.

                        MR. SNYDER
            You really have faith in those kids,
            don't you?

                        GILES
            Yes, I do.

                        MR. SNYDER
            Weird.

He goes, leaving Giles alone.

                                            CUT TO:

38 INT. LIBRARY - EVENING   38

    The sun is just fading as our team researches. Giles crosses
    to the center of the room, book in hand.

                        GILES
            All right, I've got something. It's
            latin, so bear with me. Um, to
            revive the vampire, they need his
            bones,
                    (sheepishly looks at
                     Buffy)
            which they have... and, uh, the
            blood... this is very unclear...of
            the closest person, someone connected
            to the vampire.

                        BUFFY
            That'd be me.

                        GILES
            Perhaps...

                        BUFFY
            We were close. Way close. We killed
            each other, okay? It really promotes
            togetherness.

                                            CONTINUED

38 CONTINUED: 38

                        XANDER
          Well, is there anything on WHEN the
          ceremony might take --

A rock SMASHES through the window behind his head. He
ducks -- everyone moves, alarmed. Buffy just spins and
catches the rock.

Wrapped around it is Cordelia's necklace, and a note.

                        BUFFY
          This is Cordelia's.

Everyone looks at each other. Buffy takes the note, opens
it. It reads:

                        BUFFY (cont'd)
          "Come to the Bronze before it opens,
          or we make her a meal".

                        XANDER
          They're gonna cook her dinner?
                    (gets it)
          Please pretend I didn't ask that.

                        WILLOW
          What do we do?

                        BUFFY
          I go to the Bronze and save the day.

                        XANDER
          I don't like this.

                        GILES
          Nor I.

                        BUFFY
          Well, you guys aren't going.

                        WILLOW
          What do you mean?

                        BUFFY
          I can't be looking out for you three
          while I'm fighting.

                        WILLOW
          What about the rest of the note?

                        BUFFY
                    (looking it over)
          What rest?

                                              CONTINUED

38 CONTINUED: (2)   38

                         WILLOW
              The part where it says "PS this is a
              trap"?

                         GILES
              You'll be playing right into their
              hands.

                         BUFFY
              And their hands are gonna get slapped.

                         XANDER
              We should at least go in force.
              Stock up on stakes.

                         BUFFY
              I can handle it.

                         WILLOW
              Stop saying that! God, what's wrong
              with you?

                         XANDER
              Cordelia may be dead.

         Buffy stops, looking at them.

                         BUFFY
              This is my fight.

         She takes off, leaving them to look at each other.

                                             CUT TO:

39 EXT. ALLEY BY THE BRONZE - NIGHT   39

         Buffy is almost at the Bronze when Angel approaches. She   *
         turns to him, exasperated.

                         BUFFY
              You know, being stalked isn't really
              a big turn-on for girls.

                         ANGEL
              You need help. Someone to watch your
              back.

                         BUFFY
              You sure you don't mean my neck?

                         ANGEL
              Why are you riding me?

                                             CONTINUED

39 CONTINUED: 39

> BUFFY
> Because I don't trust you. You're a
> vampire. Or is that an offensive
> term? Should I say "undead
> American"?

> ANGEL
> You have to trust someone. You can't
> do this alone.

> BUFFY
> I trust me.

> ANGEL
> You're not as strong as you think.

> BUFFY
> You think you could take me?

> ANGEL
> What?

> BUFFY
> Come on, you must have wondered... a
> vampire, the Slayer, I know you've
> thought about it. If it came down to
> a fight... could you take me? Why
> don't we find out?

> ANGEL
> I'm not gonna fight you.

> BUFFY
> No? Big strong vampire like yourself?

> ANGEL
> Buffy...

> BUFFY
> Come on. Kick my ass.

The smile in her eyes is tending towards the crazed. He
growls, low.

> BUFFY (cont'd)
> Now we get to see who we're really
> dealing with.

He stops, controlling himself.

> ANGEL
> Don't you have somewhere to be?

CONTINUED

She remembers Cordelia. Hiding a flash of guilt, she replies.

> BUFFY
> I do.

> ANGEL
> Well, you're wasting time.

She looks to the Bronze, back to him.

> BUFFY
> Just stay out of my way.

> ANGEL
> Happy to oblige.

She goes off. After a beat, he follows.

                                                    CUT TO:

40 INT. THE BRONZE - A MINUTE LATER - NIGHT   40

Buffy enters, walking slowly, looking about her. Not as
confident as she was around the others. She pulls out a
stake, walks.

She hears CRYING. Looks near the stage and finds:

41 ANGLE: A GIRL   41

Huddled on her knees, back to Buffy, and wearing Cordelia's
coat. Her eyes narrow suspiciously as she takes a slow step
forward.

42 ANGLE: BUFFY   42

From far off, heading toward us. Angel appears off to the
side, also approaching the figure.

> BUFFY
> That's not Cordelia.

And the figure rises into frame right before us -- (it had
been huddled close to camera) -- and no, it's not Cordelia.
It's a grinning vampire. Female, yes, but definitely not
Cordy. She laughs, turns to Buffy.

> TARA
> Cordelia... she didn't come...

> BUFFY
> Where is she?

                                                    CONTINUED

                    TARA
I'm not supposed to tell...

                    ANGEL
I don't like this.

                    BUFFY
What?

                    ANGEL
There's the bait. Where's the hook?

Buffy looks around -- and the vampire JUMPS her!

She instinctively rolls, flips the vampire over. Comes up
onto her feet and steps on the vampire's neck. She looks
around some more.

                    BUFFY
You're right. Why would they send
just one?

                            CUT TO:

43   INT. LIBRARY - NIGHT   43

Willow and Xander talk as Giles continues to puzzle over his
books.

                    WILLOW
I still think we should have gone
with her.

                    XANDER
Buffy's about to lose it. I think we
should be trying to reach minimum
safe distance.

                    WILLOW
Xander, you know it was a trap!

                    GILES
Aha! This Latin is translated from
the Sumerian, and rather badly, which
makes it difficult. But the person
closest to the Master actually
translates as nearest -- physically.
The person or persons who...

He realizes what he's saying when he says it.

                            CONTINUED

> GILES (con't)
> ... were with him when...

> WILLOW
> When what?

He looks at the two of them, dead certainty on his face.

> GILES
> It IS a trap...

She comes toward him and as we pan with her we see two
vampires standing there. Smiling, needless to say. Willow
almost walks right into them. SCREAMS, stepping back.
Xander and Giles look around -- there are four of them in
here, surrounding our three.

> GILES (cont.)
> ... it just isn't for her.

> BLACK OUT.

END OF ACT THREE

ACT FOUR

44 INT. THE BRONZE - NIGHT   44

Buffy has just finished tying the vampire's hands behind her
back with Angel's belt. She hands her off to him.

                    BUFFY
          Watch her. Don't kill her if you
          don't have to.

                    ANGEL
          Buffy, what's going on?

                    BUFFY
          I'll be back.

She takes off at top speed.

                                        CUT TO:

45 INT. LIBRARY - NIGHT   45

Buffy runs in, finds much overturned. Stops, then spots:

                    BUFFY
               Xander!

She runs over to him as he is struggling to get up. He is
beaten and bloody.

                    BUFFY (cont'd)
          Where are the others? What happened?

She moves to help him up, but he violently shakes off her
hand.

                    XANDER
          Vampires. The ones you could handle
          yourself.

                    BUFFY
          Where did they take Giles and --

                    XANDER
          I don't know! I don't know what your
          problem is -- what your "issues" are,
          and as of now I officially don't
          care! If you'd worked with us for
          five seconds you could have stopped
          this.

                                        CONTINUED

45 CONTINUED: 45

Buffy takes the words hard -- she knows he's right. She
tries to gather her wits, to keep from breaking down...

                    BUFFY
          We have to think. Why did they take
          them?

                    XANDER
          If they hurt Willow I'm gonna kill
          you.

                    BUFFY
               (realizes)
          Why did they take them and not you?

This stops him. He thinks as well.

                    XANDER
          Giles said the ritual was, um.. they
          needed people close to the Master...
          physically close, when he...

                    BUFFY
          The ones who were with him when he
          died.

                    XANDER
          Giles, Willow... Cordelia.

                    BUFFY
               (nodding)
          And Ms. Calendar.

                    XANDER
          Odds are, they've got the complete
          set by now.

                    BUFFY
          We just have to find out where.

                    XANDER
          How?

                                        CUT TO:

46 INT. THE BRONZE - NIGHT   46

Xander and Angel stand watching something happen out of
frame. Suddenly the girl vampire falls into frame, much
closer to camera. Her hands are still tied behind her back,
and she lands hard.

                                        CONTINUED

46 CONTINUED: 46

                         BUFFY
              One more time.

She hauls the vampire up.

                         BUFFY (cont'd)
              Where are they?

                         TARA
              You're too late. Your friends are
              dead.

                         BUFFY
              Tell me where they are.

                         TARA
              What are you gonna do, kill me?

                         BUFFY
              As a matter of fact, yes.

She PUNCHES the vampire in the face. She flies back, landing
on top of the pool table. Buffy comes around the table,
calmly unhooking her cross necklace. She holds it above the
vampire's face and as the vampire moans in pain, **Buffy drops
the necklace into the vampire's mouth.** Clamps it shut with
her hands.

The vampire writhes, SMOKE pouring out of her mouth.

                         BUFFY (cont'd)
              But since I'm not gonna kill you any
              time **soon,** the question becomes, how
              do we pass the time till then?

47 ANGLE: XANDER AND ANGEL   47

Look on, obviously uncomfortable with Buffy's methods.

Buffy pulls the cross out by the chain.

                         BUFFY
              So. One more time.

                                          CUT TO:

48 EXT. THE FACTORY - NIGHT   48

CAMERA moves slowly towards the factory. It looks large and
forbidding in the darkness.

                                          CUT TO:

49   INT. FACTORY CELLAR - NIGHT   49

Cordelia is tending to a still unconscious Ms. Calendar. The
door opens, Cordelia starting back as a big vampire enters.

                    CORDELIA
          Please... go away... what do you --

He SLUGS her, knocking her cold. Starts dragging both women
up the stairs.

50   INT. THE FACTORY - NIGHT   50

The Anointed One walks past the old, rusted surgical table in
the middle of the room. He holds a box in his hands. As we   *
track with him, we see the Master's skeleton laid out on it.
He reaches the head of the table, and Absalom. On either   *
side of the table are two floorlength wooden torches.

The Anointed One hands him the box. Absalom looks up at   *

51   ANGLE: THE BALCONY   51

                    ABSALOM   *
          Begin.   *

Two vampires start hauling on a chain.   *

52   CLOSE ON: THE CHAIN   52

on a pulley, moving across the ceiling.

And we finally go WIDE to reveal the four bodies of BUFFY's
friends HUNG UPSIDE DOWN on meathooks attached to the chain.
They are all unconscious as they are positioned directly
above the Master's skeleton.

                                                                  *
                                                                  *

The other vampires form a semi-circle around the side of the
table.   *

53   ANGLE: UNDER THE BALCONY   53

Buffy, Xander and Angel have snuck in.

The three of them creep along in the dark until they can see
the center of the room.

They see the skeleton laid out on the table. Above it, their
four friends. The vampires in a semi-circle, six quietly
chanting figures. Absalom and the Anointed One at the head.

                                                        CONTINUED

53 CONTINUED: 53

    Buffy can't move. Her eyes widen with fear and remorse.

                                                        CONTINUED

53 CONTINUED: (2)   53

The vampires gather around the table.   *

                    ANGEL
          Buffy. Buffy!

She snaps out of, looks at him.

                    XANDER
          We gotta do something **now**.

                    BUFFY
          You two get the others out of here.

                    ANGEL
          We'll need you to distract the
          vampires.

                    BUFFY
          Right.

She starts toward the ceremony.

                    XANDER
          What are you gonna do?

She stops, turns back.

                    BUFFY
          I'm gonna kill them all.
                (walking away)
          That oughta distract them.

54 ANGLE: ABSALOM   54

Opens the box, takes out a knife, and gives the box back to   *
the Anointed One.   *

                    ABSALOM
          For the Old Ones. For his pain. For
          the Dark.

They repeat the words solemnly, one after the other.   *

                    VAMPIRE BOB
          For the Dark.

Absalom brings the knife to the first throat -- that of
Willow.

                    VAMPIRE JANE
          For the Dark.

                                                CONTINUED

54 CONTINUED: 54

                          VAMPIRE WALT   *
                    For the -- GYEHNNNNGH!

-- eyes popping wide as the tip of a stake pops out his
chest. A moment of gasping, then he EXPLODES INTO DUST,
revealing Buffy right behind him.

There's actually a moment of quiet.

Then Absalom SCREAMS, an inhuman shriek that galvanizes the
vampires (BOB, JANE and NED) into action. They effectively   *
flank our girl, and Jane and Ned rush her simultaneously.   *

She roundhouses them both in the jaw, staggering them back as
Bob gets her from behind but she elbows him in the throat.   *

55 ANGLE: XANDER AND ANGEL   55

    are sneaking up to the second level.

56 ANGLE: THE ANOINTED ONE   56

    is slowly backing out of the room, eyes on the fight.

57 ANGLE: BUFFY   57

    They are trying to surround her -- full frontal assault
    hasn't paid off. She dodges about the boxes and machines,
    quick and alert.

58 ANGLE: ABSALOM   58

    Sees she's occupied. Roughly he grabs Willow's face, brings
    the knife to her throat --

    -- when the four bodies start moving away, towards the   *
    balcony.

59 ANGLE: XANDER AND ANGEL   59

    Are hauling on the chain that holds the bodies, pulling them
    closer.

                          ABSALOM
                The sacrifices! Stop them!

                                                    CONTINUED

59   CONTINUED: 59

Ned peels off upstairs, leaving Buffy with Jane and Bob.   *

60   ANGLE: BUFFY   60

She is on one side of a pile of boxes, Jane behind her, Bob   *
on the other side of the boxes. She kicks Jane, then jumps,   *
grabbing the top box and flipping herself over the pile,
landing on her feet -- and still holding the box, she brings
it over her head and SMASHES it over Bob's head.   *

The guy's effectively wearing a box helmet. Buffy powers out
a side kick to the face, smashing through the box to hit it.   *
Bob flies back into the corner.   *

Jane slams into her and they both go down.   *

61   ANGLE: XANDER AND ANGEL   61   *

They're pulling the bodies to the safety of the Balcony.   *
Calendar and Cordy are lying nearby as they pull the third   *
one off. It's Giles, who's lust starting to waken.   *

Ned crests the stairs -- and Angel turns, his VAMPIRE FACE   *
now on. Ned charges -- Angel throws himself at him. They   *
grapple, stepping onto some rotted boards covering a hole.   *
It breaks, the two of them falling down to the lower level.   *

62   ANGLE: BUFFY   62

is under Jane, struggling to keep him from biting her. Her   *
hand sweeps the floor, coming up with a box shard. She slams
it into her back, pushing her off right before she's dusted.   *

A63 ANGLE: BOB   A63   *

Gets the box off his head and climbs swiftly to the ramp   *
above Buffy's head, trying to escape.   *

Buffy sees him. She runs, jumps -- grabs a pipe under the   *
ramp and swings her legs up --   *

--and THROUGH the wooden slats, tripping him up, sending him   *
flying to the ground. He lands hard.   *

63   ANGLE: ANGEL   63

as Ned shoves a shard of wood at his heart -- Angel grabs it   *
and shoves harder, sending it backwards through HIS.   *

64   ANGLE: XANDER   64

Gets Willow, the last one, off the chain. A dazed Giles is
helping Ms Calendar.

CONTINUED

64 CONTINUED: 64

                         GILES
              Are you all right?

                                        CONTINUED

64   CONTINUED: (2)   64

                         JENNY
              I think so. My head...   *

                         GILES
                     (to xander)
              Where's Buffy?

Xander looks down at:

65   ANGLE: BUFFY FROM XANDER'S POV   65   *

Pummeling her remaining opponent, Bob.   *

                         XANDER
              She's working out her issues.   *

A66 ANGLE: BOB   A66   *

flies into the corner under the balcony from the force of one   *
of Buffy's blows.   *

                         ABSALOM (O.S.)   *
              Enough!   *

B66 ANGLE: ABSOLOM   B66   *

Steps out of the shadows by where the Anointed One exited.   *
He is holding a sledgehammer.   *

                         ABSALOM   *
              Your day is done, girl. I'll grind   *
              you into a sticky paste. And I'll   *
              hear you beg before I smash in your   *
              face.   *

Buffy stands by the big torch, listening. Finally: *

                         BUFFY   *
              So, are you gonna kill me? Or are   *
              you just making small talk?   *

That tears it. Absalom rushes her, swinging back the hammer.   *
At the same time, Bob does as well, from the opposite   *
direction.   *

Buffy stands by the torch, waiting. Doesn't even look at   *
them.

At the last second she SWEEPKICKS the base of the torch,
splintering it and flipping it up --

-- the pointy end IMPALES Bob -- he's dusted --   *

                                                        CONTINUED

B66   CONTINUED: B66

     -- as the burning end IGNITES Absalom. He reels back, then   *
     comes at her, arms aflame, swinging --   *

     -- then stops as the flames literally consume him (FX).   *

     The sledgehammer drops to the ground in front of Buffy.   *

     66 OMITTED   66   *
   THRU   THRU
     69   69

                                                         CONTINUED

B66   CONTINUED: (2)   B66

        She takes a moment, breathing hard. Quiet in victory. Looks   *
        at something, her expression changing.

        She picks up the sledgehammer.

  70 ANGLE: THE OTHERS   70

        watching from above, in various stages of wakefulness.
        Xander helps Willow to her feet.

                            WILLOW
                It's over.

                            XANDER
                No, it's not.

71   ANGLE: BUFFY   71

As she approaches the table, we TRACK BACK to reveal it, the
Master's bones laid out before her. She stares at it quietly
for a moment, then swings the sledgehammer and SMASHES the
skull in. She swings again, smashing the Master to powder,
the grunts of her efforts rising to a roar, still she swings
it, again, again, out of control --

Angel approaches, slowly. His face is human once again. He
touches her shoulder and she stops. Drops the hammer,
shaking. She starts crying just before he folds her into his
arms.

                    ANGEL
          It's okay.... it's okay...

72   ANGLE: XANDER   72

Watches Angel hold her, silently. PAN OVER to find Willow
watching Xander with much the same emotion.

73   WIDE ON. THE FACTORY   73

As Buffy continues to sob, small in the giant, dark space.

                              DISSOLVE TO:

74   EXT. PALM COURT - MORNING   74   *

Amidst the bustle, we see Cordelia and Ms. Calendar walking
together.

                    CORDELIA
          What an ordeal. And you know the
          worst part: It stays with you
          forever. No matter what they tell
          you, none of that rust and blood and
          grime comes out. You can dry-clean
          till judgement day; you're living
          with those stains.

                    JENNY
               (dead pan)
          Yes. That's the worst part of being
          hung upside down by a vampire that
          wants to slit your throat. The
          stains.

                    CORDELIA
          I hear you.

As they cross out of frame we pick up Buffy walking with
Giles. The swagger has gone out of her step a bit.

                                                    CONTINUED

74 CONTINUED: 74

                    BUFFY
          I don't think I can face them.

                    GILES
          Of course you can.

                    BUFFY
          I can't! What am I gonna say?
          "Sorry I almost got your throats cut.
          What's the homework?"

                    GILES
          Punishing yourself like this is
          pointless.

                    BUFFY
          It's entirely pointy! I was a moron.
          I put my best friends in mortal
          danger -- on the second day of school!

                    GILES
          What are you going to do, crawl into
          a dark cave for the rest of your life?

                    BUFFY
          Would it have cable?

He stops, turns to her.   *

                    GILES
          Buffy, you acted wrongly, I admit,
          but believe me, that was hardly the
          worst mistake you'll ever make.
                    (a beat)
          That wasn't nearly as comforting as
          it was meant to be.

                    BUFFY
          Well, points for effort. I'll see
          you.

She heads inside.   *

                                        CUT TO:

75 INT. CLASS - CONTINUOUS   75

She slowly makes her way to the back row, where Willow and
Xander sit, talking. The seat next to Willow is empty.
Hesitantly, Buffy approaches. Willow turns and looks up at
her.

                                        CONTINUED

                         WILLOW
            Buffy.

                         BUFFY
            Hey.

                         WILLOW
            We saved you a seat...

Buffy smiles gratefully, sits. Xander leans over to say:

                         XANDER
            There's a rumor going around that Mr.
            Cox is the most boring teacher in the
            entire world. Like I think he won a
            belt or something.

                         BUFFY
            Lucky us.

                         WILLOW
            Well, I hear he nods off a lot, so
            that's a plus.

                         XANDER
            So, are we bronzing tonight?

                         WILLOW
            Wednesdays it's kind of beat.

                         XANDER
            Well, we could grind our enemies into
            talcum powder with a sledgehammer,
            but, gosh, we did that **last** night.

Buffy laughs, relaxing. As they continue to talk -- Buffy
joining in -- we dolly away, leaving them to their
conversation.

                                              CUT TO:

76 INT. THE FACTORY - DAY   76

Through the wreckage walks the Anointed One, his expression
calm but gloomy. He stops, looks about him for a while.

                         ANOINTED ONE
            I hate that girl...

                                              BLACK OUT.

                         THE END

BUFFY THE VAMPIRE SLAYER

"Some Assembly Required"

Written By

Ty King

Directed By

Bruce Seth Green

<u>SHOOTING SCRIPT</u>

July 7, 1997
July 8, 1997   (Blue Pages)
July 15, 1997 (Pink Full Script)
July 16, 1997 (Yellow Pages)
July 21, 1997 (Green Pages)
July 25, 1997 (Goldenrod Pages)

BUFFY THE VAMPIRE SLAYER

"Some Assembly Required"

CAST LIST

BUFFY SUMMERS............................ Sarah Michelle Gellar
XANDER HARRIS............................ Nicholas Brendon
RUPERT GILES............................ Anthony S. Head
WILLOW ROSENBERG......................... Alyson Hannigan
CORDELIA CHASE........................... Charisma Carpenter
ANGEL................................... David Boreanaz

MS. CALENDAR............................*Robia La Morte
CHRIS................................... Angelo Spizzirri
ERIC.................................... Michael Bacall
DARYL................................... Ingo Neuhaus
CHRIS' MOM.............................*Melanie MacQueen
FIRST CHEERLEADER....................... Amanda Wilmhurst

BUFFY THE VAMPIRE SLAYER

"Some Assembly Required"

SET LIST

INTERIORS

SUNNYDALE HIGH SCHOOL
        HALL
        LIBRARY
        LOUNGE
        CHEERLEADER PREP ROOM
        LAB (OLD SCIENCE BUILDING)
        *HALL BY PREP ROOM
        *SCIENCE CLASSROOM

CHRIS'S HOUSE
        LIVING ROOM
        STORAGE ROOM/BASEMENT/DARYL'S LAIR

EXTERIORS

SUNNYDALE HIGH SCHOOL
        FOUNTAIN QUAD
        PARKING LOT
        ALLEY(DUMPSTER)
        FOOTBALL FIELD
        STADIUM BLEACHERS
        SCHOOL GROUNDS/OLD SCIENCE BUILDING

CEMETERY

BUFFY THE VAMPIRE SLAYER

"Some Assembly Required"

TEASER

1 EXT. CEMETERY - NIGHT   1

CLOSE ON: A HEADSTONE

The engraved rock tells us that STEPHAN KORSHAK died within
the last couple of days and now rests below.

Then, a **YO-YO** DROPS DOWN INTO FRAME in front of the death
stone, spins, then reels BACK UP AND OUT OF FRAME.

A beat, then the YO-YO RETURNS. This time, WE GO BACK UP
WITH IT to BUFFY, atop the tombstone, keeping a bored vigil
with the stringed toy in one hand and a stake in the other.

BEHIND HER, ANGEL approaches through the cemetery, UNNOTICED.

                    BUFFY
                (to the grave below)
          Come on, Stephan, rise and shine.
          Some of us have a ton of trig
          homework waiting.

                    ANGEL
          Hey--

Caught off guard, Buffy SPINS, startled.

                    BUFFY
          Ack!

                    ANGEL
          Is this a bad time?

                    BUFFY
                (steps off the stone)
          Are you crazy? You don't just sneak
          Up on people in a graveyard. You
          make noise when you walk. You...
          stomp, or... yodel.

                    ANGEL
          I heard you were on the hunt.

                    BUFFY
          Supposed to be. But lazybones here
          doesn't wanna come out and play.

                                              CONTINUED

1 CONTINUED: 1

                         ANGEL
               When you first wake up, it's a little
               disorienting. He'll show.

                                                    CONTINUED

                         BUFFY
               It's weird to think of you going   *
               through that.   *

                         ANGEL
               It's weird to go through. You're   *
               here alone?

                         BUFFY
               Yeah, why?

                         ANGEL
               I just thought you'd have somebody
               with you... Xander or someone.

                         BUFFY
               Xander?

                         ANGEL
               Or someone.

                         BUFFY
               No, no Xander. Why, are you jealous?

                         ANGEL
               Of Xander? Please. He's just a kid.

                         BUFFY
               Is it 'cause I danced with him?

                         ANGEL
               "Danced with" is a pretty loose term.
               "Mated with" might be a little
               closer --

                         BUFFY
               Oh, you're shocking! One little
               dance and you know I just did it to
               make you crazy which by the way
               behold my success!

                         ANGEL
               I am not jealous!

          Neither of them notice as they argue that **Stephan starts
          crawling out of his grave**, looking at them with ravenous glee.

                         BUFFY
               Oh, you're not jealous. What,
               vampires don't get jealous?

                                                         CONTINUED

1 CONTINUED: (3)   1

                    ANGEL
          See? W henever we fight, you always
          bring up the vampire thing.

                    BUFFY
          I didn't come here to fight.

Stephan **leaps** on her, knocking her to the ground. She throws
him off.

                    BUFFY (cont'd)
          Oh, right. I did.
                    (looks around,
                     getting up)
          Where's my stake?
                    (to Angel)
          What'd you do with my stake?

                    ANGEL
                    (looking around)
          I didn't touch your stake...

2 ANGLE: STEPHAN   2

He grabs a shovel. Grins.

Angel charges him and he WHACKS him in the head. Angel flies
back, lands hard as Buffy moves in --

-- Stephan swings at her but she gets inside it, raises her
arm and the shovel -- CRACK - splinters in half as it hits
her forearm. With the other arm she wrenches the half he's
holding out of his grasp and SHOVES it into his heart.

He turns to DUST.

Angel rises, rubbing his head.

                    BUFFY
          And what do you mean, "He's just a
          kid." Does that mean I'm just a kid
          too?

Angel starts to answer, then just shakes his head.

                    ANGEL
          Look, obviously I made a mistake
          coming here tonight...

Angel turns and starts away, going around the tree. Buffy
quickly starts after him, working to catch up.

                                                   CONTINUED

2 CONTINUED: 2

                         BUFFY
              Oh, no you don't. You can't just
              turn and walk away. It takes more
              then that to get rid of me...

And suddenly, BUFFY DROPS OUT OF FRAME.

3 ANGLE: LOOKING DOWN INTO AN OPEN GRAVE   3

Buffy lays in an open, silk-upholstered coffin at the bottom
of the six foot hole.

                         ANGEL (O.S.)
              You okay?

Buffy looks up at Angel, who crouches at the edge of the
grave above, looking down. She sits up slowly, stiffly.

                         BUFFY
              I wish people wouldn't leave open
              graves laying around like this.

She rises from the box, looking to Angel for a hand up and
out. But he's standing again, scanning the cemetery.

                         ANGEL
              So another vampire has risen tonight.

4 ANGLE ON: BUFFY STIL IN THE HOLE   4

At eye level with the ground around the open grave.

                         BUFFY
                      (soberly)
              I don't think so.
                      (creeped)
              Whoever was buried here didn't <u>rise</u>
              from this grave...

RACK FOCUS:

To two shallow depressions in the grass. We don't need to   *
know what they are -- Buffy does. She jumps out of the grave.   *

BUFFY'S POV - AT GROUND LEVEL

Tracking fast through the grass (and the depressions) to a   *
WHITE, FORMAL WOMAN'S SHOE, left behind. A hand enters frame,   *
picks up the shoe, takes us to Buffy: *

                                                    CONTINUED

                             BUFFY (cont'd)
... she was <u>dragged</u> from it.

                                      BLACK OUT

          END OF TEASER

ACT ONE

5 INT.   LIBRARY - DAY   5

     Buffy and XANDER enter. GILES, his back toward them, doesn't
     notice their entrance. He's busy TALKING TO AN EMPTY CHAIR.

                    GILES
          So, what I'm proposing... and I don't
          mean to appear indecorous... is a
          social engagement... a date, if you
          will. If you're amenable..
               (then, edgy)
          Idiot!

                    BUFFY
          Boy. I guess we just never realized
          how **much** you liked that chair.

                    GILES
               (turns, frustrated)
          Oh, I, uh, I was just working on--

                    BUFFY
          Your pick-up lines?

                    GILES
               (busted)
          In a manner of speaking, yes.

                    BUFFY
          Then, if you don't mind a little Gene
          and Roger, I would leave off the
          "idiot" part. Being called an idiot
          tends to take a person out of the
          dating mood.

                    XANDER
          Actually, it kind of turns me on.

                    BUFFY
               (to Xander)
          I fear you.
               (to Giles)
          I'd also avoid words like "amenable"
          and "indecorous." Speak English, not
          whatever they speak in...

                    GILES
          England?

                                                        CONTINUED

                         BUFFY
          Yeah. Just say, "Hey, I got a thing,
          you're maybe feeling a thing, and
          there could be a thing."

                         GILES
          Well, thank you, Cyrano.

                         BUFFY
          I'm not finished. Then you say, "How
          do you feel about Mexican?"

                         GILES
          About Mexicans?

                         BUFFY
          Mexican! Food. You take her for
          food. For which you then pay.

                         GILES
          Right.

                         XANDER
                 (to Giles, re: chair)
          So, this "chair" woman? We are
          talking Ms. Calendar, right?

                         GILES
          What makes you think that?

                         XANDER
          Simple deduction: Ms. Calendar is
          reasonably dollsome, especially for
          someone in your age bracket; she
          already knows you're a school
          librarian, so you don't have to worry
          about how to break that embarrassing
          news to her...

                         BUFFY
          And she's the only woman we've ever
          actually seen speaking to you. Add
          it all up, it spells "duh."

                         XANDER
          Now, is it time for us to talk about
          the facts of life?

                         GILES
          I am suddenly deciding that this is
          none of your business.

                                        CONTINUED

5 CONTINUED: (2)   5

                    XANDER
          'Cause that whole stork thing is a
          smokescreen...

Giles pointedly changes the subject.

                    GILES
          So, how did things go last night?
          Did Mr. Korshack show up on schedule?

                    BUFFY
          More or less. Angel and I took care
          of him.

                    XANDER
               (snorts)
          Angel.

                    BUFFY
          There's something else, though. I
          found an empty grave.

                    GILES
          Another vampire?

                    BUFFY
          No, no. It was dug up, and the body
          was taken out.

                    GILES
               (into it)
          Grave robbing. Well, that's new.
          Interesting.

                    BUFFY
          I know that you meant to say "gross
          and disturbing".

                    GILES
               (sheepish)
          Yes of course. Terrible thing. Must
          put a stop to it.
               (feebly adds)
          Dammit.

                    XANDER
          So why does someone rob graves?

                    GILES
          I'll collate some theories. Might
          help to know who the body belonged to.

                                          CONTINUED

5 CONTINUED: (3)   5

                          BUFFY
                Meredith Todd. Ring a bell?

Xander shakes his head.

                          BUFFY (cont'd)
                She died very recently. And she was
                our age.

                          XANDER
                Drawing a blank.

                          GILES
                Well, perhaps Willow can fire up the   *
                machine   *
                          (points at computer)   *
                and track Meredith down.   *

6 INT. SCHOOL LOUNGE - DAY   6

    A table is set up beneath a banner: "SCIENCE FAIR SIGN-UP."
    WILLOW is writing on one of the clipboards. She looks up to
    see:

7 ANGLE: A CAMERA   7

    Going off in her face. ERIC is an annoying, aggressive
    science nerd who right now is taking pictures of every pretty
    girl who passes by.

    He turns the lens on a passing senior, looking her up and
    down.

                          ERIC
                Look at those legs...

                          WILLOW
                No thank you.

                          CHRIS
                Eric, knock it off.

    Willow glances over at CHRIS EPPS, who picks up the clipboard
    next to her. He's shy and brainy, but he has a quiet
    authority.

    Chris glances up to see Willow watching him write. She
    reacts.

                          WILLOW
                Hey, Chris. I was just wondering
                what you're going to do this year.

                                                        CONTINUED

7 CONTINUED: 7

                         CHRIS
                    (smiles awkwardly)
          Why?

                         WILLOW
          Well, every year, you win and I place
          second. I just thought I'd see what
          I'm up against.

                         CHRIS
          You know what the key is? If Dr.
          Clark doesn't understand your
          experiment, he gives it higher marks
          so it looks like he understands your
          experiment.
                    (reads Willow's
                     clipboard)
          "Effects of Subviolet Light Spectrum
          Deprivation on the Development of
          Fruit Flies."
                    (smiles, friendly)
          That should do the trick.

CORDELIA steps up beside Willow, picks up a clipboard, starts
writing. She is not radiating sunshine.

                         CORDELIA
          Okay, I'm doing this under protest.
          It is not fair that they're making
          participation in the Science Fair
          mandatory this year. I don't think
          anyone should have to do anything
          educational at school if they don't
          want to.

                         WILLOW
                    (reading from
                     Cordelia's entry)
          "The Tomato: Fruit or Vegetable?"

                         CORDELIA
          I want something I can finish in a
          weekend, okay?

Just then, Eric appears and begins aggressively snapping
photos of Cordelia.

                         CORDELIA (cont'd)
          What do you think you're doing?!
          Stop it! We're under fluorescent
          lights, for god's sake!

Cordelia turns away.

                                                    CONTINUED

>   ERIC
>   Come on. The camera loves you.
>
>   CORDELIA
>   I thought yearbook nerds didn't come
>   out of hibernation till the spring.
>
>   ERIC
>   It's for my private collection.
>
>   CHRIS
>   Eric, will you quit it?

Buffy enters. Eric snaps her picture.

>   BUFFY
>   Coming through.
>   (then, to Willow)
>   Hey, Willow, sorry to interrupt,
>   but.. it's the Bat Signal.
>
>   WILLOW
>   Sure, okay.
>   (smiles to Chris)
>   See you, Chris. Thanks for the tip.

Chris smiles at Willow as she leaves with Buffy. Cordelia
lingers, but when she sees Eric's leer, she quickly follows.
Eric watches her go, with a malevolent grin.

>   ERIC
>   Cordelia is so fine. You know, she'd
>   be just perfect for us...
>
>   CHRIS
>   (sternly)
>   Don't be an idiot.
>   (turns away)
>   She's alive.

Chris crosses off, leaving Eric to continue watching Cordelia
walk away. Eric's creepy smile returns.

8 INT. LIBRARY - DAY   8

Willow settles in at the computer. Buffy et al. hover.

>   WILLOW
>   This shouldn't take long. I'm
>   probably the only girl in school who
>   has the Coroner's Office bookmarked
>   as a "favorite place."

                                                        CONTINUED

8 CONTINUED: 8

     Willow starts her web search as Cordelia enters.

                         CORDELIA
               Hi. Sorry to interrupt your little
               undead play group, but I need to ask
               Willow if she'll help me with my
               Science Fair project.

                         WILLOW
                    (not looking up)
               It's a fruit.

                         CORDELIA
               I would ask Chris for help, but...
                    (a little emotional)
               ... it would bring back too many
               memories of Daryl.

                         WILLOW
               I found it...

     The gang gathers around Willow at the computer screen,
     ignoring Cordelia.

                         WILLOW (cont'd)
               According to this, Meredith Todd died
               in a car accident last week.

                         CORDELIA
               Of course, I've learned to deal with
               my pain...

                         BUFFY
               And how was her neck?

                         WILLOW
               Fine... except for being broken.

                         CORDELIA
               Hello? Can we deal with my pain
               please?
                                                                    *

                                                                    *

                         XANDER
               There there.
                                                                    *
     Xander, without looking at Cordelia and without feeling, pats   *
     her shoulder.   *

                                                       CONTINUED

8 CONTINUED: (2)   8

                         WILLOW
          It says Meredith and two other girls
          in the car were killed instantly.
          They were all on the pep squad at
          Fondren High, on the way to a game.

                         BUFFY
          You know what this means...

                         XANDER
          That Fondren might actually beat
          Sunnydale in the cross-town body
          count competition this year?

                         BUFFY
          It means she wasn't killed by
          vampires. So somebody did dig up her   *
          corpse.

                         CORDELIA
          Eeuw. Why is it that every
          conversation you people have has the
          word "corpse" in it?

                         XANDER
          So, okay, we got us a body snatcher.
          What does that mean?

                         GILES
          Here's what I've come up with: demons
          who eat the flesh of the dead to   *
          absorb their souls.   *

                                                          *

                                                          *

                                                          *

                                            CONTINUED

8 CONTINUED: (3)   8

                    GILES (cont'd)
          Or it could be a voodoo   *
          practitioner--

                    WILLOW
          You mean, making a zombie?

                    GILES
          More likely, zombies. For most
          traditional purposes, a voodoo priest
          would need more than one.

                    BUFFY
          So we should see if the other girls
          from this accident are AWOL, too.
          Might help figure out what this creep
          has in mind if we know whether he's
          dealing in volume.

                    XANDER
          So we dig up some graves tonight?   *

                    WILLOW
          Oh boy, a field trip!   *
               (to Buffy)   *
          Are you gonna call Angel?   *

                    BUFFY
          I don't think so.

                    XANDER
          Yeah, why bother him?

                    BUFFY
          We've been sort of... never mind. As
          far as Angel knows, I'm taking the
          night off. Okay?

                    XANDER
          So, we're all set, then. Say
          nine-ish, B.Y.O. shovel.

                    WILLOW
          I'll pack some food. Who likes those
          little powdered donuts?

                                                    CONTINUED

8 CONTINUED: (4)   8

Xander raises his hand.   *

                    WILLOW (cont'd)
            Cordelia?

                    CORDELIA
            Darn, I have Cheerleader practice
            tonight. Boy, I wish I'd known you
            were gonna be digging up dead people
            sooner; I would have cancelled.

                    XANDER
            All right. But if you do run into
            the army of zombies, could you page
            us before they eat your flesh?

Trying not to be affected by that idea, Cordelia exits.

                    GILES
            Xander, Zombies don't eat the flesh
            of the living.

                    XANDER
            I know, but did you see her face?

9 ANGLE ON: THE LIBRARY'S COMPUTER SCREEN   9

With an article and NEWS PHOTO OF THE THREE DEAD GIRLS, all
smiles in their pep squad outfits. The caption below,
identifies them as Meredith Todd, Jane Atkins and **CATHY RYAN.**

                                        CUT TO:

10 EXT. CEMETERY - NIGHT   10

CLOSE ON: A HEADSTONE

With the name CATHY RYAN, her birth and death dates: she was
17.

11 WIDER ANGLE: CEMETERY - NIGHT   11

Buffy with her back to a tombstone next to Willow. Before
them, Xander and Giles wield shovels, already pretty deep
into the ground, and way grimed from the effort. As they
talk, Willow munches a little powdered donut.   *

                    BUFFY
            He was getting all jealous and he
            wouldn't even admit it.

                                                       CONTINUED

11 CONTINUED: 11

                         WILLOW
          Jealous of what?

                         BUFFY
          Of Xander.

                         WILLOW
          'Cause you did that sexy dance with
          him?

                         BUFFY
               (sheepishly)
          Am I ever gonna live that down?

                         WILLOW
               (blithely)
          Nope.

                         BUFFY
          Anyway, Angel's being totally
          irrational

                         WILLOW
          Love makes you do the wacky.

                         BUFFY
          That's the truth.

                         XANDER
               (sticks his head out)
          You know, this might go faster if you
          fems picked up a shovel, too.

                         BUFFY
          Sorry, but I'm an old-fashioned girl.
          I was raised to believe the men dig
          up the corpses and the women have
          the babies.
               (to Willow)
          Speaking of the wacky, what was
          Cordelia's whole riff about painful
          memories? Who's Daryl?

                         WILLOW
          Daryl Epps. Chris's older brother.
          He was a big football star. All-
          State two years ago. A running...
          someone that runs and catches.

                         BUFFY
          Was he a studly?

                                                      CONTINUED

                         WILLOW
          Big time. All the girls were crazy
          for him.

                         BUFFY
          And he broke Cordy's heart? Thus
          possibly proving its existence...

                         WILLOW
          He died. Rock climbing, or
          something. He fell.

                         BUFFY
          Oh, man. That's lousy. Poor Chris.

                         WILLOW
               (nodding)
          He really looked up to his brother.
          It was tough. Ever since then he's
          been... real quiet. Kind of in his
          own world. And I hear his mother
          doesn't even leave the house anymore.

THUNK.

                         GILES
          I think we're there.

Buffy and Willow peer over the edge of the open grave as
Giles and Xander quickly clear the top of the coffin.

                         WILLOW
          By the way, are we hoping to find a
          body, or no body?

                         XANDER
          Call me an optimist, but I'm hoping
          to find a fortune in gold doubloons.

                         BUFFY
          Well, "body" could mean flesh eating
          demon or corpse-mutilating pagan
          ritual. "No body" points more toward
          the army of zombies thing. Take your
          pick.

Everyone looks on in anticipation as Giles and Xander each
wait for the other to do the honors.

                         GILES
          Go ahead.

                                        CONTINUED

11   CONTINUED: (3)   11

                         XANDER
                You're closer.

                         BUFFY
                Pathetic much?

Buffy agilely drops down, takes a deep breath and reaches for   *
the latch that will open the top half of the hinged coffin
lid.

12   BLACK, INSIDE THE COFFIN.   12

As the lid is opened and WE LOOK up at our quartet, who look
back at us.

                                        CUT TO:

13   EXT. SCHOOL PARKING LOT - NIGHT   13

Cordelia and TWO OTHER CHEERLEADERS in full uniform talk as
they cross the school student parking lot after practice.

                         CORDELIA
                Guys, if we don't have it down by
                tomorrow then no one will be led by
                our cheers. Practice.

The other cheerleaders get in their car and drive off,
leaving Cordelia to cross to her car several yards away.

She feels like someone's watching. She stops, scans the lot.

                         CORDELIA (cont'd)
                Hello?

No answer. She digs her keys from her purse as she quickens
her pace to her car. She looks around again. No one.

She puts the key in the lock, then hears a WHOOSH sound.

                         CORDELIA (cont'd)
                Xander Harris, if this is your idea
                of a joke...

Another SOUND. Closer.

Cordelia juggles her keychain, fumbles it to the ground. The
keys glance off her shoe and skitter under the car.

Cordelia, at maximum wig now, crouches to try to retrieve her
keys. But as she looks beneath the car, she sees--

                                                  CONTINUED

13 CONTINUED: 13

FEET, two, standing right on the other side of her car.

Cordelia freaks, leaves her keys and takes off running, away
from the car, toward the nearest school building.

We see the FORM of SOMEONE coming around the car after her.

14 EXT. SCHOOL/AROUND THE CORNER - NIGHT   14

An alleyway formed by the wall of a separate building and the
main school building. It's deserted, save for a couple of
FOOTBALL BLOCKING SLEDS and orange DRIVER'S ED. CONES stored
there beside a GARBAGE DUMPSTER.

A SHADOW, Cordelia's pursuer, drifts slowly past the objects,
pausing for only a moment before moving along.

Then, all is quiet.

15 CLOSER ON: THE DUMPSTER   15

As Cordelia slowly, tentatively sticks her head up and looks
left, then right into the eyes of--

ANGEL

Cordelia screams, falls back. Angel smiles.

                    ANGEL
          Cordelia. This is the last place I
          expected you to hang out.

                    CORDELIA
                  (recovering, slowly)
          Oh, god... oh, god, it's you. Why
          were you following me?

                    ANGEL
          I wasn't sure it was you at first.
          I'm looking for Buffy.

                    CORDELIA
          Buffy? Well, she's -- big shock --
          at the graveyard.

                    ANGEL
          She said she'd be home.

                    CORDELIA
          Oh, she lied. Isn't she a rascal?

Angel reacts, affected by this, betrayed.

                                                        CONTINUED

15 CONTINUED: 15

                        CORDELIA (cont'd)
              But, luck is on your side, it just so
              happens my night's free...

Cordelia holds out her hand. Angel, somewhat reluctantly,   *
takes it, to help her climb out. The back of her dress gets   *
stuck on something.   *

                        CORDELIA (cont'd)   *
              Hold on, my dress is caught...   *

She reaches behind her, pulls something loose.   *

                        CORDELIA (cont'd)   *
              There, that's...   *

Cordelia sees what she just pulled loose behind her: a **human**   *
hand, severed a ways below the wrist. Cordelia holds it at   *
the wrist. Cordelia screams.   *

                        BLACK OUT.

                   END OF ACT ONE

ACT TWO

16 INT. LIBRARY - (SAME) NIGHT   16

WE HEAR VOICES approaching from the hallway. The doors open
as Buffy, Willow, Xander and Giles return from the cemetery.

                    XANDER
          So, both coffins empty, that makes
          three girls signed up for the army of
          zombies.

                    WILLOW
          Is it an army if you just have three?

                    BUFFY
          Well, Zombie drill team then --

                    ANGEL'S VOICE (O.S.)
          You're back...

Angel steps from the shadows, Cordelia clinging to him with
a hermetic seal, her head buried in his chest. Buffy reacts.

                    BUFFY
          Angel...?

She stops, standing right by Xander, a fact not lost on Angel.

                    ANGEL
               (greeting him)
          Xander.

                    XANDER
               (equally enthused)
          Angel.

                    ANGEL
               (to Buffy)
          I thought you were taking the night
          off.

                    BUFFY
          I was... going to. But, at the last
          minute--

                    ANGEL
          Cordelia told me the truth.

                    XANDER
          That's gotta be a first.

                                        CONTINUED

16 CONTINUED: 16

                          BUFFY   *
              We were investigating... somebody's   *
              been stealing the bodies of dead   *
              girls.   *

                          ANGEL
              I know. We found some of them.

                          BUFFY
              You mean like two of the three?   *

                          ANGEL
              I mean, like some of them. Like
              parts.

                          CORDELIA
                    (finally looking up)
              It was horrible. Angel saved me from
              an arm.

Another look between Angel and Buffy.

                          CORDELIA (cont'd)
              God, there were parts everywhere.
              Why do these terrible things always
              happen to me?

                          XANDER
                    (coughing the word in
                     to his fist)
              Karma!

                          WILLOW
              Well, so much for the zombie theory.

                          GILES
              So much for all our theories.

                          BUFFY
              I don't get it. Why dig up three   *
              bodies, just to chop them up and   *
              throw them away again?   *

                          ANGEL
              What I saw didn't add up to three
              whole girls. I think they kept some
              parts.

                                                 CONTINUED

16 CONTINUED: (2)   16

                    BUFFY
          Could this get yuckier?

                    WILLOW
          They probably kept the other parts to
          eat.

                    BUFFY
          Question answered.

                    GILES
          But why dispose of the remains here   *
          at the school?   *

                    BUFFY
          Maybe whoever did it had other
          business in the neighborhood. Like,
          say... classes.

                                                       *

                                                       *

                    ANGEL
          This was no hatchet job. Whoever
          made those incisions really knew what
          they were doing.

                    GILES
          Yes, what student here would be that
          well-versed in physiology?

                    WILLOW
          I can think of maybe five or six guys
          in the science club.   *

                                                       *

                    BUFFY
          Why don't you get their locker   *
          numbers, and we'll check 'em out.   *

                                          CONTINUED

16 CONTINUED: (3)   16

                        CORDELIA
                      (pitifully)
               No, I want to go home now. I have to
               bathe and burn my clothes.

                        XANDER
               Everybody wave bye-bye.

                        CORDELIA
               I don't want to go alone. I'm still
               fragile.
                      (to Angel)
               Can you take me?

                        ANGEL
               I...

Angel turns toward Buffy. She looks away. Cordelia quickly
wraps an arm around Angel.

                        CORDELIA
               Great! I'll drive.

With a look back, Angel is dragged from the library by
Cordelia.

                        XANDER
               How about that? I always pegged him
               as a "one woman" vampire.

                        WILLOW
               Xander!

Willow nudges Xander, gestures toward Buffy.

But Buffy is staring at the library door. She hasn't heard
a word said since the doors closed behind Angel.

17 INT. CHRIS'S LIVING ROOM - NIGHT   17   *

CHRIS'S MOM, in a loose floral house dress, sits in a worn
arm chair. A cigarette, burning a quarter inch into the
filter, hangs from her lips. Her empty gaze is fixed on a
television set OFF CAMERA. The house is unkempt, dark and
depressing.

Chris enters from downstairs, carefully shutting the cellar
door behind him. On the door we see a sign that says: NO
TRESPASSING - KEEP OUT! (Typical of a teenager, it's
cluttered with other signs as well, and stickers and whatnot.)

                        CHRIS
               I'm going out, mom.

                                                    CONTINUED

17 CONTINUED: 17

Chris's Mom doesn't react, doesn't even acknowledge him.

                          CHRIS (cont'd)
               I'll be back later, okay? Mom...?   *

Still nothing but cigarette smoke from Chris's Mom. After a
beat, Chris finally goes, leaving his Mom in her smoking
world.

18 ANGLE: THE TV   18

We see a home vid of a football game -- a victorious Daryl
Epps running up to the camera, smiling.

19 INT. HALL - NIGHT   19

Willow and Xander are opening lockers using info from copies
of a computer print-out. Giles sort of hovers behind them.

                          GILES
                       (officious)
               I hope you understand that as a
               school official, I can not condone
               this unauthorized search.

                          BUFFY
               Okay, your butt's covered. You want
               to grab a locker?

                          GILES
               Yes of course.

Giles takes a sheet from Buffy and crosses to a locker. Buffy
crosses to Eric's, saying:

                          BUFFY
               Okay, Eric, let's see what's on your
               mind.

Willow opens a locker. It's full of magazines.

                          WILLOW
               Nothing but back issues of
               "Scientific American."
                       (lights up)
               Ooh, I haven't read this one.

                          GILES
               Nothing remarkable here...

                                                     CONTINUED

19 CONTINUED: 19

                        XANDER (O.S.)
              Guys...

Giles and Willow cross to Xander.

                        XANDER
              Your friend, Chris Epps' locker.

He opens the door wider, revealing a stack of books inside.

                        WILLOW   *
              "Gray's Anatomy", "Mortician's Desk   *
              Reference", "Robicheaux's Guide to   *
              Muscles and Tendons".   *

MOVE DOWN THE BOOKS' SPINES, with titles like "Gray's
Anatomy", "Mortician's Desk Reference", "Robicheaux's Guide
to Muscles and Tendons", etc.

Giles reaches in, pulls out a folded section of the local
newspaper, open to the story and NEWS PHOTO OF THE THREE DEAD
PEP SQUAD GIRLS we saw on Willow's computer screen before.

                        GILES
              Fair to say, Chris is involved.

                        XANDER
              He's into corpses, all right, but we
              still don't know why.

                        BUFFY
              Yes we do.

She is staring at Eric's locker. Taped inside that locker
door--

THE PICTURE OF A WOMAN

Actually, it's a COLLAGE, with various facial features and
body parts torn from different MODELS in magazine ads and
pasted together to form a grotesque image of an "ideal" woman.

                              DISSOLVE TO:

20 INT. LAB (OLD SCIENCE BUILDING) - NIGHT   20

21 ANGLE: BIRD'S EYE VIEW OF AN OPERATING TABLE   21

There is a body clearly defined under the sheet on this
table, (framed to match the size and angle of the locker
collage).

                                                    CONTINUED

21 CONTINUED: 21

Walking around the table is Chris. He lifts part of the
sheet, hooks an electrode to a foot.

22 ANGLE: ERIC   22

Emerges from a small darkroom off the lab, a few still-dripping photos in his hands. He is singing to himself:

> ERIC
> (sings)
> I GUESS, YOU'D SAY, WHAT CAN MAKE ME   *
> FEEL THIS WAY. MY GIRL...   *
> (to Chris)
> How's my baby?

> CHRIS
> She's not your baby.

> ERIC
> She's not gonna be anyone's baby if
> we don't finish her soon.

> CHRIS
> I'm working on it.

> ERIC
> So am I, friend. So am I.

As he says this he hangs the photos on a line with some others. They are all photos of Sunnydale girls, including Buffy, Willow and Cordelia.

He goes back into the dark room, passing the body and for the first time we see up close:

23 HER LEG   23

Which has clearly been sewn together.

                                           CUT TO:

24 A DREAM GIRL   24

That is, a fantastic looking SENIOR GIRL as she walks across--

25 EXT. QUAD - THE NEXT MORNING   25

A TRIO of GEEKISH GUYS worshipfully watch her every step.

ANGLE ON: XANDER AND WILLOW

As they sit together on the front steps of the school. Buffy joins them, watching the geek trio watching the dream girl.

> XANDER
> Any sign of our suspects?

> BUFFY
> Not yet.

She sits, still looking at the people around her.

> BUFFY (cont'd)
> I don't get it, why would anyone want
> to make a girl?

> XANDER
> You mean, when there's so many pre-
> made ones just lying around?
>   (shrugs)
> The things we do for love...

> BUFFY
> Love has nothing to do with this.

> XANDER
> Maybe not, but I'll tell you this:
> People don't fall in love with
> what's right in front of them. People
> want the dream. What they can't
> have. The more unattainable, the
> more attractive.

Buffy reacts. This notion strikes a chord -- actually with
all three of them.

> WILLOW
> And for Eric the unattainable would
> include everyone. That's alive.

> BUFFY
> Eric's sick enough to do something
> like this, but what's up with Chris?
> He seems like a human person.

> WILLOW
> I don't know. The thing with his
> brother was really hard on him. He
> talked a lot about death. Maybe he
> just wants to get one up on it.

> BUFFY
>   (hesitantly)
> But, it's not... doable, is it? I
> mean, making someone from scraps?
> Actually making them live?

> WILLOW
> If it is, my science project's
> definitely coming in second this year.

CONTINUED

25 CONTINUED: (2)   25

> Giles emerges from the school. He scans the ARRIVING CROWD, not noticing Buffy and company.

> > XANDER
> > And speaking of love...

> > WILLOW
> > We were talking about the reanimation
> > of dead tissue.

> > XANDER
> > Do I deconstruct your segues? Yeesh.

> > BUFFY
> > Hey, Giles.

> > GILES
> > Oh. Yes. Hello.

> > BUFFY
> > Still no sign of our mad doctors.

> > GILES
> > What? Oh. Corpses. Evil. Very
> > good.

> Buffy turns, sees what Giles sees. MS. CALENDAR is coming.

> > BUFFY
> > Okay, Giles, just remember. "I'm
> > feeling a thing, you're feeling a
> > thing." But personalize it.

> > GILES
> > (nervously)
> > Personalize it?

> > BUFFY
> > She's a techno-pagan, right? Ask her   *
> > to bless your laptop or something.
> > (to the others)
> > Come on, guys.

> She nudges the other two and they take off. Giles turns as the trio disappears into the school.

> > GILES
> > No! Don't leave me! Oh, dear.

> And Ms. Calendar is there, passing Giles on her way inside.

                                                      CONTINUED

                         MS. CALENDAR
              Good morning, Rupert.

                         GILES
                    (nods, nervously)
              Ms. Calendar.

                         MS. CALENDAR
                    (stops, turns back)
              Please, call me Jennie. "Ms."
              Calendar is my father.

                         GILES   *
              Jenny, then.   *

     They head:

A26 INT. SCHOOL CORRIDOR - DAY   A26

                         GILES
              You know, uh, Jenny, I don't mean to   *
              appear indecorous... no, not
              indecorous...

                         MS. CALENDAR
                    (smiles expectantly)
              Yeah...?

                         GILES
              Oh, dear... I, uh... that is...

                         MS. CALENDAR
                    (a beat, then)
              Rupert, look, I have to get inside to
              set up the computer lab...

                         GILES
              Well, what I am proposing is...

     The SCHOOL BELL RINGS, and PEOPLE start moving inside.

                         MS. CALENDAR
              Sorry, but I really have to go.

     Giles nods and Ms. Calendar turns and crosses to the door.

                         GILES
                    (to himself)
              Idiot...

     Giles is startled as Ms. Calendar reappears beside him.

                                                  CONTINUED

A26 CONTINUED: A26

                     MS. CALENDAR
              Listen, if it's important, why don't
              you just tell me at the game?

                     GILES
              You're going to the football game?

                                             CONTINUED

BUFFY THE VAMPIRE SLAYER "Some Assembly Required"(Pink)7/15/97   31.

A26   CONTINUED: (2)   A26

                        MS. CALENDAR
              You seem surprised.

                        GILES
              I guess I just assumed you spent your
              evenings downloading incantations...
              casting bones.

                        MS. CALENDAR
              On game night? Are you nuts? I
              assume you're going, too.

                        GILES
              Oh, uh, of course.

                        MS. CALENDAR
              So, why don't we just go together?
              I could pick you up after school, we
              could get something to eat on the
              way, if you like. How do you feel
              about Mexican?

              Giles can manage no better than a twitchy nod.

                        MS. CALENDAR (cont'd)
              And whatever it is you want to tell
              me, you can tell me then. Okay?

                        GILES
              Okay... tonight, then.

              Ms. Calendar smiles, then drifts inside. Giles lingers a
              beat, before a self-satisfied smile crosses his face.

                        GILES (cont'd)
              That went well. I think.

26   INT. SCIENCE CLASSROOM - AFTERNOON   26

     Xander is playing with a visible head as Willow pores over
     volumes.

                        WILLOW
              I still don't get how Chris could do
              it. Arresting the cell deterioration
              is one thing, but...

     Xander makes the head talk.

                        XANDER
              Hello... I want to get ahead!

                                                          CONTINUED

26 CONTINUED: 26

                              WILLOW
                    Maybe an electrical current combined
                    with an adrenaline boost...

                              XANDER
                         (as the head)
                    For the love of God, somebody scratch
                    my nose!

Buffy enters, all business.

                              BUFFY
                    Well, it's official. Chris and Eric
                    didn't come to school today.

                              XANDER
                    That's not a coincidence.

                              WILLOW
                    Maybe they finished their project.

                              BUFFY
                    God, what if it worked, what if that
                    poor girl is walking around...

                              XANDER
                    Uh, poor **girls**, technically.

                              BUFFY
                    What could she be thinking?   *

                              WILLOW
                    And what are they... going to do with
                    her?

                              GILES
                    I don't think we have to worry about
                    that just yet.

All turn as he enters.

                              GILES (cont'd)
                    I contacted the police this morning
                    about the remains. They've just
                    finished sorting through them.
                    Apparently, there were three heads in
                    the dumpster.

                                                          CONTINUED

BUFFY THE VAMPIRE SLAYER "Some Assembly Required"(Pink)7/15/97   32A*.

26 CONTINUED: (2)   26

                    BUFFY
          And they only had three girls.

                    WILLOW
          So they don't have the whole, uh,
          package.

                    XANDER   *
          Heads must be no good. Hmmmm, they   *
          seemed attractive enough to me...   *
                    (off their looks,   *
                     with some pride)   *
          ...obviously I'm not as sick as Chris   *
          and Eric.   *

                                        CONTINUED

26 CONTINUED: (3)   26

                         GILES
              Based on what the police put
              together, they're one step away from
              completing their masterpiece.

                         WILLOW   *
              One step...

         As the four of them contemplate this, the camera ARMS DOWN,
         the visible head filling the frame.

27 ANGLE: THE DOOR TO CHRIS'S BASEMENT   27

         We track slowly in at the sign that says: NO TRESPASSING -
         KEEP OUT! (A.D.'s beware, Chris' mom may be in the shot.)   *

                         ERIC (V.O.)
              We're running out of time!

28 INT. STORAGE ROOM/BASEMENT - DAY   20

         Chris and Eric are in a dark, cramped, cluttered room filled
         with dust-covered pieces of furniture, boxes, etc. The room
         is lit only by a single bare light bulb and a shaft of light
         angling down from a small clerestory window above.

                         ERIC
              If we wait too long, the onset of
              atrophy in the limbs will be
              irreversible.

                         CHRIS
              We can turn up the current. That'll
              buy us a day at least.

                         ERIC
              We'll lose the entire body if we
              don't attach the head soon!

                         CHRIS
              We have time!

                         ERIC
              We don't! The crash with the girls
              was lucky. But we can't keep waiting
              for another lucky accident to just
              drop a head in our laps. You know
              what we have to do! Hell, it's just
              one lousy girl!

                                                      CONTINUED

                         CHRIS
            I won't do it... I can't
                    (softer, cracking)
            I can't... kill anyone.

Chris turns toward a DARK, SHADOWY RECESS of the storage room
behind them.

                         CHRIS (cont'd)
                    (to the shadows)
            Please understand. I can't do that.
            Please don't make me.

                         VOICE FROM THE SHADOWS
                    (low, eerie)
            But, you gave me your word... you
            promised me, little brother...

THE VOICE slowly steps forward from the shadows.

This big, hulking THING has ONE GREEN EYE AND ONE BROWN EYE.
His face - all of him that we can see - has been stitched
together. The guy's a walking jig-saw puzzle.

Meet DARYL EPPS.

                         DARYL (cont'd)
            ...that I wouldn't be alone.

                                        BLACK OUT.

                    END OF ACT TWO

ACT THREE

29   INT. STORAGE ROOM/BASEMENT - CONTINUOUS - DAY   29

Daryl paces around the cluttered room like a caged animal.
Chris leans against a wall, a bit intimidated. Eric watches
Daryl with the pride of a parent watching his offspring.

                    ERIC
          The body is perfect. And if we
          harvest a head tonight, she'll be
          ready by sunrise.

Daryl goes to Chris, crouches down to his brother's eye level.

                    DARYL
          When you brought me back, you
          promised you'd take care of me. I
          need this, Chris. I need someone.

                    CHRIS
          Please don't ask me to do this.
          Don't ask me to take a life.

                    ERIC
          I tried to tell him, if you take a
          life to make a new life, the whole
          thing's a wash. No harm, no foul.

                    CHRIS
          Maybe you could... you could go out,
          let people know --

                    DARYL
          No! Can't see me.

His fury is sudden -- and suddenly gone. He approaches his
brother.

                    DARYL (cont'd)
          Chris, you've always been smarter
          than me. You were the brains.
          You're the only one who can do this
          for me.

Chris stares at him, uncertain. Daryl begins an old chant,
one that sounds odd and forlorn down here:

                    DARYL (cont'd)
          Third and long, seconds to go, where
          do you throw, where do you throw...

                                              CONTINUED

29 CONTINUED: 29

                         CHRIS
                       (quietly)
           Number five, Daryl's gonna drive.   *

                         DARYL
           Help me, brother.

Chris nods silent acquiescence.

                         DARYL (cont'd)
           Thank you.

Daryl gently kisses the top of Chris's head, then turns to
Eric.

                         DARYL (cont'd)
           Show me!

Eric takes his girl pix from his backpack, fans them out on
a chest of drawers as Daryl starts leafing through them. As
Eric smiles a malignant smile back toward the still bowed
Chris, Daryl selects one of the photos and hands it to Eric.

                         DARYL (cont'd)
           This one.

                         ERIC
                       (smiles at photo)
           A man of taste.

Eric uses scissors to begin cutting the chosen photo <u>of
Cordelia</u>.

30 OMITTED   30

                         ERIC (O.S.)
                       (sings)
           TALKIN' 'BOUT MY GIRL.   *
                                                                      *

31 INT. LIBRARY - (THAT) AFTERNOON - DAY   31

    Willow is at the computer. Buffy paces, impatient.

                                                    CONTINUED

BUFFY THE VAMPIRE SLAYER "Some Assembly Required"(Pink)7/15/97   37.

31 CONTINUED: 31

                    WILLOW
          Well, I've checked the obits.
          Nothing that would make for a likely
          candidate.

                    XANDER
          They're kinda picky for guys who had   *
          three heads to begin with.   *

                    WILLOW
          Formaldahyde.

                    XANDER
          Come again?

                    GILES
          Yes of course. It accelerates neural
          decay in the brain cells.

                    WILLOW
          A couple days and they're useless
          They're gonna need something really
          fresh.

                    BUFFY
               (quietly alarmed)
          How fresh?

                    WILLOW
          As fresh as possible...
               (gets it)
          Buffy, you don't think they'd...

                    BUFFY
          I think anyone who cuts dead girls
          into pieces does not get the benefit
          of any doubt. Let's end this thing.

                    GILES
          Seconded.

                    BUFFY
               (to Xander and Willow)
          You two head to Eric's. I'll try
          Chris's. We can meet back here.

                    GILES
          I'm supposed to be at the, uh, the
          big game, I believe it's called.

                    BUFFY
          You go ahead. We can handle this.

                                        CONTINUED

31 CONTINUED: (2)   31

                         GILES
          Well, I really should --

                         BUFFY
          Okay, we'll meet up there. Report
          back.

                         GILES
          All right.

The kids start to leave.

                         WILLOW
          Buffy, don't be too hard on Chris.
          I mean, he's not a vampire...

                         BUFFY
          No. He's just a ghoul.

                                        CUT TO:

32 INT. CHRIS'S HOUSE - AFTERNOON   32

As CHRIS'S MOM, with housedress and ever-present cigarette,
stands inside the door. She is looking at:

                         BUFFY (O.S.)
          I'm a friend of Chris's. Is he home?

Without a word, she turns, waddles away. Buffy steps inside
and tentatively looks about her.

Buffy sees a small, musty room where Chris's mom has already
settled back into her well-worn armchair two feet in front of
the television screen, Buffy all but forgotten.

The walls of the room are papered with photos of Daryl in his
football uniform, articles about Daryl's triumphs clipped
from the sports page, Daryl's framed letter sweaters, etc.

Buffy looks around, takes it all in: Daryl Epps was a good-
looking kid who apparently had a full and active life.

And this room is his SHRINE.

                         BUFFY
                    (a beat, then)
          So... is Chris home?

                                             CONTINUED

32 CONTINUED: 32

                    CHRIS'S MOM
                (points to TV screen)
        Westbury game. November 17, 95.   *
        Daryl rushed 185 yards that night -   *
        four TDs. He was MVP and made All   *
        City that season--.   *

Buffy looks at the TV. An amateur videotape of a high school
football game plays on screen. A stack of videotapes labeled
with dates and names of opponents sits atop the set.

                    BUFFY
                (a bit wigged)
        Yea, that was a great one... but is
        Chris home?

                    CHRIS'S MOM
        I don't know... is today a school day?
                (leans toward
                 screen/intense)   *
        Watch - watch this move. Daryl takes   *
        the kick off, sheds one - two - three   *
        defenders! He breaks into the open   *
        field for a 95 yard touch down.   *
                (matter-of-fact)
        He would have been nineteen next
        week, you know.

Buffy looks down at Chris's Mom, who has never taken her eyes
off the television screen or taken the cigarette from her
lips. After a beat, Buffy starts to back out of the room.

(NOTE: HEATING GRATE OMITTED)

Buffy looks about her, going to head further into the house
when she sees the sign:

33 NO TRESPASSING - KEEP OUT!   33

One last look to make sure Mom is oblivious, and she opens
the door.

34 INT. BASEMENT/DARYL'S LAIR - SAME TIME - DAY   34

Dark, deserted looking. Buffy comes down the steps slowly.

                                                            CONTINUED

34 CONTINUED: 34

She scans the room, spots Eric's GIRL PHOTOS atop the chest
of drawers. She picks them up, starts looking through them.   *
One of the photos has the head cut off. Then she sees: *

A35 A MEDICAL DRAWING   A35   *

Chris's work: it's of a woman's body, with muscles, joints ,   *
all kinds of equations and science type stuff (English major   *
much?) scribbled all over it. And pasted over the head is the   *
photo of CORDELIA.   *

BEHIND HER, (right behind her if possible) Daryl emerges from   *
the blackness. Buffy doesn't see him, intent upon the drawing: *

                    BUFFY
                (under her breath)
            Cordelia...   *

Daryl is about to grab her when he HEARS a CREAKING   *
FLOORBOARD upstairs. Footsteps approaching. Daryl backs into   *
the blackness from whence he came. Buffy looks up towards the   *
cellar door then leaps, spins off an overhead water pipe and   *
zips out an open clerestory window.   *

Hold the darkness, finding for a moment Daryl's tortured face   *
in it.   *

35 INT. CHEERLEADING PREP ROOM AT THE STADIUM - NIGHT   35

The two cheerleaders we saw the night before in the parking
lot with Cordelia are dressed and ready. Cordelia is doing
last minute touch-ups at one of the make-up mirrors.

                    FIRST CHEERLEADER
            Cordelia, you coming?

                    CORDELIA
            I'll be right out.

The cheerleaders exit, leaving Cordelia alone. She looks in
the mirror, then glances down to her make-up tray. When she
looks back up into the mirror again, she sees--

CHRIS

--standing slumped back by the lockers behind her. She
jumps, then recognizes him.

                    CORDELIA (cont'd)
            Oh, Chris! Hi. God, you scared me.
                (concerned)
            What are you doing in here?

                                                        CONTINUED

35 CONTINUED: 35

    Chris winces, turns his head as if to avoid seeing something.

                    CORDELIA (cont'd)
      Is something wrong...?

                                              CONTINUED

35 CONTINUED: (2)   35

     THE CLOTH SACK that SLAMS down over Cordelia's head seems to
     come out of nowhere.

36 INT. HALL BY PREP ROOM - SAME TIME - NIGHT   36

     The two cheerleaders head towards double doors, through which
     we can hear the cheering of a good-sized crowd.

     Buffy runs up to them.

                         BUFFY
                    (with urgency)
               Joy, Lisa, where's Cordelia?

                         FIRST CHEERLEADER
                    (haughty)
               Cordelia's got a game to think about.
               She doesn't need losers like you --

     Buffy slaps a hand against the wall on either side of the
     first cheerleader's head, pinning the wide-eyed girl.

                         BUFFY
                    (sweetly)
               I'm sorry... where, did you say?

37 INT. CHEERLEADING PREP ROOM - MOMENTS LATER - NIGHT   37

     The door collapses as Buffy charges into the room. Eric
     looks up from tying up the struggling Cordelia on the floor.

     Buffy leaps, heel kicks Eric off her, against a wall. In no
     mood to fight, he beats a quick retreat out a back door.

     Buffy turns back, quickly removes the cloth sack hood from a
     nearly hysterical Cordelia.

                         BUFFY
               It's okay, you're okay. He's gone.

                         CORDELIA
               Oh, my god, Buffy...!

                         BUFFY
               He's gone. What happened?

                         CORDELIA
               I don't know. I was just about to go
               to the field when Chris came in, and
               then somebody just jumped me.

                                                          CONTINUED

37 CONTINUED: 37

            Buffy quickly looks around the room. No sign of anyone here.

                              BUFFY
                    Well, it's okay now. You're fine.
                    Just relax, take your time...   *

            Cordelia rises, works to compose herself. It looks like this
            could take awhile. But the sound of the--

            MARCHING BAND

            --playing the SUNNYDALE FIGHT SONG out on the field drifts
            into the room, instantly perking Cordelia.

                              CORDELIA
                    Oh, my god! That's the fight song.
                    It's time for the cheerleader pyramid
                    at mid-field. I have to go.

                              BUFFY
                    You sure you're okay to go out there?

                              CORDELIA
                         (sense of duty)
                    You don't understand, I have to go.
                    I'm the apex.

            A re-energized Cordelia grabs her pompoms and springs out of
            the room, leaving Buffy alone. After a beat--

                              BUFFY
                         (calls out)
                    I know what you're trying to do,
                    Chris... you and Eric...

            A beat. Nothing.

                              BUFFY (cont'd)
                    I know about the bodies from the
                    cemetery. But you haven't hurt anyone   *
                    yet, you can still do the right   *
                    thing...   *

            Finally, Chris steps from behind the row of lockers.

            Buffy sees him. He looks so small at the moment. So
            tortured. He doesn't make eye contact with Buffy.

                                                        CONTINUED

37 CONTINUED: (2)   37

                    BUFFY (cont'd)
          Listen, I don't know what it's like
          to lose someone close to you like
          your brother, but I know what you're   *
          trying to do is wrong.

                    CHRIS
          I have to do it for him... He needs
          someone...

                    BUFFY
          Who, Eric? He needs industrial
          strength therapy.

                    CHRIS
          He always looked out for me... stood
          up for me... he's all alone...
          everybody loved him and now he's all
          alone...

                    BUFFY
          Who are you --

She stops.

                    BUFFY (cont'd)
          Oh my God.

                                        CUT TO:

38 INT. BASEMENT/DARYL'S LAIR - SHORT TIME LATER - NIGHT   38

CRASH!

A raging Daryl is trashing the place, smashing heavy objects
into other heavy objects as Eric stands back, staying out of
harm's way.

                    DARYL
                 (raging)
          He promised me! Promised!
                 (smash)
          I wouldn't have to be alone!

                    ERIC
                 (tentatively)
          It's not too late...

A seething Daryl turns on Eric, lifts him by the collar and
massively slams him against the wall, holding him there.

                                        CONTINUED

                         ERIC (cont'd)
                      (a glimpse of fear)
            Nothing's changed. We can still do
            this. You and me.

Daryl breathes heavily as he doesn't loosen his grip on Eric.
It's touch and go whether Eric will survive.

                         ERIC (cont'd)
            Your brother's not the only one who
            can create life... what do you say...?

Then, the fear in Eric's eyes slowly turns in something
darker... a creepy enthusiasm. Daryl lets him go.

                         ERIC (cont'd)
            Let's go scare you up a date.

                                        BLACK OUT.

                 END OF ACT THREE

ACT FOUR

39 INT. BASEMENT/DARYL'S LAIR - SAME TIME - NIGHT   39

The basement is totally trashed now. Buffy bolts down the   *
stairs, followed by Chris.

                    BUFFY
          Daryl...? Daryl!

Buffy slowly checks through the wreckage, lifting smashed
furniture as Chris, in borderline shock, shadows her.

                    BUFFY (cont'd)
          Okay, he's not here. Where else
          could he be?

                    CHRIS
          But he would never go out... Unless...

                    BUFFY
          He's gonna pick up where you left off.

                              CUT TO:

40 CLOSE ON: CORDELIA   40

Leading cheers on the sideline at the football field.

41 EXT. STADIUM BLEACHERS - SAME TIME - NIGHT   41

With Giles and Ms. Calendar amongst the fans.

                    MS. CALENDAR
          I don't know what it is about
          football that does it for me. It
          lacks the grace of basketball and the
          poetry of baseball. At its best,
          it's unadorned aggression. It's just
          such a rugged contest...

                    GILES
               (amused)
          Rugged? American football?

                    MS. CALENDAR
          What's funny about that?

                                        CONTINUED

41 CONTINUED: 41

                         GILES
              Well, I do find it odd that a nation
              that prides itself on its virility
              feels compelled to strap on forty
              pounds of protective gear just to
              play rugby.

                         MS. CALENDAR
                    (surprised)
              Is this your normal strategy for a
              first date: dissing my country's
              national pastime?

                         GILES
                    (a beat, then)
              Did you say... "date"?

                         MS. CALENDAR
                    (smiles)
              You noticed that, huh?

But before the silly, schoolboy grin has a chance to spread
all the way across Giles' face--

                         WILLOW (O.S.)
              Hi, Ms. Calendar. Hey, Giles.

Hey, look. Willow and Xander have joined us!

                         MS. CALENDAR
              Hi, guys. What's up?

                         WILLOW
              Buffy get back yet?

                         GILES
              No.
                    (hinting)
              But perhaps you should circulate down
              nearer the field to find her.

                         WILLOW
              Eric's was a bust. Nothing there.

                         XANDER
                    (looks around)
              Yeah, nothing but a lot of computer
              equipment and a pornography
              collection so prodigious it even
              scared me.

And, to Giles' chagrin, Xander and Willow settle in for the
duration. It's become a date with children.

                                                    CONTINUED

41 CONTINUED: (2)   41

                        XANDER (cont'd)
               So... what's the score?

42 STRANGE NEW ANGLE ON: THE FOOTBALL FIELD - NIGHT   42

    At ground level. The SOUNDS of the CROWD, the BANDS, the
    REFEREES' WHISTLES and the GRUNTING and TACKLING of the
    PLAYERS are strangely muted here as we look out beyond the
    CHEERLEADERS and BENCHWARMERS to the excitement of the game
    just beyond. We are--

43 UNDER THE BLEACHERS OF THE FOOTBALL STADIUM - NIGHT   43

    In the dark and shadowy web of metal crossbeams that stripe
    the cavity below the thousands of SPECTATORS.

    Daryl watches the High School football game through the
    slotted openings and legs of the paying FANS above.

    He's mesmerized by the deja vu sights and sounds of the
    stadium. This used to be his world. He drinks in every
    sensory image.

    There's a Phantom of the Opera quality to his reaction.

44 REVERSE ANGLE: ON THE CHEERLEADERS - NIGHT   44

    As they face the bleachers, urging the home team on.

    At the end of the cheer, Cordelia crosses to a cooler near
    the edge of the bleachers and draws a paper cup of water.

    Daryl GRABS her, jerking her into the dark below the stands.

    Her SCREAM is absorbed by the CHEER of the stadium full of
    people as the Razorbacks score a touchdown on the field.

45 EXT. BY THE STANDS - MINUTES LATER - NIGHT   45

    Buffy and Chris move quickly toward the far end, where the
    Sunnydale Cheerleaders are finishing a post-touchdown cheer.

    But as they draw near, it becomes apparent that Cordelia is
    not among the leaping and cheering squad.

                        BUFFY
               I don't see her. Do you?

                                        CUT TO:

46   INT. LAB (OLD SCIENCE BUILDING) - NIGHT   46

The gutted room with boarded up windows still bears the
carbon streaks from the fire a year earlier.

The sheet-draped Body is now joined by a second table.
Cordelia (blindfolded) is thrown on it by Daryl. Eric straps   *
her in immediately.

                    CORDELIA   *
          Please... what's going on... take off   *
          the blindfold, I won't scream, I   *
          promise...   *

                    DARYL (O.S.)
          She's beautiful...

Eric turns to see Daryl, his back to Cordelia, lifting the
sheet to check out the inanimate, piecemeal body.

                    ERIC
          No! It's bad luck for the groom to
          see the bride before the wedding.

Eric hastily crosses to Daryl.

                    CORDELIA
          Please... just take off the   *
          blindfold, I promise I won't --   *

                    DARYL
          Cordelia...

Daryl removes the blindfold. Cordelia takes one look at him   *
and screams bloody murder.   *

                    ERIC   *
          You can scream all you want - we're   *
          in an abandoned building...   *
                    (scream continues; he   *
                     picks up a blunt   *
                     object)   *
          ...okay, that's enough.   *

Daryl just looks at Cordelia with his sad, mangled eyes.   *

                    DARYL
          You were always good to me. Always
          noticed me, but I ignored you. I'm
          sorry. I'm glad that I got this
          second chance to tell you that.

                    CORDELIA
                    (stunned)
          D-Daryl...?

                                                        CONTINUED

46 CONTINUED: 46

                         DARYL
          I was thoughtless, I know that now.
          But I've changed, I've learned to
          appreciate how much it meant that you
          wanted to be with me.

                         ERIC
          We're ready.

                         CORDELIA
          Ready?   Ready for what?!

                                              CONTINUED

46 CONTINUED: (2)   46

                         ERIC
             You're going to feel a little pinch,
             maybe a little discomfort around the
             neck area. But when you wake up,
             you'll have the body of a seventeen
             year old. In fact...

Eric lifts the sheet so that Cordelia can see the Body on the
adjacent table. (We're angled so we can't however.)

                         ERIC (cont'd)
             ... you'll have the body of several.

47 EXT. STADIUM BLEACHERS - SAME TIME - NIGHT   47

Buffy runs right behind the cheerleaders to Cordelia's place.
She spots the two POMPOMS lying on the ground several feet
away at the edge of the bleachers...

                         BUFFY
             He was here. Chris, where did he
             take her?

                         CHRIS
             To the rest of the body. To the lab.

                         BUFFY
             Where is that?

                         CHRIS
             I promised him...

                         BUFFY
             He'll kill Cordelia.
                   (desperate)
             You can't just give and take lives
             like that. It's not your job.

Chris looks up at Buffy. This hits home.

                         CHRIS
             Please try not to hurt him. He's in   *
             the old science building. Everything
             is set up there.

                         BUFFY
             Okay, find Willow and Xander and Mr.
             Giles. Tell them what's going on.

Buffy heads off. Chris watches her for a beat, worried about   *
his brother, then moves off.   *

48   INT. LAB (OLD SCIENCE BUILDING) - NIGHT   48

Eric finishes pouring gas from a five gallon drum into the
generator. He turns on the generator. All around the room,
jerry- rigged machines hum to life. Eric holds a surgical   *
saw over a bunsen burner.

                    CORDELIA
          Daryl, please... you don't have to
          do this.

                    DARYL
          I have to. So we can be together.

                    CORDELIA
               (frantic now)
          We can be together anyway. I'll be
          with you. I promise.

He leans in to Cordelia. She can't help looking away.

                    DARYL
          Is that right? You see anything you
          like?

He turns away, to the unfinished girl.

                    DARYL (cont'd)
          When you're finished, you won't go
          out. You won't go away. We'll hide
          together.

Tears start to flow down Cordelia's face.

                    CORDELIA
          Please...

Eric pulls the shiny surgical saw out of the flame, steps
forward.

                    ERIC
          Sterile enough for government work...

He lowers the blade towards Cordelia's neck. Cordelia SCREAMS.

Just as the door CRASHES open and Buffy steps inside.

                    CORDELIA
          Buffy! Help me!

As Buffy looks down at Cordelia, Eric heaves the surgical saw
across at her. Buffy neatly catches it by the handle in mid-
air.

                                              CONTINUED

48 CONTINUED: 48

>   Eric, ever the coward, flees into a corner, ducking. Buffy   *
>   ignores him, turns to Daryl.   *

                         BUFFY
               Daryl, listen, I know who you are.
               Your brother sent me to stop this.

                         DARYL
               He wouldn't do that. He loves me.

                         CORDELIA
               Buffy, they're crazy!

                         BUFFY
               It's okay, Cordelia, I'm getting you
               out of here.

                         DARYL
               No, I'm not finished with her.

Daryl picks up another blade from the surgical tray, starts
toward Cordelia. Buffy runs, somersaults over the table with
the Body, kicking Daryl back and away from Cordelia.

He's up again in an instant. He punches Buffy hard - she
goes back into the gurney, sends it rolling across the room.

It hits the gas can and generator -- the can topples,   *
spilling gas.   *

                         CORDELIA
               Buffy!

                         DARYL
               I won't live alone!

At that moment, Eric makes a break for the door. Daryl grabs
him by the scruff of the neck.

                         DARYL (cont'd)
               You have to help me!

                         ERIC
               Let go!

Furious, Daryl hurls Eric into the wall by the door, knocking
him unconscious.

Buffy starts toward Cordelia again, but Daryl lunges at her.

She catches him with a roundhouse kick that sends him
reeling. He plows into a table, knocking the bunsen burner to   *
the ground.   *

49 ANGLE: THE POOL OF GAS   49

As the bunsen burner flame ignites it, setting a fire in the   *
middle of the room.   *

                         XANDER
          Buffy!

Xander runs in, susses the sitch.

                         BUFFY
          Get Cordelia!

He goes to the gurney, skirting around the flames. He starts
to untie Cordelia --

Daryl grabs a huge bottle of chemicals and hurls it at Buffy.
She ducks but the chemicals hit the wall and burst into
flame, creating a wall of fire, cutting Xander and Cordelia   *
off from the door.   *

Buffy rains blows on Daryl.   *

50 ANGLE: THE DOOR   50

The rest of the group arrive. They react to the carnage and   *
flames. No way can they get to Xander and Cordelia on the   *
gurney. Willow and Giles pull the unconscious Eric out of
the room.

Xander looks around, thinking. He grabs the gurney, gives it
a massive shove --   *

                         CORDELIA   *
          No!   *

-- then dives on top of Cordelia as the table rolls back   *
through the wall of flames (saving her life) and to the door   *
with Giles and the others.

                         MS. CALENDAR
          Buffy, get out!

But Daryl strikes again, knocking her against a wall. He   *
picks up a student desk, to bash Buffy's head with, when--   *

                         CHRIS
          Daryl! Don't!

Daryl looks across at his brother standing in the doorway.   *
Looks down at Buffy, some remaining human instinct preventing   *
him from unloading the desk.   *

Then he looks across through the fire to see the flames   *
whirling up around the sheet covered Body. He freaks.

                                                  CONTINUED

BUFFY THE VAMPIRE SLAYER "Some Assembly Required"(Pink)7/15/97   52A*.

50 CONTINUED: 50

                        DARYL
          No!   She's mine!

                                                    CONTINUED

50   CONTINUED: (2)   50

        Daryl barrels into the fire, which quickly engulfs him as he
        falls onto the sheet-covered Body to shield it from the
        flames.

                        DARYL (cont'd)
                Mine!

                        CHRIS
                Daryl!

        Chris bolts toward his brother, but Buffy grabs him, wraps
        him up, holds him back.

51   ANGLE ON: THE FLAMES   51

        As the photo chemicals fuel the conflagration to greater
        intensity. Daryl is draped over the Body, motionless now as
        the fire engulfs them.

                                                DISSOLVE TO:

52   EXT. SCHOOL GROUNDS - LATER - NIGHT   52

        We see most of the combatants, bathed in fire trucks'
        flashing lights. The fire seems to be over by now.

53   ANGLE: CHRIS AND BUFFY   53

        Are staring at the old science building together. After a
        time...

                        CHRIS
                The first time he woke up, after...
                he said I shouldn't have brought him
                back. I was just trying to look out
                for him. Like he would have done for
                me.

        Buffy decides against saying anything. Just puts her hand on
        his shoulder.

        Angel approaches, goes up to Buffy, concerned.

                        ANGEL
                I saw the fire, figured you'd be
                here. Is everyone okay?

                        BUFFY
                Yeah. We're okay.

54 ANGLE ON GILES AND MS. CALENDAR: 54

                         GILES
          I am sorry about all this.

                         MS. CALENDAR
          That's okay. Although a good rule of
          thumb for a first date is don't do
          anything so exciting that it will be
          hard to top on the second date.

                         GILES
                    (ruefully)
          Believe it or not, since I've moved
          here to live on top of the Hellmouth,
          the events of this evening actually
          qualify as a slow night.
                    (stops)
          Did you say, "second date"?

                         MS. CALENDAR
          Ah, you noticed that too?

55 ANGLE ON: XANDER AND WILLOW   55

     As they watch Buffy and Angel, Giles and Ms. Calendar
     together.

                         XANDER
          Well, I guess that makes it official.
          Everyone's paired off. Vampires can
          get dates. Hell, even the school
          librarian is seeing more action than
          me.
                    (shakes his head)
          You ever feel like the world is a
          giant game of musical chairs, and the
          music has stopped and you're the only
          one who doesn't have a chair?

     Cordelia steps up behind the two, summons her nerve.

                         WILLOW
          All the time.

                         CORDELIA
          Xander, I, uh, just wanted to say
          thanks for saving my life in there.
          It was... really brave and heroic and
          all. And if there's ever anything I
          can do to repay you...

                         XANDER
          Do you mind? We're talking here.

                                                   CONTINUED

55 CONTINUED: 55

Cordelia reacts, turns and crossing off.

                    XANDER (cont'd)
                    (to Willow)
          So, where were we?

                    WILLOW
          Wondering why we never seem to have
          dates.

                    XANDER
          Oh, yeah. So, why do you think that
          is?

56 EXT. CEMETERY - NIGHT   56

Buffy and Angel walk along together.

                    BUFFY
          The whole thing was creepy. But at
          the same time... I mean, he did do it
          all for his brother...

                    ANGEL
          Sounds like he took it a little over
          the edge.

                    BUFFY
          Love makes you do the wacky...

                    ANGEL
          The what?

                    BUFFY
          Crazy stuff.

                    ANGEL
          Oh. Crazy like a 241 year old being
          jealous of a high school junior?

                    BUFFY
                    (charmed)   *
          Are you fessing up?   *

                    ANGEL
          I thought about it. Maybe he bothers
          me a little.

Buffy turns, close to Angel.

                    BUFFY
          I don't love Xander.

                                                    CONTINUED

                          ANGEL
         But he's in your life. He gets to be
         there when I can't. Take your
         classes, eat your meals, hear your
         jokes and complaints. He gets to see
         you in the sunlight.

                          BUFFY   *
         I don't look all that great in direct   *
         light...   *

He half-smiles at that, looks out into the sky a moment.   *

                          ANGEL
         It'll be morning soon. I should   *
         probably...   *
                  (motions: go)   *

                          BUFFY   *
         ...yeah. I've got things to...   *

She looks up at him for a beat. A little despair coursing   *
through both of them.   *

                          BUFFY (cont'd)
         I could walk you home...   *

He holds out his hand. She takes it. They walk off.   *

The camera holds them a while, until a headstone comes into   *
the foreground and we focus on that, the camera finally
settling. The headstone reads:

                   DARYL EPPS

                   1978 - 1996

                   REST IN PEACE

                                        BLACK OUT.

                        END OF SHOW

BUFFY THE VAMPIRE SLAYER

"School Hard"

Story By

Joss Whedon and David Greenwalt

Teleplay By

David Greenwalt

Directed By

John Kretchmer

<u>SHOOTING SCRIPT</u>

July 25, 1997
July 29, 1997 (Blue Pages)
July 30, 1997 (Pink Pages)

BUFFY THE VAMPIRE SLAYER

"School Hard"

CAST LIST

BUFFY SUMMERS............................ Sarah Michelle Gellar
XANDER HARRIS............................ Nicholas Brendon
RUPERT GILES............................. Anthony S. Head
WILLOW ROSENBERG......................... Alyson Hannigan
CORDELIA CHASE........................... Charisma Carpenter
ANGEL.................................... David Boreanaz

JOYCE.................................... Kristine Sutherland
JENNY CALENDAR........................... Robia La Morte
MR. SNYDER............................... Armin Shimerman
ANOINTED ONE............................. Andrew J. Ferchland
SPIKE.................................... James Marsters
DRUSILLA................................. Juliet Landau
SHEILA................................... Alexander Johnes
BIG UGLY................................. Gregory Scott Cummins
LEAN BOY................................. Andrew Palmer
CHIEF.................................... Brian Reddy
PARENT................................... Keith Mackechnie
VAMP 5...................................

THE BAND..................................*Nickel

BUFFY THE VAMPIRE SLAYER

"School Hard"

SET LIST

INTERIORS

SUNNYDALE HIGH SCHOOL
    NORTH HALL
    SOUTH HALL
    HALL OUTSIDE SNYDER'S OFFICE
    LIBRARY
    SCHOOL LOUNGE
    SCIENCE CLASSROOM
    SNYDER'S OFFICE
    UTILITY CLOSET
    CRAWLSPACE

BUFFY'S BEDROOM

THE BRONZE

THE FACTORY
    SPIKE AND DRUSILLA'S ROOM

EXTERIORS

SUNNYDALE HIGH SCHOOL

THE BRONZE
    ALLEY BY THE BRONZE

THE FACTORY

ROADSIDE

THE FISHTANK
    ALLEY NEXT TO FISHTANK

BUFFY THE VAMPIRE SLAYER

"School Hard"

TEASER

1 EXT.   SUNNYDALE HIGH - DAY - ESTABLISHING   1

                    MR. SNYDER (V.O.)
          A lot of educators tell students:

2 INT. SNYDER'S OFFICE - DAY   2

                    MR. SNYDER
          ...think of your principal as your
          "pal". I say think of me as your
          judge, jury and executioner.

SHEILA MARTINI (17, sexy, slovenly and somewhat dangerous)
faces SNYDER across his desk.

                    MR. SNYDER (cont'd)
          Tell me, who do you think is the most
          troublesome student in this school?

Sheila studies Snyder, pops her gum, and jerks her head to
the right, indicating BUFFY whom we now discover sitting next
to her. Snyder smiles.

                    MR. SNYDER (cont'd)
          Well, it is quite a match between you
          two.

Snyder opens two THICK FILES on his desk.

                    MR. SNYDER (cont'd)
          On the one hand, Buffy hasn't stabbed
          a horticulture teacher with a trowel,
          yet.

                    SHEILA
          I never stabbed anyone with a trowel!

Sheila stabs the file in front of Snyder with her finger, he
involuntarily edges back.

                    SHEILA (cont'd)
          It was pruning shears. It should say
          pruning shears.

                    MR. SNYDER
               (to Buffy)
          On the other hand, Sheila's never
          burned down a school building.

                                                    CONTINUED

                         BUFFY
          That was never proved... the fire
          marshal said it could have been...
          mice...

                         MR. SNYDER
          Mice?

                         BUFFY
          Mice that were smoking?

                         MR. SNYDER
                    (looking at file)
          And the two of you seem to be tied in
          the class-cutting and fight-starting
          events. You're really neck and neck
          here. It's very exciting.

                         SHEILA
          What does the winner get?

                         MR. SNYDER
          Expelled.

This registers with Buffy. Less so with Sheila.

                         MR. SNYDER (cont'd)
          This Thursday is parent teacher
          night. Your parents --
                    (to Buffy)
          assuming you have any --will meet
          your teachers --
                    (to Sheila)
          assuming you have any **left**. I have
          decided to put you two in charge of
          this event. You have three days to
          prepare the refreshments, make the
          banners, and transform the school
          lounge into a habitable place for
          adults. This will incur my goodwill,
          and may even affect what I tell your
          parents when I meet them. Are we
          clear?

                         BUFFY
          We're clear.
                    (to Sheila)
          Don't you feel clear?
                    (to Snyder)
          We're very clear.

CONTINUED

2 CONTINUED: (2)   2

                    MR. SNYDER
          Good. Because you mess up this time,
          and your parents will be coming to
          clean out your lockers.

3 EXT. SCHOOL - DAY - AFTER SCHOOL   3

Buffy walks with Sheila as Xander and Willow approach.

                    BUFFY
          It really shouldn't be that hard.
          We'll work on banners tomorrow at
          lunch and we can figure out
          refreshments then.

                    SHEILA
          Yeah, sure, whatever.

She calls out to an older, slovenly, tattooed guy.

                    SHEILA (cont'd)
          Hey, Meatpie! Wait up!

And she's off, Xander and Willow watching her go.

                    XANDER
          Heard Snyder's got you guys making
          party favors.

                    BUFFY
          Yeah, his two worst students.
                    (watching Sheila)
          When my Mom looks at me, that's what
          she sees. A Sheila.

                    XANDER
          Sheila's definitely intense. That
          guy with her? That's the one she CAN
          bring home to mother.

                    WILLOW
          She smoked when we were in fifth
          grade. Once I was lookout for her.

                    XANDER
          You're bad to the bone.

                    WILLOW
          I'm a rebel.

CONTINUED

3 CONTINUED: 3

                         BUFFY
          It's just not fair. I'm the Slayer,
          which requires a certain amount of
          fighting and cutting. What's Sheila's
          excuse?

                         XANDER
          Homework. She won't do it. And most
          of the teachers respect that now.
          You'll probably want to keep her away
          from sharp implements while you're
          working.

                         BUFFY
          Do you think any of the other Slayers
          ever had to go to high school?

                         XANDER
          Hey, it's no biggie. You'll put on
          a nice little affair. The parents'll
          love it. As long as nothing really
          bad comes along between now and then,
          you'll be fine.

Both girls turn, appalled.

                         BUFFY
          Are you nuts? What'd you say that
          for? Now something bad is gonna
          happen!

                         XANDER
          What do you mean? Nothing is gonna
          happen!

                         WILLOW
          Not until some dummy says "As long as
          nothing bad happens..."

                         BUFFY
          That's like the ultimate jinx!

                         WILLOW
          What were you thinking? Or were you   *
          even thinking?   *

                         XANDER
                    (defensively)
          Well, you don't know. Maybe this
          time is different.

                                        CUT TO:

4 EXT. ROADSIDE - NIGHT   4

We see a sign proclaiming WELCOME TO SUNNYDALE. See it for
a good few seconds before the black caddy roars out from
behind camera, smashing the sign flat.

The caddy screeches to a halt. The door opens.

We see his foot first, stepping out in a shitkicker steel-
toed boot. As he walks in front of the car the camera ARMS
UP, revealing his punkish outfit, his long coat. As he puts
a cigarette to his lips we reach his face. He looks young,
his eyes sparkling with anarchy. He smiles as he lights the
cigarette. And, oh yeah. He's a vampire.

This is SPIKE.

He looks down at the sign sticking partially under his wheel.
Looks at the row of houses in the near distance.

                    SPIKE
          Home sweet home.

                              BLACK OUT.

          END OF TEASER

ACT ONE

5 INT.   THE FACTORY - NIGHT   5

The ANOINTED ONE holds court from his throne-like chair with
several vampires. Two in particular do the talking: a big
ugly one and a skinny, intense one. Nobody looks too happy.

                    BIG UGLY
          The Master is dead. Someone has to
          take his place.

                    LEAN BOY
          As long as the Slayer is alive,
          whoever takes his place will be
          sharing his grave!

                    BIG UGLY
          Then let the soul who kills her wear
          his mantle.

                    ANOINTED ONE
          Can you do it?

                    BIG UGLY
          Yes. This weekend, the Night of
          Saint Vigeous, our power shall be at
          it's peak! When I kill her, it'll be
          the greatest event since the
          crucifixion. And I should know. I
          was there.

                    SPIKE
          You were there? Oh please.

He strolls in, eyeing everyone with amusement. He gets in
Big Ugly's face.

                    SPIKE (cont'd)
          If every vampire who said he was at
          the crucifixion was actually there,
          it would have been like Woodstock!

                    BIG UGLY
          I ought to rip your throat out.

Spike wrinkles his nose.

                    SPIKE
          Would it kill ya', little mouthwash
          every couple hundred years?

                                        CONTINUED

5 CONTINUED: 5

Spike moves on, purposefully turning his back on Big Ugly,
looking at the others, glancing at a METAL CAGE, some meat
hooks and old chains hanging from pulleys in the ceiling.

                    SPIKE (cont'd)
          I was actually at Woodstock. That
          was a weird gig. Fed off a flower
          person and spent six hours watching
          my hands move.

Big Ugly comes at him from behind. Spike rips a chain from
the pulley whips it around Big Ugly's neck and yanks,
bridling Big Ugly, chaining his face against the iron bars of
the cage. This all happens REAL FAST. And Spike isn't even
out of breath.

                    SPIKE (cont'd)
          So, who do you kill for fun around
          here?

                    ANOINTED ONE
          Who are you?

                    SPIKE
          Spike. You're that anointed guy. I
          read about you. And you got Slayer
          problems. You know what I find works
          real good with Slayers? Killing
          them.

                    ANOINTED ONE
          Can you?

                    SPIKE
          A lot faster than fatboy here.
                    (to Big Ugly, who
                     chokes and grunts)
          Doncha' think?
                    (more gagging: to the
                     Anointed)
          He agrees. Where was I? Oh yeah, I
          did a couple Slayers in my time.
          Don't like to brag. Oh, who am I
          kidding, I love to brag. There was
          one Slayer, during the Boxer
          Rebellion --

DRUSILLA wanders in as he speaks, looking at everything with
the quiet wonder of a child. Spike sees her and his whole
face changes. Literally, as he resumes his human visage.

                    SPIKE (cont'd)
          Drusilla!

                                                           CONTINUED

He lets go of Big Ugly, goes to her. His manner becomes
surprisingly gentle and solicitous with her.

                    SPIKE (cont'd)
          You shouldn't be walking around.
          You're weak.

                    DRUSILLA
          Look at all the people. Are these
          nice people?

                    SPIKE
          We're getting along.

She goes over to the Anointed One.

                    DRUSILLA
          This one has power. I could feel it
          from outside.

                    SPIKE
          Yeah, he's a big noise in these
          parts. Anointed, and all that.

                    DRUSILLA
                (to the Anointed One)
          Do you like daisies? I plant them
          but they always die. Everything I
          put in the ground withers and dies.
          Spike, I'm cold.

He whips off his coat and lays it around her shoulders,
holding her as he does.

                    SPIKE
          I got you.

                    DRUSILLA
          I'm a princess...

                    SPIKE
          That's what you are.

She runs her finger along his cheek. We see that her
fingernail has drawn blood. It trickles down Spike's face.
He doesn't flinch, and Drusilla gently licks it off.

He turns to the others.

                                              CONTINUED

                         SPIKE (cont'd)
          Me and Dru, we're moving in. Anyone
          wanna test who's got the biggest
          wrinklies around here, step on up.
                    (to the Anointed One)
          I'll do your Slayer for you. You
          keep your flunkies from trying
          anything behind my back. Deal?

The Anointed One nods. Drusilla suddenly grabs Spike's arm.

                         DRUSILLA
          I can't see her. The Slayer. I
          can't see. It's dark where she is...
          Kill her! Spike! Kill her for me!

                         SPIKE
          It's done, baby.

                         DRUSILLA
                    (calm, but shaking)
          Kill her for princess?

                         SPIKE
          I'll chop her into messes.

                         DRUSILLA
          You are my sweet.

                         SPIKE
                    (to the Anointed One)
          So, how about this Slayer. Is she
          tough?

6 INT. BUFFY'S BEDROOM NIGHT   6

                         BUFFY
          Ow!

She's dressed for bed, brushing tangles out of her hair in
front of the vanity. JOYCE appears in the doorway.

                         JOYCE
          What's wrong?

                         BUFFY
          I spent half my allowance on that new
          cream rinse and it's neither creamy
          nor rinsey.

                         JOYCE
          Life is hard, dear.

CONTINUED

                         BUFFY
          Don't I know it. Look at these split
          ends!

                         JOYCE
          I got the mail.

                         BUFFY
          Oh good.

                         JOYCE
          Which included a reminder notice
          about parent teacher night Thursday.

                         BUFFY
          Oh less good.

                         JOYCE
          Which you were planning on telling me
          about...?

                         BUFFY
          For the last two weeks. I've been
          working up my nerve.

                         JOYCE
          Uh huh. So what do you think your
          teachers will tell me about you?

                         BUFFY
          Well... I... think they'd all agree
          I always bring a pen to class, ready
          to absorb the knowledge.

                         JOYCE
          And this absorption rate, how is it
          reflected in your homework and test
          scores?

                         BUFFY
          What can you really tell about a
          person from a test score?

                         JOYCE
          Whether or not a she's ever going out
          with her friends again.

                         BUFFY
          Oh that.

                         JOYCE
          What about your principal?

                    BUFFY
          He put me in charge of the banners
          and refreshments for the whole
          evening. If that's not a sign of
          respect I don't know what is.

                    JOYCE
          I look forward to meeting him.

                    BUFFY
          Won't that be something.

                    JOYCE
          Look, sweetheart, life is more than
          grades and test scores and not
          getting kicked out of school.

                    BUFFY
          You are so right.

                    JOYCE
          But we moved once because of you
          getting in trouble. And I had to
          start a new business -- not to
          mention a new life -- in a whole new
          town.

                    BUFFY
          And you don't want to do that again.

                    JOYCE
          What I don't want is to be
          disappointed in you again.

Beat.

                    BUFFY
          Mom, believe me, that's the last
          thing I want, too. I'm trying, I've
          just got a lot of... pressure right
          now.

                    JOYCE
          Wait till you have a job.

She gives Buffy a little kiss on the head.

                    JOYCE (cont'd)
          Sleep tight.

Joyce goes. Buffy tries one more tangle, tugs open a drawer
to drop the brush in, sees the vampire stake in the drawer.

                                        CONTINUED

6 CONTINUED: (3)   6

                         BUFFY
          I **have** a job.

7 EXT. SCHOOL - DAY - ESTABLISHING   7

8 INT. SCHOOL LOUNGE - DAY   8

     Morning.   Buffy has a big banner laid out over a long table.
     Willow is helping her paint "WELCOME PARENTS" on it.   Xander
     is painting "PARENT TEACHER NIGHT" on another banner next to
     them.

                         WILLOW
          Sheila's a no show?
                (Buffy nods)
          She goes to this really rank bar, the
          Fish Tank, sometimes they have raids
          and... other things that could make
          you tardy.

                         BUFFY
          Can you help me cram some French
          tonight? I don't want Mr. DeJean
          telling my mother I'm an...
                (big French accent)
          ...imbecile!

                         WILLOW
          I thought we were going to the Bronze
          tonight. 'Cause of how you thought
          Angel might show.

                         XANDER
          If he does he'll meet some other nice
          girl. Studying comes first.

                         BUFFY
          We're going to the Bronze. I can
          study and party and do parent teacher
          night and make my mother proud as
          long as I don't have to...
                (sees Giles and Jenny
                 coming; deflates)
          ...fight vampires.

     GILES and JENNY CALENDER join the group, in mid-discussion.

                         GILES
          There's nothing in the Chronicles
          about an extraneous lunar cycle.

                                                           CONTINUED

                JENNY
The Order never accurately calculated
the Mesopotamian calendar! Rupert,
you have to read something that was
published AFTER 1066.

                XANDER
What's the up, guys?

                BUFFY
I don't suppose this is something
about happy squirrels?

                GILES
Vampires.

                BUFFY
That was my next guess.

                GILES
Ms. Calendar has been researching
surfing on her computer. According
to her calculations, this Saturday is
the Night of Saint Vigeous.

                BUFFY
Lemme guess. He didn't make balloon
animals.

                GILES
He led a crusade. Of vampires. They
swept through Edessa, Harran, and
points east.

                JENNY
They didn't leave much behind.

                XANDER
So Saturday's kind of a big doo for
bloodsuckers.

                JENNY
It's a Holy Night of Attack. They'll
come in numbers.

                BUFFY
If I survive parent teacher night
tomorrow...
        (nods at banner)
...I'll see what I can do about
Saturday.

CONTINUED

                         GILES
          You're being a tad flip, don't you
          think? This is serious.

                         BUFFY
          And being kicked out of school is
          laffs aplenty?

                         GILES
          You know what happens when you let
          your life interfere with your slaying.

                         BUFFY
          Yes, I found that out that last time
          I had a date, back in the Restoration
          era.

                         GILES
          You just need to keep the two things
          separate.

                         BUFFY
          Yes, well, if my slaying doesn't get
          me expelled, I promise my banner
          making won't get me killed. Just let
          me get through the week.

                         GILES
          Saturday will require a great deal of
          preparation.

                         WILLOW
          Well, we'll help.

                         XANDER
          Yeah! I can whittle stakes!

                         WILLOW
          And I can research stuff.

                         XANDER
                   (to Willow)
          While I'm whittling, I plan to
          whistle a jaunty tune.

                         GILES
          Your help will be appreciated. But
          when it comes to Battle, Buffy must
          be prepared to fight alone. You are,
          after all, a slay--

          He sees Snyder approaching, quickly adjusts:

                    GILES (cont'd)
          slay....ve. Slave. You're all
          slaves to the... television. You
          young people nowadays. Goodbye.

Giles and Jenny take off. Snyder turns to Xander and Willow.

                    MR. SNYDER
          You wouldn't be helping Buffy in
          Sheila's place would you?

                    XANDER
                 (brush behind back)
          No.

                    WILLOW
          We're hindering.

                    MR. SNYDER
          She ditched. Mmm-mmmm, I feel an
          expulsion coming on.

                    BUFFY
          She's been helping for hours. She's
          just out getting more paint...

Buffy follows Snyder's gaze to the door as SHEILA stumbles
through in last night's party dress, dark glasses: Marilyn
Monroe after a hard night Kennedying. Buffy rushes to
Sheila, guides her to Xander's banner, under:

                    BUFFY (cont'd)
          No more teal in the art room? I know
          you wanted it to be perfect, but
          let's just keep going with the green.

She plops (Xander's) brush in Sheila's hand.

                    MR. SNYDER
          Just make sure everything is perfect
          on Thursday.

He goes off.

                    SHEILA
          Thanks for covering. Guy's a serious
          rodent.

                    BUFFY
          No problem.

                                              CONTINUED

8 CONTINUED: (4)   8

                         SHEILA
          Did you really burn down school
          property one time?

                         BUFFY
          Well, not actually ONE time...

                         SHEILA
          Cool.

                         BUFFY
          But I didn't feel good about it or
          anything. I mean, I don't condone...
          So. We're gonna Bronze it tonight,
          if you wanted to come...

                         SHEILA
          I can't go there. You threaten one
          bartender with a broken bottle and
          they like ban you for life.
                    (snorts)

                         BUFFY
          Ahhh.

9 INT. BRONZE - NIGHT   9

    Buffy and Willow at a table. Buffy thinks hard, composing a
    sentence. Willow's got a French book.

                         BUFFY
          <La vache doit me touche de la jeudi>
                    (off Willow's
                     furrowed brow)
          Is that wrong? Should I use the
          plural?

                         WILLOW
          No, but... you just said that "the
          cow should touch me from Thursday".

                         BUFFY
          Well, maybe that's what I was feeling.

                         WILLOW
          And you said it wrong.

                         BUFFY
          Oh. Je stink.

                                                          CONTINUED

9 CONTINUED: 9

> WILLOW
> You're just not focussed. It's Angel
> missage.

> BUFFY
> Well he didn't say for sure, it was
> a maybe see you there kind of deal.

Xander comes off the dance floor.

> XANDER
> Guys! I'm all alone out there!
> Somebody has to dance with me.

> WILLOW
> Well, we are studying...

> XANDER
> Come on, one dance! You've been
> studying for nearly twelve minutes!

> BUFFY
> No wonder my brain is fried.

They get up, hitting the floor as a fairly rocking song
begins. The three of them dance together, Buffy occasionally
repeating french phrases to herself.

In the b.g. we see a LONE FIGURE in the dark watching Buffy.
Is it Angel?

The figure steps out of he shadows. It's not Angel, it's
Spike. He circles through the dancers, moving closer and
closer, staying out of Buffy's line of sight, never taking
his eyes off her. A hunter stalking his prey.

Spike circles. Buffy is oblivious to the danger. He's
closer and closer... and suddenly gone.

10 AT THE BAR - SPIKE   10

Joins Big Ugly (without a vamp face on.)

> SPIKE
> Go get something to eat.

Big Ugly nods, obediently moves off. Spike looks back at

11 BUFFY   11

On the floor. We discover Spike behind them, speaking to
some other folk, but so Buffy will hear:

CONTINUED

11 CONTINUED: 11

                         SPIKE
              Where's a phone? I need to call the
              police. There's some big guy out
              back trying to bite someone.

Buffy reacts and is gone in a flash.

12 EXT. ALLEY BEHIND BRONZE - NIGHT   12

    A HELPLESS GIRL backs away from Big Ugly (who now has his
    vamp face on.) He gets his huge hand around her dainty neck,
    closes in for the kill as --

13 BUFFY'S TWO HANDS   13

    Locked together, slam down on his wrist, breaking his hold.

                         BIG UGLY
              Slayer.

                         BUFFY
              Slay-ee.

    And Buffy spin kicks him in the head. He takes it well,
    grabs her and hurls her against a wall. He charges, she
    ducks, pivots under his arm and away. He moves after her but
    we DRIFT RIGHT and discover Spike, calmly watching the melee
    from the shadows.

14 BUFFY AND BIG UGLY   14

    Trade punches. Willow and Xander race out the back door.

                         BUFFY
                    (re: girl)
              Get her out of here!

    Buffy ducks a punch, kicks. Willow grabs the girl.

                         BUFFY (cont'd)
              And...
                    (punch)
              ...a stake...
                    (duck)
              ...would be nice.
                    (kick)

    Xander races back inside on the heels of Willow and the
    freaked girl.

15 SPIKE   15

Watches her every move, enjoying himself immensely.

16 INT. BRONZE - NIGHT   16

Xander races to the table. Upends Buffy's purse, claws
through lipstick, make-up, hair brush, a tampon!

                    XANDER
          Ahhh!

He drops it like a hot tampon, finally finds a stake, runs.

17 EXT. ALLEY BEHIND BRONZE - NIGHT - BUFFY   17

Big Ugly swings and connects. Buffy goes down. He looms
over her.

                    BIG UGLY
          I don't need to wait for Saint
          Vigeous. You're mine!

He comes at her, but she knocks him back.

Xander races out the back door, hurls the stake at Buffy who
catches it sharply on the spin in mid-air. Willow peeks out
from behind Xander.

                    BIG UGLY (cont'd)
          Spike, give me a hand.

Xander and Willow look around the dark alley: who's he
talking to?

18 SPIKE - UNSEEN IN THE SHADOWS   18

Just watches, makes no move to help.

19 BUFFY SINKS THE STAKE   19

Goodbye Big Ugly. Spike applauds slowly, steps out of the
darkness. Right next to Willow and Xander who both jump.

                    SPIKE
          Nice work, baby.

                    BUFFY
          Who are you?

                    SPIKE
          You'll find out on Saturday.

                                                  CONTINUED

19 CONTINUED: 19

                              BUFFY
                  What happens on Saturday?

                              SPIKE
                  I kill you.

He smiles, slides back into the shadows and is gone. Xander
and Willow are wigged. So is Buffy.

                                        BLACK OUT.

                  END OF ACT ONE

ACT TWO

20 EXT. SUNNYDALE HIGH - NIGHT - ESTABLISHING   20

                    GILES (O.S.)
          Spike...

21 INT. LIBRARY - NIGHT   21

Vamp books and diaries on the table. The gang is assembled:
Buffy, Giles Willow, Xander and Jenny who is dragging a
staggering amount of weaponry out of the book cage as:

                    GILES
          ...that's what the other vampire
          called him?
                    (Buffy nods)
          Sounds a little unorthodox.

                    BUFFY
          Maybe he's reform.

                    GILES
                    (thumbing through
                     diaries)
          He may have gone by a different name
          in times past...

                    JENNY
          Whoever he is, we'll need all the
          help we can get come this Saturday.

Xander eyes THE ATTACK OF SAINT VIGEOUS engraving in a huge
old tome. (Medieval vamp crusade mayhem.)

                    XANDER
          This Night of Saint Vigeous deal, if
          they're gonna attack in force
          shouldn't we be thinkin': vacation?

                    WILLOW
          We can't run, that would be wrong.
          Could we hide? I mean if that Spike
          guy is leading the attack...
                    (shudders loudly)
          ...sorry, was that audible?

                    GILES
          I'm sure he's no worse than any other
          creature you've faced --

CONTINUED

21 CONTINUED: 21

                              ANGEL (O.S.)
                    He's worse.

          Angel is suddenly standing inside the doorway. Xander jumps.

                              BUFFY
                    Angel.

                              GILES
                    You know him?

          Instead of answering that directly, Angel says to Buffy:

                              ANGEL
                    Once he starts something he doesn't
                    stop, until everything in his path is
                    dead. Stay away.

          A beat as this sinks in.

                              XANDER
                    So he's thorough, goal oriented...
                    okay, someone else lighten the mood.

                              BUFFY
                    We were at the Bronze before. I
                    thought you said you might show.

                              ANGEL
                    You said you weren't sure if you were
                    going.

                              BUFFY
                    I was being cool. You been dating
                    for what, two hundred years, you
                    don't know what a girl means when she
                    says maybe she'll show? Work with me
                    here.

          Angel gives her a small smile. The nice moment is broken by:

                              WILLOW
                    Wow, two centuries of dating. If you
                    only had two a year that'd still be
                    like four hundred dates with four
                    hundred different --
                              (suddenly interested
                              in weapons)
                    -- why do they call it a mace?

                                                              CONTINUED

21 CONTINUED: (2)   21

                         GILES
                    Yes, well we've slightly more urgent
                    things to discuss.

                         BUFFY
                         (turning away from
                          Angel)
                    Like keeping my mom away from
                    Principal Snyder tomorrow night.

                         JENNY
                    And not dying Saturday.

                         GILES
                    Angel, do you know if this Spike
                    fellow has any other names?

Giles looks up from the diaries. Angel is gone. They all
look around.

                         XANDER
                    That's it, I'm puttin' a collar with
                    a little bell on that guy.

Off Buffy,

22 EXT. THE FISH TANK - NIGHT   22

A rank dive. Just horrible, mind-numbing industrial music
pounds within. Next to the sign: Fish Tank, a door opens and
Sheila emerges with TWO LOW-LIFES. They're older than her
and hoping to get some.

23 ANGLE - ALLEY NEXT TO THE FISH TANK   23

Sheila trips down the alley with the low-lifes. Both guys
wear tank tops and are covered in tattoos.

                         SHEILA
                    All right, which one is Dwayne and
                    which one is Dell -- don't tell me,
                    Dell's the one with the tattoo!

Sheila laughs at her joke as they move on.

24 ANOTHER ANGLE - TWO SHOT, SHEILA AND DELL   24

                         SHEILA
                    You guys weren't lying about havin'
                    a cadillac, were ya'? Cause I'm
                    crazy about a cad. Just the feel of
                    the leather makes me wanna...

CONTINUED

24 CONTINUED: 24

    Sheila looks around. Dwayne is gone.

                    SHEILA (cont'd)
        What happened to your friend?

25 CLOSE ON SHEILA   25

                    SHEILA
        Hey, illustrated man, over here.

    And as the CAMERA circles her we discover Dell is gone now,
too, and she is alone.

                    SHEILA (cont'd)
        What's going on?

    She looks up and down the alley, getting spooked.

                    SHEILA (cont'd)
        Where are you guys?

    She moves further down the alley. We creep after her.

                    SHEILA (cont'd)
        Not funny...

    Sheila moves on. More than a little freaked now. She looks
behind her. Nothing. Looks the other way. Nothing. Then
Spike, out of nowhere, is just standing right in front of
her. She SCREAMS.

                    SHEILA (cont'd)
        Who are you?

                    SPIKE
        Who do you want me to be?

    She's half-scared, half-mesmerized by his presence.

                    SHEILA
        Did you see...?

                    SPIKE
        Those two losers who thought they
        were good enough for you?

    She half-smiles.

                    SHEILA
        What happened to 'em?

                    SPIKE
        They got sleepy.

                                        CONTINUED

25 CONTINUED: 25

                         SHEILA
               Huh?

                         SPIKE
               And you got something a whole lot
               better.

He holds her gaze, hypnotic.   Then he turns and walks on.

                         SHEILA
               Hey, wait up. What's your name?

She goes after him.   And we PAN DOWN to the dark floor of the
alley. Where two bodies lie. Dwayne and Dell. Way dead.

26 INT. THE FACTORY - NIGHT   26

Spooky.   Lit by torches.   Spike and Drusilla are noticeably
absent

Vampires are chanting, whipping themselves and each other.
The Anointed One sits in the shadows.   Standing near him and
speaking for him is:

                         LEAN BOY
               Saint Vigeous, you who murdered so
               many, we beseech you, cleanse us of
               our weaknesses: mercy, compassion and
               pity.

                         OTHERS
               We will bathe in their blood.

The Anointed One, like a little Godfather, motions to Lean
Boy who leans down close to him.

                         ANOINTED ONE
               Where is he?

                         LEAN BOY
               Spike? He, uh, said he doesn't go
               for religion.

                         ANOINTED ONE
               He should be here.

                         LEAN BOY
               He's with the woman. He's always
               with the woman.

The Anointed One looks displeased.   CAMERA TRACKS PAST the
ceremony, into the darker recesses of the factory.

                         LEAN BOY (cont'd)
                          (to vamps)
                    Lambs to the slaughter!

                         OTHERS
                    Bathe in their blood!

We discover a narrow passageway, stairs leading down.

                                        DISSOLVE TO:

27 INT. SPIKE AND DRUSILLA'S ROOM - NIGHT   27

The stairs lead down into their little dungeonesque suite,
their furniture now moved in. The medieval feel of the room
is sharply contrasted by an old black and white TV, showing
nothing but snow. Lined up on an old trunk by the wall are
five victorian dolls, gags of old linen tied around their
mouths, their eyes wide and innocent.

Drusilla takes one of the dolls and turns it toward the wall.

                         DRUSILLA
                    Miss Edith speaks out of turn. She's
                    a bad example and will have no cakes
                    today.

Spike comes up behind her, slides his arms around her.

                         SPIKE
                    Darling, are you gonna eat something?

                         DRUSILLA
                    I'm not hungry. I miss Prague.

                         SPIKE
                    You nearly died in Prague, Baby.
                    That idiot mob... this is the place
                    for us. The Hellmouth'll restore
                    you. Put color in your cheeks.
                    Metaphorically speaking.

                         SPIKE (cont'd)
                    And in a few weeks time...

                                        CONTINUED

                         DRUSILLA
               The stars will align, and smile down
               on me.

                         SPIKE
               And then, God, this town will burn.

                         DRUSILLA
               A pretty fire.

                         SPIKE
               But baby, none of that's gonna happen
               unless you EAT.

And on that word, the camera WHIP-PANS to the corner of the
room, where sits Sheila, trussed, gagged and absolutely
terrified. No longer the bad girl.

The noise of CHANTING drifts down from upstairs. Spike and
Drusilla look up as they settle on the bed.

                         DRUSILLA
               They're preparing.

                         SPIKE
               St. Vigeous is coming up. Should be
               a party. And I need a party. Man,
               I'm restless. Can't wait to ice that
               Slayer.

                         DRUSILLA
               You should go up with them and
               cleanse.

                         SPIKE
               Dru...

                         DRUSILLA
               The boy doesn't trust you. They
               follow him. I sometimes think that
               my hair will fall out.

                         SPIKE
               Never happen. Alright, I'll go get
               chanty with the fellahs. But you
               have to do me one favor.

He grabs Sheila and hands her to Drusilla. The two lovers
exchange a smile, then Spike heads upstairs.

Drusilla looks at Sheila, then past her, to the dolls.

                                                    CONTINUED

27 CONTINUED: (2)   27

                         DRUSILLA
            See, Miss Edith, if you'd been good,
            you could watch with the rest.

28 CLOSE ON: DRUSILLA   28

    Now has Vampire face on. It is pale, horrible, and eerily
    beautiful.

    She buries dripping fangs in Sheila's neck.

29 EXT. SCHOOL - DAY - ESTABLISHING   29   *

    A hand painted banner across the entry: PARENT TEACHER NIGHT.

30 INT. LIBRARY - DAY   30   *

    Hectic. Cordelia and Xander are sharpening stakes, Jenny and
    Willow sights arrows, tightening screws on the crossbow and
    other weapons. Camera moves past them to find Buffy in
    equally frantic preparation: chopping carrots. She's laying
    out an impressive platter of crudites. She has a nice I'm-a-
    model-student dress on.

                         WILLOW
            Do you think Sheila will show?

                         BUFFY
            I doubt it. She doesn't seem to care
            about getting kicked out - about
            anything. I sort of envy that.

                         WILLOW
            I don't think she's very happy.

    Giles crosses in, Book in hand.

                         GILES
                  (re: diaries)
            For three nights the unholy ones
            scourge themselves into a fury,
            culminating in a savage attack on the
            Night of Saint Vigeous.

                         XANDER
            Anyone still remember when Saturday
            night meant date night?

                         CORDELIA
            You sure don't.

                                                         CONTINUED

> BUFFY
> (glances at clock)
> The parents start arriving in an
> hour. Okay, banners are in place,
> the lounge is comfy, what am I
> forgetting...?

> WILLOW
> Punch?

> BUFFY
> Punch! I need punch.

> XANDER
> The important thing in punch is the
> ratio of Vodka to Schnapps.
> (off looks)
> That was obviously far too
> sophisticated a joke for this crowd.

Cordelia drops a stake, exhausted.

> CORDELIA
> My fingers are cramping, how long
> have I been doing this?

> XANDER
> Three minutes.

> CORDELIA
> So can I go now? She's not gonna
> need that many stakes, I mean if this
> Spike guy's as mean as you all said,
> it should be over pretty fast.
> (to Buffy, off their
> looks)
> We're still rooting for you Saturday.
> I'd be there myself but I've got a
> leg wax.

Buffy is up and on her way out.

> BUFFY
> You guys hold the fort. I'm punch
> bound.

She goes out. There is a beat, then both Xander and Cordelia
reach for some of the food Buffy has prepared.

Buffy's back in the door in a flash.

> BUFFY (cont'd)
> No!

CONTINUED

30 CONTINUED: (2)   30

And gone again.

31   INT. SCHOOL LOUNGE - NIGHT   31

CLOSE - A HUMONGOUS PUNCH BOWL.

The lounge looks clean. Extra chairs lined up. Pretty,
freshly painted banners hung. Refreshments laid out. Willow
joins Buffy as she stirs the punch up.

                    WILLOW
          What kind of punch did you make?

                    BUFFY
          Lemonade.

Willow takes a cup, pleased.

                    BUFFY (cont'd)
          I made it fresh and everything.

                    WILLOW
          How much sugar did you use?

                    BUFFY
                    (worried)
          Sugar?

And as she says it, Willow sips. The catastrophic face she
makes indicates a total lack of sugar.

                    WILLOW
                    (hardly able to speak)
          It's very good...

She puts the cup down, still face making.

                    BUFFY
          Now if we can just keep my mother and
          Snyder from crossing paths for the
          next three hours...

                    WILLOW
                    (sees Joyce arriving)
          Hi Mrs. Summers.

                    JOYCE
          Hi Willow.
                    (to Buffy)
          Hi honey. Did you do all this?

CONTINUED

31 CONTINUED: 31

                         BUFFY
          I did. How 'bout some lemonade --

Behind Joyce, Buffy sees Snyder (wearing a name tag) heading
down the hall towards them.

                         BUFFY (cont'd)
          -- after Willow shows you the library.
                    (steering them away
                     from Snyder)
          I have to stay here and hostess.

                         WILLOW
          Yeah, the library -- no, because
          Giles and everyone...

                         BUFFY
                    (steering them down
                     another hall)
          ...are locked inside studying.
          French class it is

Willow disappears with Joyce as Snyder walks up.

                         MR. SNYDER
          Was that your mother?

                         BUFFY
          Oh hi. Yeah, I wanted to introduce
          you. She wouldn't have said too
          much, she doesn't speak a word of
          English.

Snyder gives her a look, moves off to greet some parents,
Buffy looks up at

32 THE CLOCK ON THE WALL   32

It reads: 6:14.

                                        DISSOLVE TO:

33 THE CLOCK ON THE WALL   33

It now reads 8:45. Parents and teachers (with name tags)
mingle. Buffy stands near the refreshments keeping a wary
eye out for her mother and Snyder. Cordelia walks up, fuming.

                         CORDELIA
          Giles has us locked in that library
          working on your weapons. Even slaves
          get minimum wage.

                                        CONTINUED

Cordelia stares at Buffy's skin.

                    BUFFY
          What?

                    CORDELIA
          You're starting to look pretty
          slagged. What are you, just skipping
          foundation entirely now?

                    BUFFY
          Cordelia, I have at least three lives
          to contend with and none of them
          really mesh. It's like oil and water
          and... a third unmeshable thing.

                    CORDELIA
          Yeah. And I can see the oil.
               (re: Willow and Joyce
                approaching)
          Is that your mom? Now that's a woman
          who knows how to moisturize. Did it
          like skip a generation?

                    JOYCE
          Well I believe I've seen every
          classroom on campus. And in each one
          your teachers had miraculously just
          stepped out.

Buffy shoots Willow a discreet thumbs up, sees Snyder heading
their way.

                    BUFFY
          But you didn't see the boiler room.
          And that's really interesting because
          of the boiler being right there in
          the room and all --

Joyce ignores Buffy's efforts and offers her hand to Snyder.

                    JOYCE
          Hello. I'm Joyce Summers, Buffy's
          mother.

                    MR. SNYDER
          Principal Snyder. I'm afraid we need
          to talk. My office is down here.

Buffy deflates as they walk away.

                    BUFFY
          He didn't look very happy.

                                                   CONTINUED

                    WILLOW
    But you did such a good job...

                    CORDELIA
    When they're done talking...

                    BUFFY
    What?

                    CORDELIA
    My guess? Tenth high school reunion?
    You'll still be grounded.

                    WILLOW
    Cordelia... Have some punch.

34 INT. LIBRARY - NIGHT   34

Jenny sees Giles, studying a diary, looking concerned and
intrigued.

                    GILES
    Well, there you are...

                    JENNY
    There who is?

                    GILES
             (re: diaries)
    Our new friend Spike. "Known as
    William the Bloody, earned his
    nickname by torturing his victims
    with railroad spikes..." Ahh, but
    here's some good news, he's barely
    two hundred, not even as old as
    Angel... oh...

His face darkens again.

                    XANDER
    That's a bad look, right?

                    GILES
    I think your suggestion of running
    away this Saturday may have been a
    good one. Spike has fought two
    Slayers in the last century. And
    killed them both.

35 INT. SCHOOL LOUNGE - A BIT LATER   35

    With the exception of FIVE PEOPLE (two PARENTS, two TEACHERS,
    one STUDENT) everyone else is gone. Willow tries to console
    Buffy.

    Snyder and Joyce return. Buffy doesn't have to ask: Joyce
    looks at Buffy like she wishes she were never born.

                    JOYCE
          In the car. Now.

    Snyder gives Buffy a "gotcha" look, starts flicking off hall
    lights. Buffy hangs her head, moves off with her mom.
    Snyder, by the platform in front of the big picture window,
    flicks off that light as (possible slow mo) the huge window
    shatters and Spike crashes through it. Dressed for killing.
    Flanked by Lean Boy and FIVE other vampires.

    Pandemonium erupts, Snyder and others scream and run. Only
    Buffy stands still as Spike locks eyes with her way across
    the room.

                    SPIKE
      What can I say? I couldn't wait.

                                BLACK OUT.

                  END OF ACT TWO

ACT THREE

36   INT. SCHOOL LOUNGE - NIGHT   36

     As before: chaos. Snyder, the two parents, two teachers and
     one student run for their lives.

37   SPIKE   37

     Makes a beeline for Buffy. She grabs a chair, swings it
     around in a 360 and lets fly. It hits him SOLID in the head,
     knocking him back.

                         BUFFY
               Run!

     Buffy grabs Joyce, drags her toward an exit. Sees Vamp 1
     blocking it. Pivots back toward the hall.

                         BUFFY (cont'd)
               They've got the exits, this way!
               Everybody, this way!

     Buffy hustles her mother, Snyder, Parent 1, the two teachers
     and the student down the NORTH HALL towards the library.

38   SPIKE BOUNDS UP, HIS HAND SHOOTS OUT   38

     Grabs Parent 2 by the neck. Looking for the Slayer.

                         SPIKE
               No one gets out! Especially the girl!

39   CORDELIA AND WILLOW   39

     Run for their lives in the opposite direction Buffy went,
     towards the SOUTH EXIT where Vampire # 2 leaps out, gets a
     hold of Cordelia who screams. Willow grabs the heavy bust of
     Flutie, clonks him with it, they cut left, down the SOUTH
     HALL. Lean Boy sees them, gives chase. Meanwhile:

40   INT. NORTH HALL - NIGHT - BUFFY, JOYCE, SNYDER   40

     And the others race towards the library. Giles, Xander and
     Jenny fly out of the library doors, see them coming. Buffy
     shouts to Giles:

                         BUFFY
               It's Spike and a small army! Look out!

     Vampire 3 rounds the corner.

                                              CONTINUED

40 CONTINUED: 40

    Buffy spots Vampires # 4 and 5 closing from the hall that
    leads back toward the lounge. She hustles her charges into
    the SCIENCE CLASSROOM.

                        BUFFY (cont'd)
                In here! Go, go!

    Giles, Jenny and Xander hightail it back into the library, as
    Vamp 3 pounds on the door.

41 INT. SCIENCE CLASSROOM - NIGHT   41

    The one with the big metal slats covering the high windows.
    The best fortress Buffy could find on short notice. She
    hustles everyone in, being none to gentle with Snyder, locks
    the door just as Vamp 4 gets there.

                        BUFFY
                Barricade --

                                               SMASH CUT TO:

42 INT. LIBRARY - NIGHT - GILES   42

                        GILES
                -- the door!

    Giles, Xander and Jenny do just that.

43 INT. SCIENCE CLASSROOM - NIGHT   43

    Joyce and the others slide desks and cabinets in front of the
    door as Buffy vaults across the room and locks the door at
    the opposite end of the room. That's when the lights go out.

                        MR. SNYDER
                Oh my god!

44 INT. LIBRARY - SAME TIME   44

    Lights go out here, too. (Note: from here on out only
    emergency lights and Gersh-light.)

45 SPIKE IN THE LOUNGE   45

    His hand still firmly around poor Parent 1's neck. Lean Boy
    runs up:

                        LEAN BOY
                We cut the power, nobody got out.

                        SPIKE
                And the Slayer?

                                                    CONTINUED

45 CONTINUED: 45

                         LEAN BOY
              She either went that way...

Lean Boy points down the North Hall. We see Vamps 3 and 4
trying to break down the door to the classroom.

                         LEAN BOY (cont'd)
                    (points to South Hall)
              ...or that way. I saw two others --

                         SPIKE
                    (tightens death grip
                     on parent's neck)
              You don't know?

Spike sighs, turns to the terrified parent.

                         SPIKE (cont'd}
              I'm a veal kinda guy, you're too old
              to eat...

He eases up on the guy's neck. The Parent starts to breath
again. Until Spike snaps his neck and he drops out of frame.

                         SPIKE (cont'd)
              ...but not to kill.
                    (to Lean Boy)
              I feel better.

46 INT. LIBRARY - NIGHT   46

Giles clicks the hook switch on the phone. Dead.

                         GILES
              They cut the phones.
                    (to Xander)
              There's an old boarded up cellar
              behind the stacks. You can get out
              that way. Find Angel. He knows
              about Spike, we need him.

                         XANDER
              I'm not going anywhere until I know
              Buffy and Willow are all right.

                         GILES
              No one's going to be all right if we
              don't get some help.

Off Xander, realizing the truth of that,

47 INT. SCIENCE CLASSROOM - NIGHT   47

Buffy stands next to her mom, thinking hard about her next
move. Snyder is losing his shit. The two teachers, the
parent and the student are freaked. O.S. we hear VAMPIRES
hurl their shoulders into the doors.

                    PARENT
          Who are those people, what do they
          want?

                    JOYCE
          I didn't get much of a look but, is
          there something wrong with their
          faces?

                    MR. SNYDER
          Yes!
               (Buffy looks over)
          P.C.P. It's a gang on P.C.P.! We've
          got to get out of here.

Snyder climbs up on a chair, claws at the metal slats on the
windows. Buffy moves to him. Speaks softly but firmly.

                    BUFFY
          You can't go outside. They'll kill
          you.

                    MR. SNYDER
          YOU DON'T TELL ME, I TELL YOU!

Buffy pulls him off the chair. Gets in his face. Never
loses her cool:

                    BUFFY
          They will kill everyone in this room.
          Nobody goes out. Nobody comes in.
          Until I say so. Do you read me?

It's clear to everyone in the room that she knows what she's
talking about. Snyder is not about to admit it.

                    MR. SNYDER
          Who do you think you are?

                    BUFFY
          I'm the one who knows how to stop
          them.

Buffy turns to go. Joyce grabs her.

                                              CONTINUED

                        JOYCE
            Buffy, are you crazy? I know you've
            been...
                    (re: Snyder)
            ...accused of fighting and other
            things but those guys are serious...
            you can't go out there.

                        BUFFY
            I know. That's why I'm going up
            there.

Buffy points up, puts a foot on a chair and jumps.

ANGLE - THE CEILING TILE

Buffy moves it aside, climbs into the cramped space above.
She looks back down.

                        BUFFY (cont'd)
            Don't worry, Mom.

And she's gone. Off Joyce,

                                            CUT TO:

48 INT. SOUTH HALL - NIGHT   48

The hall where Cordelia and Willow ran. Spike strolls down
the hall, humming a merry tune. Lean Boy searches in the
b.g.

                        SPIKE
            Slayer... here kitty, kitty...

WHAM! Spike kicks down a door.

                        SPIKE (cont'd)
            I find one of your friends first, I'm
            gonna suck 'em dry...

49 DISTANT ANGLE   49

Spike is full in the frame.

                        SPIKE
            ...and use their bones to bash your
            head in.

WHAM! Another door kicked open. CAMERA PANS off Spike to a
door marked UTILITY CLOSET. CAMERA PUSHES IN:

50 INT. UTILITY CLOSET - NIGHT   50

Willow and Cordelia huddle inside. Plenty scared. They hear:

                        SPIKE (O.S.)
            Are you gettin' a word picture here?

                        CORDELIA
            Oh god, oh god, oh god --

Willow clamps her hand over Cordelia's mouth.

51 INT. SOUTH HALL - NIGHT   51

Spike's about to kick in the Utility Closet when:

                        LEAN BOY
            Spike!

Spike lowers his foot.

52 LEAN BOY - AT THE FAR END OF THE HALL   52

As Spike arrives. Skinny points up to a VENT REGISTER near
the ceiling.

                        LEAN BOY
            Listen.

Faint SOUND of someone crawling. Spike smiles.

                        SPIKE
            Someone's in the ceiling.

53 INT. CRAWLSPACE - NIGHT   53

Buffy crawls through the claustrophobic space. She HEARS
something behind her. Tries to look. Too tight to see for
sure if anything's coming up behind her. She move on. We
creep with her for a few tense beats.

54 INT. LIBRARY - NIGHT   54

Giles pockets several stakes, hefts a stabbing axe as he
heads to the doors (with cabinets piled high in front of
them) peers through a piece of the little round window.
Starts to pull a cabinet back.

                        JENNY
            What are you doing? There's at least
            three vampires in that hall and god
            knows how many others in the building.

                                                    CONTINUED

> GILES
> I'm the Watcher, I'm responsible for
> her, I have to go.

Jenny puts her hand on his arm.

> JENNY
> Be careful.

Giles looks at her hand for a beat, emotions churning, then
grabs the cabinet.

> GILES
> Push them back the minute I'm --

CRASH! The ceiling tile above his head gives way -- a body
fall through. Giles raises his axe. Stops.

> GILES (cont'd)
> Buffy!

It's Buffy, already on her feet. Dusty and dirty. But fine.

> GILES (cont'd)
> You're all right.

> JENNY
> How are the others?

Buffy is already loading her book bag with a throwing ax,
stakes, etc.

> BUFFY
> Snyder, my mom, and four others are
> locked in the science room across the
> hall. Cordelia and Willow ran the
> other way, I don't know if they're...
> where's Xander?

> GILES
> He got out through the stacks. He's
> getting Angel.

> BUFFY
> Good. After I take out the vamps in
> the hall you two can get my mom and
> the others out that way, too.

Buffy grabs the pack, kicks a chair under the hole in the
ceiling.

> GILES
> I should go with you and fight.

CONTINUED

54 CONTINUED: (2)   54

                         BUFFY
               Giles, my mother is in that
               classroom. If I don't make it, I
               know you'll make sure she does.

                         GILES
               Bloody well right I will. What's
               your plan?

                         BUFFY
               They split up to hold us here. So I
               can take 'em one on one. Set 'em up,
               knock 'em down.

          They share a look, and Buffy's up on the chair and back in
          the ceiling vent.

                         GILES
               Watch your back...

55 INT. SCIENCE CLASSROOM - NIGHT   55

          Snyder paces, growing more feverish by the moment. The
          others look pretty freaked. Vamps (O.S.) still POUNDING on
          doors. Joyce tries to calm Snyder.

                         JOYCE
               Why don't you sit down...

          He looks at her with wild eyes.

                         MR. SNYDER
               This is my school. What I say goes.
               And I say this isn't happening.

                         JOYCE
               Well then I guess the danger is over.

                         PARENT
               I'm not waiting for them to break
               down the doors. I'm getting out.

                         JOYCE
               Don't be an idiot!

                         MR. SNYDER
               I'm beginning to see a certain mother-
               daughter resemblance.

                         JOYCE
               OH yeah.

                                                         CONTINUED

55 CONTINUED: 55

He climbs up on a chair, starts pulling like crazy at the
metal bands that cover the high windows.

                        JOYCE (cont'd)
            No! You heard what Buffy said --

                        MR. SNYDER
            She's a student, what does she know?

And Snyder climbs up next to the parent, starts helping him
yank on the metal.

56 INT. NORTH HALL - NIGHT   56

Vamp 5 (at door closest to library) hurls his shoulder one
more time, stands there breathing hard. On the wall behind
him is a fire ax in a glass box. Suddenly Spike is next to
him.

                        VAMP 5
            Doors are solid.

Spike gently puts a hand on 5's head.

                        SPIKE
            Use your head...

Spike slams 5's head into the glass, breaking it. Drops the
fire ax into 5's hand, moves back down the hall towards the
lounge telling 3 in route:

                        SPIKE (cont'd)
            You. Come with me.

Vamp 5 raises the ax and CHOPS INTO THE DOOR!

57 INT. SCIENCE CLASSROOM - NIGHT   57

Joyce and the others react to the new assault. Parent and
Snyder have one metal band peeled off and now they get a
second one. Just enough room to crawl out the high window.

                        MR. SNYDER
            I did it!

Snyder tries to get out. Parent pushes him aside -- every
man for himself -- and lunges through first. He's a big guy,
trying to squeeze himself through the little opening.

And the ax is still chopping at the door.

                                                      CONTINUED

57 CONTINUED: 57

    And suddenly the parent gets a big boost -- from outside! We
    don't see it, but something gets him and starts pulling.

                          PARENT
              He's got me! Help! Help!

    And WHOOSH! he's gone. Right out the window. His HORRIBLE
    SCREAMS quickly fade to silence. Snyder jumps down, backing
    away as Joyce climbs up, pounds the metal back in place.

58 INT. LOUNGE - NIGHT - TRACKING SHOT   58

    Looking up as the ceiling moves past us. Then we see a duct
    register. This is SPIKE'S POV. ANGLE DOWN down to Spike
    looking up at the vent, listening. Vamp 3 stands nearby,
    listening, too.

59 INT. CPAWLSPACE - NIGHT   59

    Buffy crawls along. Cautious. Her pack o' weapons making a
    little scraping NOISE.

60 EXT. SCHOOL - NIGHT   60

    The dead body of the Parent lies on the ground. Angel and
    Xander run past it. Xander looks down, freaked. Angel looks
    ahead, grim and determined.

                          XANDER
              You know about this Spike guy so, uh,
              you got a plan?

    Angel grabs him and drags him out of frame.

                          XANDER (cont'd)   *
              Good plan.   *

61 INT. UTILITY CLOSET - NIGHT   61

    Willow and Cordelia huddle in the corner. Cordelia whispers:

                          CORDELIA
              I think he's gone.

    She starts to reach for the door knob.

                          WILLOW
              He could come back.

                                                          CONTINUED

61 CONTINUED: 61

    Cordelia drops her hand. Fast.

CONTINUED

61 CONTINUED: 61

                              CORDELIA
                    What are we gonna do?

                              WILLOW
                    Pray.

62 INT. SCHOOL LOUNGE - NIGHT   62

    Spike pulls two long metal support bars out of the rubble of
    the broken window. Tosses one to Vamp 3. Walks around the
    lounge never taking his eyes off the ceiling. Suddenly he
    thrusts the metal spear up right through the ceiling.
    Hunting Buffy. Takes a few steps. Stabs again. Vamp 3 gets
    the idea. Does likewise.

63 INT. CRAWLSPACE - CONTINUOUS - NIGHT   63

    Buffy is moving cautiously forward when a rod comes shooting
    up right in front of her. A moment, and she slowly crawls
    backwards.

64 INT. LIBRARY HALL - NIGHT   64

    Vamp 5 chops away. He's seeing holes in the door now. And
    the terrified faces of Joyce and Snyder within. A couple of
    more chops and it'll all be over.

                              VAMP 5
                         (calls to vamp 4)
                    Guard that door. I'm almost in.

    VAMP 4 - AROUND THE CORNER AND DOWN THE HALL - nods, he heard.

    VAMP 5 - raising the ax, hears something. Looks left. Looks
    right. Nothing there. Starts to bring the ax down into the
    door when the ceiling bursts above him and Buffy stakes him
    quicker and quieter than you can say WHOOSH! Buffy moves to
    the door, her mom sees her through one of the ax holes.

                              JOYCE
                    Buffy! Are you okay?

                              BUFFY
                         (sotto voce)
                    I'm fine, Mom.

                              JOYCE
                    Buffy, get out of here! We'll be
                    okay.

                                                      CONTINUED

64 CONTINUED: 64

                              BUFFY
                   Just hang on for one more minute,
                   till I tell you to open the door.

Buffy peers around the corner, looks down the hall. Vamp 4
is dutifully standing guard at the other door.

Buffy steps back from the corner. Selects a sharp stake for
his demise. Senses someone behind her. Spins. It's Sheila,
who's just come in from the outside door.

                         BUFFY (cont'd)
                   Sheila! Where've you --?

                              SHEILA
                   Sorry I'm late. There's some pretty
                   weird guys outside...

                              BUFFY
                   They're trying to kill us.

                              SHEILA
                         (picks up fire ax)
                   This should be fun.

Buffy smiles: she's got an ally. She turns away to look and
Sheila stares at her with dead contempt.

65   INT. SCHOOL LOUNGE - NIGHT   65

Spike and 3 stab the ceiling. The door bursts open. Angel
enters, Xander in tow. Spike recognizes:

                              SPIKE
                   Angelus. I'll be damned.

We see that Angel has VAMP FACE on. Xander sees it too, and
jumps. Spike drops his bar. Spike and Angel (never letting
go of Xander) hug. Then:

                              ANGEL
                   I taught you to always guard your
                   perimeter.
                         (re: door he entered)
                   You should have someone out there.

                              SPIKE
                   I did. I'm surrounded by idiots.
                   What's new with you?

                              ANGEL
                   Everything.

                                                    CONTINUED

65 CONTINUED: 65

                         SPIKE
          Come up against this Slayer yet?

                         ANGEL
          She's cute. Not too bright, though.
          Gave the puppy dog, I'm-all-tortured
          act. Keeps her off my back when I
          feed.

                         SPIKE
          People still fall for that Anne Rice
          routine? What a world.

Xander looks from Angel to Spike.

                         XANDER
          I knew you were a lying... undead
          liar guy.

Angel silences him by grabbing his hair and his shoulder and
baring Xander's neck for Spike.

                         ANGEL
          Want a bite before we kill her?

Off Xander, about to lose his mind,

66 INT. NORTH HALL - NIGHT   66

Buffy and Sheila.

                         BUFFY
          Stay behind me.

Buffy sneaks around the corner. Sheila dutifully close
behind, ax at the ready. Buffy sees:

VAMP 4 - his back to them. Buffy raises her stake to hurl,
taking careful aim.

ANGLE - BEHIND SHEILA AND BUFFY

We now see Sheila raise her ax high over her own shoulder.
Aiming it at the back of Buffy's head. As we COME AROUND we
see that Sheila has a new face on. A vampire face.

                         BLACK OUT.

                    END OF ACT THREE

48.

ACT FOUR

67 INT. NORTH HALL - NIGHT   67

As before. Buffy about to hurl her stake. Sheila about to
cleave Buffy's head.

CAMERA ROARS PAST THEM towards the little porthole window to
the library as Giles' face appears.

                    GILES
          Buffy! Look out --

Sheila chops down. Buffy spins, grabs the ax handle under
the blade stopping it inches from her pretty head.

VAMP 4 - sees her now, runs full tilt for her from behind.

Buffy pivots the ax head into Sheila's jaw. She goes down.
Buffy spins, swinging the ax. Vamp 4 ducks. The fire ax
slices over his head, imbeds in the wall. He comes back up.
Looking cocky. Until he looks down. Stake's already in his
heart. We cut away before he's even dust.

Buffy turns to Sheila who growls and back away, pure animal
now. She runs outside.

                    BUFFY
          Mom! Now!

Joyce unlocks and opens the axed door as Giles and Jenny open
the library doors. Buffy ushers Joyce, Snyder and the others
into Giles' care.

                    BUFFY (cont'd)
          Get them out.

                    JOYCE
          You're coming, too.

                    BUFFY
          In a minute. Go!

Snyder doesn't need any coaching. He bumps a woman teacher
out of his way, makes a beeline for the library. The others
follow, Giles and Jenny helping them to safety.

                    GILES
          Right through the back...

Joyce hangs back, watching as Buffy heads down the hall
toward the lounge.

68 INT. LOUNGE - NIGHT   68

Lean Boy and Vamp 2 enter from the South hall, move next to
Vamp 3, watch as Spike's eyes move from Xander's neck to
Angel's face. Angel holds Xander in a vice-like grip.

                    SPIKE
          Haven't seen you in the killing
          fields for an age.

                    ANGEL
          I'm not much for company.

                    SPIKE
          No, you never were. So why are you
          so scared of this Slayer?

                    ANGEL
          Scared?

                    SPIKE
          Time was, youd've taken her out in a
          heartbeat. Now look at you. This
          tortured thing is an act, right?
          You're not housebroken?

                    ANGEL
          I saw her kill the Master. Hey, you
          think you can take her alone, be my
          guest.
                    (re: Xander)
          I'll just feed and run.

                    SPIKE
          Don't be silly. We're old friends.
          We'll do her together. Let's drink
          to it.

Spike nods at Xander's neck, smiles. Xander tries to break
free. Angel holds him steady. Spike holds Angel's gaze,
bends to Xander's neck.

                    XANDER
          No!

At the last moment, Spike looks down, Xander closes his eyes,
and Spike sucker punches Angel in the face.

                    SPIKE
          You think you can fool me? You were
          my sire, man... you were my Yoda!   *

                    ANGEL
          Things change.

                                              CONTINUED

                              SPIKE
                    Not us! Not demons. Man, I can't
                    believe this -- you Uncle Tom!

Spike and Angel circle each other.

                              SPIKE (cont'd)
                         (to vamps)
                    This isn't a spectator sport!

They all attack Angel and Xander. Angel shoves Xander toward
the exit. They just make it out the door.

Vamp 2, 3 and Lean Boy chase after them. Spike picks up the
rod again, ready to give chase, but-

SPIKE

Stops. Very still. CIRCLE AROUND HIM as the door behind
slowly opens. Buffy enters, twenty feet behind him, throwing
ax in hand.

                              SPIKE (cont'd)
                         (without turning)
                    Fe fi fo fum. I smell the blood of
                    a nice ripe girl.

Now he turns.

                              BUFFY
                    Do we really need weapons for this?

                              SPIKE
                    I just like 'em. Make me feel all
                    manly.

A beat, then he drops his. And she hers.

                              SPIKE (cont'd)   *
                    The last Slayer I killed, she begged
                    for her life. I don't see you as the
                    begging kind.

                              BUFFY
                    You shouldn't have come here.

                              SPIKE
                    Yeah, I messed up your doilies and
                    stuff. But I just got so bored!
                    Tell you what. As a personal favor
                    from me to you, I'll make it quick.
                    It won't hurt a bit.

                                                          CONTINUED

68 CONTINUED: (2)   68

                              BUFFY
                Wrong. It's gonna hurt **a lot.**

A moment's hesitation crosses his face, and he HURLS HIMSELF
at her. Fast.

And now the punches fly, fast and furious. Think Gross
Pointe Blanke. Two pros giving it all they've got.

69 EXT. SCHOOL - NIGHT   69

Xander and Angel fight Vamps 2, 3 and Lean Boy. They are
holding their own, as Angel knocks 2 into 3, and Xander holds
off Lean Boy with a trash can lid.

70 INT. LOUNGE - NIGHT   70

Buffy and Spike are going full tilt. They're both getting
winded, Spike is starting to give just a little better than
he's getting.

Spike closes in with a vicious combination of punches and
kicks. She pretends like the last one hurts more than it
did. He goes for the big k.o. She perks up and moves out of
the way causing Spike's hand to go right through the wall.
Buffy locks her hands and hammers him on the back of the neck.

                              SPIKE
                Now that hurt.

Spike rips his hand out of the wall -- bringing a broken two
by four stud with it.

                          SPIKE (cont'd)
                Not as much as this will -

Wallops Buffy with the stud. Buffy goes down. Winded,
nowhere to turn. She looks up at Spike, standing over her
victorious.

He raises the stud over his head. He's going to bash her
brains in. As he's about to do just that --

71 SPIKE IS HIT IN THE FACE   71

By Joyce! Wielding the blunt end of the fire ax. Spike
flies back -- hits the ground hard. Totally blindsided.
Joyce is deep in a mother's rage.

                                              CONTINUED

71 CONTINUED: 71

                         JOYCE
              You get the hell away from my
              daughter!

Spike (in the dark so Joyce can't see his face too well)
glances out the broken window:

A72 EXT. SCHOOL - NIGHT   A72   *

Angel knocks Lean Boy on his ass, saving Xander. Vamp 2 is
already on the ground. 3 turns and runs. As does Lean Boy.
Retreat time.

72 BACK TO SCENE   72

Buffy is now on her feet. Ready for blood. Standing next to
her mother whose hands grip the ax: Thelma and Louise on
crack. Spike knows it's time to run and fight another day.

                         SPIKE
                       (bitterly)
              Women.

And he leaps out the window and disappears into the night.

73 BUFFY TURNS TO HER MOTHER   73

They're both breathing hard. Physically and emotionally
drained.

                         BUFFY
              Mom... you...

                         JOYCE
              No one... lays a finger... on my
              little girl.

And Joyce drops the ax. And Buffy falls into her arms.

74 EXT. SCHOOL - NIGHT   74

Cop cars, COPS, flashing bubble lights, CORONER'S WAGON.

Giles and Jenny walk out, passing

The CHIEF OP POLICE, who moves to Snyder.

                         MR. SNYDER
              Hello Bob.

                                                          CONTINUED

74 CONTINUED: 74

                              CHIEF
                It's over. They all got away.

        Chief glances at the others, lowers his voice.   *

                                                    CONTINUED

74 CONTINUED: 74

                         CHIEF (cont'd)
              We got a body inside, another one on
              the south lawn. Looks like he was
              pulled right out the window.

                         MR. SNYDER
              I told him not to go out that window.

                         CHIEF
              I'm going to have to say something to
              the media.

                         MR. SNYDER
              So?

                         CHIEF
              So... usual story, gang-related,
              P.C.P.?

                         MR. SNYDER
              What did you have in mind, the truth?

Snyder locks eyes with the Chief. They know a lot more than
they're letting on.

                         CHIEF
              Right. Gang related. PCP.

75 XANDER AND ANGEL (NOT IN VAMP FACE)   75

Round a different corner of the building.

                         XANDER
              So when you were giving him my neck
              to chew on, how come you didn't clock
              him before he clocked you?

                         ANGEL
              I told you, I couldn't make the first
              move. I had to see if he was buying
              it or not.

                         XANDER
              And if he bit me, then what?

                         ANGEL
                     (can't resist)
              We would have known he bought it.

Angel moves off. Xander stares off after him with renewed
loathing.

                                              CONTINUED

75 CONTINUED: 75

                         XANDER
                And what was that about you bein'
                Spike's sire? What's a sire?
                         (rubs his aching neck)
                God, I could sleep for a month.

76 BUFFY AND JOYCE   76

Walk to their car together.

                         BUFFY
                So, uh... what did you and principal
                Snyder talk about anyway?

                         JOYCE
                Principal Snyder told me you were a
                troublemaker. And I could care less.
                         (turns to her)
                I have a daughter who can take care
                of herself. Who's brave and
                resourceful and thinks of others when
                there's a crisis. No matter who you
                hang out with or what dumb teenage
                stuff you think you have to do, I'm
                gonna sleep better knowing all that.

Needless to say, a moment passes between them. They start
toward the car again.

                         BUFFY
                About how long till this wears off
                and you start ragging on me again?

                         JOYCE
                At LEAST a week and a half.

                         BUFFY
                That is so cool...

Off them,

                                                    DISSOLVE TO:

77 EXT. SCHOOL - NIGHT - LATER   77

The last cop car pulls away. All is silent and still.

78 INT. SOUTH HALL - NIGHT   78

CAMERA creeps down the completely deserted hall. And stops
before the door marked UTILITY CLOSET.

55.

79 INT. UTILITY CLOSET - NIGHT   79

Willow and Cordelia are still here, forgotten in all the
turmoil. Cordelia's praying hard, whispering:

                    CORDELIA
          ...and if you get me out of this I
          swear I'll never be mean to anyone
          ever again... you know, unless they
          really deserve it...

PUSH IN on poor Willow, for whom death by Spike is beginning
to seem like a wondrous alternative,

                    CORDELIA (cont'd)
          ...or unless it's that time of the
          month in which case I don't see how
          You or anyone else can hold me
          responsible...

                    WILLOW
          Ask for some aspirin.

80 EXT. SCHOOL - NIGHT   80

                    CORDELIA (O.S.)
          ...and send us some aspi -- hey!

81 EXT. FACTORY - NIGHT JUST TURNING TO DAY   81

82 INT. FACTORY - DAWN   82

The first warm glow of sunrise is peaking through the huge
windows. Vamps 2 and 3 dutifully shut out the dreaded light
by closing huge shutters.

Spike moves across the floor looking a lot worse for wear.
Drusilla is waiting for him.

                    DRUSILLA
          Did she hurt you?

Is there just a little pleasure at that question?

                    SPIKE
          I was close, baby, but...

CONTINUED

82 CONTINUED: 82

                              DRUSILLA
                    Come here.

She strokes his head.

                              SPIKE
                    A Slayer with family and friends.
                    That sure as hell wasn't in the
                    brochure.

                              DRUSILLA
                    You'll kill her. And then we'll have
                    a nice party.

Spike is distracted, looking over at:

83 ANGLE: THE ANOINTED ONE   83

Is standing with Lean Boy and a few others, looking glum.

                              SPIKE
                    Yeah, a party.

                              DRUSILLA
                    With streamers, and songs.

                              SPIKE
                    How's the Annoying One?

                              DRUSILLA
                    He doesn't want to play.

                              SPIKE
                    Figures. Suppose I better go make
                    nice.

He crosses to them, looks down at the Anointed One. Everyone
stares at him expectantly. Begrudgingly, he goes down on one
knee.

                              ANOINTED ONE
                    You failed.

                              SPIKE
                    Yeah, I, uh... I offer penance...

                              LEAN BOY
                    Penance? You should lay down your
                    life! Our numbers are depleted. The
                    Feast of St. Vigeous has been ruined
                    by your impatience.

                                                       CONTINUED

83 CONTINUED: 83

                        ANOINTED ONE
                Should I forgive you?

                        SPIKE
                I was... rash... and if I had to do
                it all over again.... ah who am I
                kidding? I'd do it exactly the same,
                only I'd do THIS first.

Spike grabs the Anointed One. Hard. Sweeps him into the
cage, slamming the door shut.

Lean Boy makes a move. Spike doesn't even look back as he
viciously backhands him away.

Everyone else is too shocked and scared to speak. Drusilla
gives it half a beat, then smiles, jamming on Spike's balls.

Spike slings a meat hook to the top of the cage, grabs a
pulley chain and starts raising the cage.

                        SPIKE (cont'd)
                From now on we're gonna have a little
                less ritual and a little more fun
                around here.

The cage rises in the air... toward a great big old PATCH OF
SUNLIGHT shining in through the top shutters. Shutters the
vamps haven't got around to yet.

84 THE ANOINTED ONE   84

Looks from the impending sun back down at Spike. As the cage
enters the sunlight and the Anointed One cries out --

85 SPIKE GIVES A LAST FINAL TUG ON THE CHAIN   85

And ties it off. We HEAR the end of the Anointed's cry and
then a sizzling sound not unlike Mongolian bar b cue.

86 CRANE UP WIDE   86

Spike takes Drusilla's hand and they head down to their
dungeon suite...

                        SPIKE
                Let's see what on TV.

Lean Boy and the other vamps staring in disbelief after
them...

                                                        CONTINUED

86 CONTINUED: 86

     And the cage, gently swaying to and fro in the hard shaft of
     sun, no sound coming from within, no sign of a body, just a
     gentle waft of smoke curling up into the golden light of a
     brand new day.

                                         BLACK OUT.

                    THE END

BUFFY THE VAMPIRE SLAYER

"Inca Mummy Girl"

Written By

Matt Kiene

&

Joe Reinkemeyer

Directed By

Ellen S. Pressman

SHOOTING SCRIPT

July 31, 1997
August 7, 1997 (Blue Full Script)
August 8, 1997 (Pink Pages)
August 12, 1997 (Yellow Pages)
August 15, 1997 (Green Pages)
August 19, 1997 (Goldenrod Pages)

BUFFY THE VAMPIRE SLAYER

"Inca Mummy Girl"

CAST LIST

```
BUFFY SUMMERS........................ Sarah Michelle Gellar
XANDER HARRIS........................ Nicholas Brendon
RUPERT GILES......................... Anthony S. Head
WILLOW ROSENBERG..................... Alyson Hannigan
CORDELIA CHASE....................... Charisma Carpenter


JOYCE................................*Kristine Sutherland
AMPATA............................... Ara Celi
*PERUVIAN BOY (AMPATA)................ Samuel Jacobs
GWEN.................................* Kristen Winnicki
RODNEY............................... Joey Crawford
GUIDE................................ Bernard White
OZ................................... Seth Green
DEVON................................ Jason Hall
PERU MAN.............................* Gil Birmingham
SVEN................................. Henrik Rosvall
JONATHAN............................. Danny Strong

THE BAND............................. Dingoes Ate My Baby
                                     (music by Four Star Mary)
```

BUFFY THE VAMPIRE SLAYER

"Inca Mummy Girl"

SET LIST

INTERIORS

SUNNYDALE HIGH SCHOOL
    HALL
    LIBRARY
    WOMEN'S RESTROOM

BUFFY'S HOUSE
    BUFFY'S BEDROOM
    BUFFY'S KITCHEN

NATURAL HISTORY MUSEUM
    ENTRANCE LOBBY
    BURIAL CHAMBER
    THE SARCOPHAGUS

THE BRONZE
    BACKSTAGE

EXTERIORS

SUNNYDALE HIGH SCHOOL
    COURTYARD
    FOOTBALL BLEACHERS

BUFFY'S HOUSE
    BUSHES NEAR THE HOUSE

THE BRONZE

GILES' CAR

NATURAL HISTORY MUSEUM

BUS STATION

BUFFY THE VAMPIRE SLAYER

"Inca Mummy Girl"

TEASER

FADE IN:

1 EXT. NATURAL HISTORY MUSEUM - DAY   1

A museum-looking building with a sign: 'SUNNYDALE NATURAL
HISTORY MUSEUM.' Under it is a banner: CULTURAL EXCHANGE
SPECIAL EXHIBIT: TREASURES OF SOUTH AMERICA. BUFFY, WILLOW,
XANDER and other STUDENTS walk up the steps.

            BUFFY
    It's so unfair.

            WILLOW
    I don't think it's that bad.

            BUFFY
    It's the uber-suck! Mom could have
    at least warned me!

            XANDER
    Well, a lot of the parents are doing
    it this year. It's part of this
    whole cultural exchange magilla. The
    exhibit, the dance...

            WILLOW
    I have the best costume for the dance.

            BUFFY
    A complete stranger in my house for
    two weeks! I'm gonna be insane! A
    danger to myself and others within
    three days, I swear.

            XANDER
    I think the exchange student program
    is cool.
            (off their looks)
    I do. It's the beautiful melding of
    two cultures.

            BUFFY
    Have you ever **done** an exchange
    program?

                                        CONTINUED

1 CONTINUED: 1

                        XANDER
              My dad tried to sell me to some
              Armenians once, does that count?

                                              CONTINUED

1 CONTINUED: 1

    CORDELIA is near the door, looking at a facebook with some
    friends.   *

                         CORDELIA
                    (pointing)
               There's mine. Sven. Isn't he   *
               lunchable? Mine's definitely the   *
               best.   *

    REVEAL they are flipping through a yearbook-type album,
    pointing at photos of cute guys. Our three approach.

                         BUFFY
               Whatcha looking at?

                         CORDELIA
               Pictures of our exchange students.
                    (shows a picture)
               Look. One hundred percent Swedish.
               One hundred percent gorgeous. One
               hundred percent staying in my house.

    They all head into the museum.

                                             CUT TO:

2 INT. NATURAL HISTORY MUSEUM - ENTRANCE LOBBY - DAY   2

    They line up behind other students at the exhibit entrance.
    A banner above it states: 'INCA PRINCESS EXHIBIT.'

                         CORDELIA
               Buffy, how's yours? Visually, I mean.

                         BUFFY
               I don't know. Guy-like.

                         XANDER
               By 'guy-like,' you mean a big, beefy,
               guy-like girl, right?

                         BUFFY
               I was just told 'guy.'

                                             CONTINUED

2 CONTINUED: 2

> CORDELIA
> You didn't even look at him first?
> He could be dogly! You live on the
> edge.

> XANDER
> Hold on a sec. This person living in
> your house for two weeks is a man,
> with man parts? This is a terrible
> idea!

> WILLOW
> What about the beautiful melding of
> two cultures?

> XANDER
> There's no melding. Okay? He can
> keep his parts to himself.

> BUFFY
> (looking off)
> What's he doing?

They see RODNEY MUNSON, 16, walking trouble. He stands
alone, facing a wall, doing something we can't see.

> XANDER
> Rodney Munson. God's gift to the
> Bell Curve.

A STUDENT tries to see what Rodney's doing. He looks up and
sneers at the kid, revealing braces. The student backs away.

> XANDER (cont'd)
> What he lacks in smarts, he makes up
> in lack of smarts.

> WILLOW
> You just don't like him 'cause of
> that time he beat you up every day
> for five years.

> XANDER
> Yeah, I'm irrational that way.

> BUFFY
> Maybe I should stop him before he
> gets in --

> WILLOW
> I got it. The non-violent approach
> is probably better here.

CONTINUED

2   CONTINUED: (2)   2

     She goes off, Buffy looking slightly offended.

                    BUFFY
          I wasn't gonna use violence. I don't
          always use violence. Do I?

                    XANDER
          The important thing is, **you** believe
          that.

                    BUFFY
          I might have used reason. Or my
          feminine wiles.

3   ANGLE: RODNEY   3

     He uses a pen knife to scrape gold dust off an Incan Death
     mask and into a baggy.

                    WILLOW (O.C.)
          Hi Rodney.

                    RODNEY
               (snarling)
          Wha'd you...
               (then, seeing her)
          Oh, Willow. Hi.

                    WILLOW
               (re: knife)
          That's probably not something you're
          supposed to be doing. You could get
          in trouble.

                    RODNEY
               (mock horror)
          Oh, no. And they might kick me out
          of school?

                    WILLOW
          We still on for our Chem tutorial
          tomorrow?

                    RODNEY
          Yeah. I think I got almost all 14
          natural elements memorized.

                    WILLOW
          There are 103.   *

                                                  CONTINUED

3 CONTINUED: 3

                         RODNEY
               Oh. So I still got to learn...
                         (calculating)
               Uh...

                         WILLOW
               We'll do a touch-up on math, too.

                         RODNEY
               Thanks.

She smiles as Rodney puts his pen-knife away.

4 ANGLE: THE ENTRANCE TO THE BURIAL CHAMBER   4

A Museum GUIDE speaks into a microphone.

                         GUIDE
               Welcome students. We shall now
               proceed into the Incan Burial Chamber.
                         (ominously)
               The human sacrifice is about to begin.

                                             CUT TO:

5 INT. NATURAL HISTORY MUSEUM - BURIAL CHAMBER - DAY   5

The room is dark, except for spotlights illuminating Incan
artifacts on the walls. They enter.

                         XANDER
               Typical museum trick. Promise human
               sacrifice, deliver old pots and pans.

                         GUIDE
               500 years ago, the Incan people chose
               a beautiful teenage girl to become
               their princess...

In the room is a STONE ZIGGURAT PYRAMID. Block steps lead up
to a flat top we can't see from the floor. They climb the
steps. Willow seems creeped.

                         WILLOW
               I hope this story ends with, 'And she
               lived happily ever after.'

Students walk past a sunken hole. Our kids PEER and see:

THE LEATHERED FACE OF A MUMMY. Macabre. Freeze-dried.
Black holes for eyes. Shrivelled lips. Ugly.

                                             CONTINUED

5 CONTINUED: 5

                         XANDER
              No. I think the story ends with,
              'And she became a scary, discolored,
              shrivelled mummy.'

                         GUIDE
              The Incan people sacrificed their
              Princess to the mountain god,
              Sebancaya. An offering, buried
              alive, for eternity in this dark tomb.

                         WILLOW
              They could have at least wrapped it
              in nice white bandages, like the ones
              in the movies.

                         GUIDE
              The Princess remained there,
              protected only by a cursed seal,
              placed there as a warning to any who
              would wake her.

The guide indicates a pictogram-covered PLATE, nestled in the
mummy's gnarled hands.

A GIGGLE. Xander turns. Sees the Cordettes down on the
museum floor, mooning, 'ooohing' and 'ahhhing' over the
pictures of their exchange students.

                         XANDER
              So, Buffy, when's exchange-o boy
              making his appearance?

WEIRD POV: from inside the sarcophagus. Looking at Buffy.

                         BUFFY
              His name is Ampata. He's showing up
              at the bus station tomorrow night.

                         XANDER
              Ooh, Sunnydale bus depot. Classy.
              What better way to say "Welcome to
              Our Country" than with the stench of
              urine.

The guide motions for the students to follow him.

                         GUIDE
              If you'll follow me this way...

                                        DISSOLVE TO:

6 INT. NATURAL HISTORY MUSEUM - BURIAL CHAMBER - DAY   6

Empty.   Silent.   Then Rodney CREEPS out from the shadows. He
looks at the Mummy, at the plate.

                    RODNEY
         Cool...

He slowly pulls the ceramic plate from the mummy's hands.
There's some resistance, and Rodney accidentally drops the
plate. It shatters.

                    RODNEY (cont'd)
         Damn.

                                                              *

THE MUMMY'S HAND suddenly GRABS Rodney's throat. Rodney
struggles. Eyes and mouth go wide.

THE MUMMY'S EYES crack open. The leathery face animates, as
it draws terrified Rodney closer.

                         BLACK OUT.

               END OF TEASER

ACT ONE

7   EXT. SCHOOL COURTYARD - THE NEXT DAY   7

    Banners everywhere proclaim 'WORLD CULTURE DANCE -- FRIDAY
    NIGHT AT THE BRONZE.'

                                        CUT TO:

8   INT. LIBRARY - DAY   8

    CLOSE ON: BUFFY

                    BUFFY
            So, can I go?

                    GILES (O.C.)
            I should think not.

    Buffy throws a mean right hook at CAMERA. WHOMP!

    REVEAL GILES as he catches her fist with his huge FIGHTING
    PAD. Xander watches them from a safe distance.

                    BUFFY
            How come?

                    GILES
            Because you are the Chosen One.

                    BUFFY
            Just this once, can't I be the
            Overlooked One?

    Giles puts down his arms, looking at her.

                    GILES
            I'm afraid that's simply not an
            option. You have responsibilities
            that other girls do not, and --

                    BUFFY
                (sarcastic)
            Oh, I can finish this one for you.
            'Slaying entails certain sacrifices
            blah blah blah-bity blah I'm so
            stuffy give me a scone.'

                    GILES
                (witheringly)
            It's like you **know** me.

                                        CONTINUED

8 CONTINUED: 8

He puts his hands back up.   WHOMP, WHOMP.

                         GILES (cont'd)
               Your secret identity is already going
               to be difficult enough to maintain
               while that exchange student lives
               with you.

                         XANDER
               Not __with__ her. In the same house as
               her. Am I the only one who's
               objective enough to make that
               distinction?

                         BUFFY
                      (to Giles)
               So then, going to the dance, like a
               normal person, is the best way to
               keep that secret.

                         GILES
                      (trapped)
               You're twisting my words.

                         BUFFY
               No, I'm just using them for good.

Giles looks at her. A beat.

                         BUFFY (cont'd)
               Come on, Giles. Budge. No one likes
               a non-budger.

                         GILES
               Fine. Go.

                         BUFFY
                      (smiling)
               Yay! I win!

                         GILES
               I think I'll go introduce my shoulder
               to an ice pack.

He limps away.

                         XANDER
               So, we're dance-bound.   *

                                                                *

                                                       CONTINUED

BUFFY THE VAMPIRE SLAYER "Inca Mummy Girl" (BLUE) 8/7/97   10*.

8 CONTINUED: (2)   8

                                                                    *

                                                                    *

                    XANDER (cont'd)
          I think I can get mom's car, so I'm
          the wheel man.

                    BUFFY
          I thought you were taking Willow.

                    XANDER
          Well, I'm gonna take Willow, but I'm
          not gonna <u>take</u> Willow. In the sense
          of "take me." See with you, we're
          three and everybody's safe. Without
          you, we're two.

                    BUFFY
          And we enter dateville. Romance.
          Flowers.

                    XANDER
          Lips.

                    BUFFY
          C'mon. All the years you've known
          Willow, you've never thought about
          her lips?

Willow enters. Unseen.

                    XANDER
          Buffy, I love Willow.

Willow smiles.

                    XANDER (cont'd)
          She's my best friend. Which makes
          her not the kind of girl who you
          think about her lips that much.
          She's the kind of girl I'm best
          friends with.

Willow steps forward not exactly smiling.

                    WILLOW
          Hey, guys.

                                        CONTINUED

8 CONTINUED: (3)   8

                    XANDER
          Willow. Hi. We were just talking
          about happy things. Like all three
          of us going to the dance together.
          See? Happy.
                    (then, worried)
          Not happy?

                    WILLOW
          No. Yes.
                    (covering)
          Rodney's missing.

Giles returns from his office, an ice pack on his shoulder.

                    GILES
          Trouble with Mr. Munson again?

                    WILLOW
          His parents said he never came home
          last night. The police are still
          looking for him.

                    XANDER
          'Police are looking for Rodney
          Munson.' There's a phrase we'll get
          used to.

                    BUFFY
          I don't remember him on the bus back
          from the field trip.

                    WILLOW
          I don't either. I hope he didn't get
          into trouble at the museum.

                    XANDER
                    (picking up on it)
          Maybe he awakened the mummy--

                    WILLOW
          Right, and it rose from its tomb...

                    BUFFY
          And attacked him...

They all chuckle a bit, then stop. They look at each other.

                                             CUT TO:

9   INT. NATURAL HISTORY MUSEUM - BURIAL CHAMBER - DAY   9

Buffy, Willow, Xander and Giles walk cautiously through the
shadows, toward the Ziggurat. Willow's creeped again.

                    WILLOW
               (hopeful)
          On the other hand, maybe Rodney just
          stepped out for a smoke.

                    XANDER
          For twenty-one hours?

                    WILLOW
          It's addictive, you know.

                    GILES
          We'll consider that idea, the moment
          we've ruled out evil curses.

                    BUFFY
          Some day I'm going to live in a town
          where evil curses are just generally
          ruled out without even saying.

                    GILES
          Where was this seal?

Buffy's already on the flat top of the pyramid. A SEAL
FRAGMENT teeters on the edge of the sarcophagus hole.

                    BUFFY
          Here. And it's broken.

                    WILLOW
          Does that mean the mummy's loose?

They peer into the hole. The mummy lies there as before.

                    BUFFY
          Nope. Still there. Comfy as ever.

                    GILES
               (studies the fragment)
          Look at this. A series of
          pictograms...

10 ANGLE: A MAN (PERU MAN)   10

murder in his eyes, rushes from the shadows, shrieking.
Long, curved KNIFE raised. (Some people call it a huge,
machete-like carving blade. We call it a long, curved knife.)

Xander ducks as the knife whizzes past. Buffy lunges for
Peru Man, who swings his knife at her head.

                                        CONTINUED

10 CONTINUED: 10

    Buffy rolls out of the way.   Suddenly, Peru Man sees
    something and stops cold.

    Xander leaps onto Peru Man.   But, instead of fighting, Peru
    Man races out of the exhibit room.   Silence.

                         XANDER
              Okay. I just saved us, right?

                         BUFFY
              Something did.

                         GILES
              Let's not fret the details. Let's
              just go. Xander, bring the fragment.

    They move to leave the pyramid.   Turn back to see Willow,
    frozen stiff, staring at the mummy.

                         BUFFY
              Willow? What is it?

                         WILLOW
              Giles. Were the Incas... very
              advanced?

                         GILES
              Yes. Yes, they were.

                         WILLOW
                   (small voice)
              Did they have orthodontists?

    They follow her gaze to see THE MUMMY'S OPEN MOUTH, filled
    with BRACES.

                                             CUT TO:

11 INT. LIBRARY - NIGHT   11

    Buffy and Xander pace around the table.   Willow sits.

                         WILLOW
              Rodney looked like he had been dead
              for five hundred years. How could
              that be?

                         XANDER
              Maybe we should ask that crazy man
              with the big ol' knife.

                                             CONTINUED

11 CONTINUED: 11

                         BUFFY
          He didn't seem overly chatty.

                         WILLOW
          The way he bolted when he saw Rodney,
          I'd say he was as freaked as we were.

                                                                    *

                         GILES   *
          This particular mummy was from the
          Sebancaya region of eastern Peru.
          Very remote. If there's an answer,
          it's locked--

                         BUFFY
          In the seal.

                         GILES
          It could take me weeks to translate
          these pictograms. Well, we'll start
          tonight with --

                         BUFFY
               (suddenly)
          Ampata!

                         GILES
          I was going to suggest hunting.

                         BUFFY
               (starting out)
          I'm late. I told my mom I'd pick him
          up.

                         XANDER
          Buffy, where are your priorities? In
          tracking down a mummifying murderer,
          or making time with some Latin lover
          whose stock in trade is the breakage
          of hearts?

                                                      CONTINUED

11 CONTINUED: (2)   11

                         BUFFY
              Ampata is there alone, and I don't
              know how good his English is. He's--
                    (realizing)
              --from South America! Maybe he could
              translate the seal.

                         XANDER
              Oh, sure. Fall for the old 'Let-me-
              translate-that-ancient-seal-for-you'
              come on. You know how many times
              I've used that?

                                        CUT TO:

12 EXT. BUS STATION - BUS ARRIVAL AREA - NIGHT   12

    Hydraulic brakes HISS. A bus pulls away, revealing AMPATA,
    a short, squat, Peruvian BOY, 16. He stands next to two beat-
    up trunks, smiling nervously. He watches as the station
    empties of PASSENGERS. Then, a female VOICE whispers:

                         VOICE (O.C.)
              Ampata!

    Ampata looks around, excited, then confused. Sees no one.

                         VOICE (cont'd; O.C.)
              Ampata!

    Ampata pulls his trunks toward the VOICE and into a DARK
    ALLEY. He stops. Searches the darkness. Suddenly his
    expression changes to horror.

13 AMPATA'S POV: A HIDEOUS MONSTER   13

    Not quite mummy, not quite human. It GRABS Ampata by the
    throat. Pulls him towards its face.

    CLOSE ON: THE MUMMY'S MOUTH as it puckers into a hideous KISS.

    Ampata is frozen in terror as the mummy plants its lips on
    his. Ampata's face begins to shrivel and decompose.   *

                                        DISSOLVE TO:

14 EXT. BUS STATION - BUS ARRIVAL AREA - LATER - NIGHT   14

    Buffy, Willow and Xander arrive at the deserted station.

                                        CONTINUED

14 CONTINUED: 14

                    BUFFY
          Forty minutes late. Welcome to
          America.

                    WILLOW
          What if he left already?

                    BUFFY
                (calling)
          Ampata? Ampata Duarte?

They walk slowly toward the alley, where Ampata disappeared.

                    XANDER
          Do we have to speak Spanish when we
          see him? 'Cause I don't know how to
          say anything much besides "Doritos"
          and "Chihuahua".

                    BUFFY
          Ampata?

                    AMPATA (O.C.)
          Here.

A GIRL appears from the dark alley. She's 16. Stunningly
beautiful, but hesitant. Vulnerable.

                    AMPATA
          I am Ampata.

Xander just stares.

                    XANDER
                (quietly)
          Hay carumba. I also know how to say
          that.

                              BLACK OUT.

                    END OF ACT ONE

ACT TWO

15 INT. BUFFY'S KITCHEN - NIGHT   15

        Buffy, Willow and Xander lead Ampata on a tour. Ampata's
        very tentative, but also awe-struck at a modern home.

                        BUFFY
                And this is the kitchen...

                        AMPATA
                It is very good.

                        BUFFY
                Oh yeah. Got your stove, your
                fridge... fully functional. We're
                very into it.

                        XANDER
                Do you want something to drink?

                        BUFFY
                    (looking into fridge)
                We've got milk, and ... older milk...
                Oh. Juice?

                        AMPATA
                Please.

        Buffy goes for glasses as Ampata sits, Xander sitting beside   *
        her.

                        WILLOW   *
                So, Ampata... You're a girl.   *

                        AMPATA
                    (smiling bemusedly)   *
                Yes. For many years now.   *

                        WILLOW
                And not a boy. 'Cause we thought   *
                that a boy was coming, and here you   *
                are in a girl way.   *

                        XANDER
                It's just one of those crazy mix ups,   *
                Will.   *

                        BUFFY
                Have you been to America before?

                        AMPATA
                I have... toured.

                                                        CONTINUED

15 CONTINUED: 15

                         XANDER
                    (as to a child)
               Where did... you go?

                         AMPATA
               I have been taken to Boston.
               Atlanta. New York.

                                             CONTINUED

15 CONTINUED: (2)   15

                         WILLOW
               New York. That's exciting. What was
               that like?

                         AMPATA
               I did not see so much.

                         XANDER
               Your English is very bueno. Muy good.

                         AMPATA
               I listen much.

                         XANDER
               Well, that works out great, 'cause I
               talk much!

They laugh together.

                                                                    *

                                                                    *

                                                                    *

JOYCE comes in, carrying sheets and blankets.

                         JOYCE
               Buffy, do you want to show Ampata up
               to your room?

                         BUFFY
               Excuse me?

                                                  CUT TO:

16 INT. BUFFY'S ROOM - MOMENTS LATER - NIGHT   16

    Buffy and Joyce make up an extra bed.   *

                         BUFFY
               You said she was staying in the study.

                         JOYCE
               That was when we thought Ampata was
               a boy. But since he's a girl, I
               thought you could double up.

                                                  CONTINUED

16 CONTINUED: 16

> BUFFY
> Mom, you think too much.

> JOYCE
> You two in a room together? Give you
> both a chance to share secrets.

> BUFFY
> I'm not a big secret sharer. I like
> my secrets. They're secret.

> JOYCE
> Oh, it'll be fun.

> BUFFY
> Fun. Yeah.
>   (smiling)
> You know, next year I ought to sign
> up for one of those 'exchange mom'
> programs.

Joyce smiles as they finish making the bed.

                              DISSOLVE TO:

17 INT. BUFFY'S BEDROOM - NIGHT   17

Buffy comes in from the hallway. They're both dressed for   *
bed.   *

> BUFFY
> Sorry about the teenyness of the   *
> room.   *

> AMPATA
> My old one was much smaller.   *

> BUFFY
> What's it like, back home?

> AMPATA
> Cramped. And very dead.

> BUFFY
> You'll feel right at home in   *
> Sunnydale.

> AMPATA
> Oh, no. You have so much here.

Ampata picks up a picture of Buffy with Willow and Xander.

                              CONTINUED

17 CONTINUED: 17

                         BUFFY
               How about friends?

                         AMPATA
               They are...
                         (sadly)
               I am just me.

                         BUFFY
               I've been there.
                         (brightening)
               But, hey. You'll meet lots of people
               tomorrow.

          Ampata climbs into bed, smiling for the first time.

                         AMPATA
               Thank you. You must teach me
               everything about your life!

          Buffy smiles uneasily.

                         AMPATA (cont'd)
               I want to fit in, Buffy. Just like
               you. A normal life.

                         BUFFY
               One normal life, coming up.

          Buffy clicks off the light.

18 EXT. BUSHES NEAR THE HOUSE - CONTINUOUS - NIGHT   18

          We see the light go off on the face of Peru Man, who is
          standing in the shadows, LOOKING UP from the hedges below.
          His long, curved knife glints ominously.

                                             DISSOLVE TO:

19 EXT. SCHOOL COURTYARD - THE NEXT DAY   19

          Banners proclaim the World Culture Dance.

20 CLOSE ON: A DRUM   20

          Bearing the logo: DINGOES ATE MY BABY.

          Two students, SAM and OZ -- by their looks, obviously members
          of the band -- load music and sound equipment into a van,
          which has their logo emblazoned on the side. Cordelia talks
          with DEVON, the band's good-looking lead singer.

                                                      CONTINUED

20 CONTINUED: 20

                         CORDELIA
          Devon, I told you I'd be at the dance
          tonight, but I'm not one of your
          little groupies. I won't be all doe-
          eyed, looking up at you, standing at
          the edge of the stage.

                         DEVON
          Got it.

                         CORDELIA
          So, I'll see you afterwards?

                         DEVON
          Sure. Where do you want to meet?

                         CORDELIA
          I'll be standing at the edge of the
          stage.

                         DEVON
          With that guy?

REVEAL SVEN, Cordelia's exchange student, stands nearby.
Hulking, blond, expressionless -- like a Swedish Lurch.

                         CORDELIA
          Sven, momento. Needa.
                  (to Devon)
          This exchange student thing has been
          a horrible nightmare. They don't
          even speak American!

Cordelia kisses Devon on the cheek.

                         CORDELIA (cont'd)
          I'll see you tonight.
                  (turns, stops)
          Sven. Come.

Sven follows. Devon turns to Oz.

                         DEVON
          Oz, man, what do you think?

                         OZ
          Of what?

                         DEVON
          Of Cordelia, man.

                         OZ
          She's a wonderland tour.

                                                      CONTINUED

20 CONTINUED: (2)   20

There's a quiet restraint and total lack of bitterness to his
sarcasm; where Devon is your typical excitable rock and
roller, Oz is completely unflappable. His is the kind of
cool that is completely unaware of itself.

                    DEVON
          You gotta admit, she's hot.

                    OZ
          Oh, yeah. Hot girl.

                    DEVON
          Let me guess. Not your type. What
          does a girl have to do to impress you?

                    OZ
          Well, it involves a feather boa and
          the theme from A Summer Place. I
          can't discuss it here.

                    DEVON
          You're too picky, man. You know how
          many girls you could have? You're
          lead guitar, Oz, that's currency!

                    OZ
          I'm not picky. You're just impressed
          by any pretty girl that can walk and
          talk.

                    DEVON
                (innocently)
          She doesn't have to talk...

Oz throws him a look.

                                        CUT TO:

21 EXT. ANOTHER PART OF THE COURTYARD - SAME TIME - DAY   21

Willow and Xander walk together, past one of the banners
advertising the World Culture Dance.

                    WILLOW
          I worked really hard on my costume.
          It's pretty cool.

                    XANDER
          Okay, but what about me? I gotta
          think.

                                        CONTINUED

21 CONTINUED: 21

                         WILLOW
               It's a celebration of cultures.
               There's lots of dress-up alternatives.

                         XANDER
               And a corresponding equal number of
               mocking alternatives, all aimed at me.

                         WILLOW
               Bavarians are cool.

                         XANDER
               No hats with feathers, no ruffled
               shirts and definitely no lederhosen.
               They make my calves look fat.

                         WILLOW
               Why are you suddenly so worried about
               looking like an idiot?
                         (a beat)
               That came out wrong.

But Xander isn't even listening. He's looking off, past
Willow, and smiling. Willow follows his gaze to see Ampata
arriving with Buffy.

                         BUFFY
               Your first day of school. Nervous?

                         AMPATA
               It is just more people than I have
               seen in a long time.

                         BUFFY
               Don't worry. You're not going to
               have any problem making friends. As
               a matter of fact, I know someone
               who's dying to meet you.

                                             CUT TO:

22 INT. LIBRARY - DAY   22

                         GILES
               How do you do? I was wondering if
               you could translate this for me.

WIDEN to reveal the gang is there. Giles holds up the seal.

                         BUFFY
               That was in no way awkward.

                                             CONTINUED

22 CONTINUED: 22

>   Ampata looks at the seal. An instant of dread crosses her
>   face. She quickly recovers.

>   BUFFY (cont'd)
>   Is something wrong?

>   AMPATA
>   No, it is... why are you asking me?

>   GILES
>   It's an artifact. From your region.
>   It's from the tomb of an Incan mummy.
>   We're trying to translate it. A
>   project for our...

>   WILLOW
>   Archaeology Club.

>   XANDER
>   'Ar-chae-ol-o-gy.' Study of old
>   stuff.

>   AMPATA
>   It is broken. Where are the other
>   pieces?

>   BUFFY
>   This is the only one we found.

>   AMPATA
>   It is very old. And valuable.
>   (thinks for a beat)
>   You should hide it.

>   GILES
>   Is there anything you recognize here?
>   (pointing)
>   This figure with the knife, for
>   instance.

>   Ampata looks at them for a beat. She turns the fragment
>   around, feigning ignorance.

>   AMPATA
>   Well, I do not know exactly. But I
>   think this represents... I believe
>   the word is... the bodyguard?

>   GILES
>   (nodding)
>   Bodyguard. Interesting.

                                                        CONTINUED

BUFFY THE VAMPIRE SLAYER "Inca Mummy Girl" (BLUE) 8/7/97   25.

22 CONTINUED: (2)   22

                    AMPATA
          Legend has it that he guards the
          mummy against those who would disturb
          her.

                    BUFFY
          By slicing them up?

                    AMPATA
          I would not know that.

                    GILES
          Yes, well. That should be a good
          starting point for our... club.

Ampata just stands there. Giles glances awkwardly at her.

                    BUFFY
          Oh, right. And as Club President, I   *
          have lots to do lots of stuff. Very   *
          dull stuff.   *
                    (re: Ampata)
          Willow, maybe you could--

Xander interjects.

                    XANDER
          --stay with Ampata for the day? I'd
          love to.

Ampata smiles, pleased.

                    AMPATA
                    (to Xander)
          Yes, that will be fun.

Xander leads Ampata out the doors.

                    GILES
          Okay, then. I'll continue with the
          translating. Buffy, you research
          this 'Bodyguard.' And... Willow?

Willow looks wistfully at the doors.

                    WILLOW
          Boy. They really like each other.

                              DISSOLVE TO:

23 EXT. FOOTBALL BLEACHERS - LATER - DAY   23

    Xander and Ampata are there. Xander reaches into a bag.

CONTINUED

23 CONTINUED: 23

                          XANDER
               And this--
                    (pulls something out)
               --is called snack food.   *

                          AMPATA
               Snack food.   *

                          XANDER
                    (unwrapping)
               It's a delicious, golden, spongy
               cake, filled with a delightful, white
               creamy substance of goodness. And
               here's how you eat it.

He shoves the whole thing in his mouth. Ampata laughs.

                          AMPATA
               Oh, but now I can not try it.

Xander reaches into the bag and pulls out another.

                          XANDER
                    (with mouth full)
               That's why you bring two.

He unwraps it and hands it to her.

                          AMPATA
                    (tentatively)
               Here goes.

She crams it in, then laughs, almost spitting out.

                          XANDER
               Good, huh? And the exciting part is,
               they have no ingredients that a human
               can pronounce. So they don't leave
               you with that heavy, **food** feeling in
               your stomach.

                          AMPATA
                    (smiling)
               You are strange...

                          XANDER
               Girls always tell me that. Right
               before they run away.

                          AMPATA
               I like it.

                                                  CONTINUED

23 CONTINUED: (2)   23

                         XANDER
            I like you like it.
                 (thinks about that)
            Please don't learn from my English.

                                          CUT TO:

24 INT. LIBRARY - DAY   24

        Buffy and Willow are looking through books, comparing   *
        pictograms with the plate. Buffy is somewhat more actively *
        involved than Willow.   *

                         BUFFY   *
            Hah! Or possible Hah... do you think   *
            this matches?   *

        Willow doesn't react for a moment.   *

                         WILLOW   *
            Oh! Yes! I'm caring about mummies.   *

                         BUFFY   *
                 (sympathetically)   *
            Ampata's only staying for two weeks.   *

                         WILLOW   *
            And then Xander will find someone   *
            else who's not me to obsess about.   *
            At least with you I knew he didn't   *
            have a shot.   *

                         BUFFY   *
            I'm sorry.   *

        As they talk, Giles enters, looks at Buffy's book, not   *
        listening.   *

                         WILLOW   *
                 (brave face)   *
            Well, you know, I have a choice. I   *
            can spend my life waiting for Xander   *
            to go with ever other girl in the   *
            world before he notices me, or I can   *
            just get on with my life.   *

                         BUFFY   *
            Good for you.   *

                         WILLOW   *
            Well, I didn't choose yet...   *

                                          CONTINUED

24 CONTINUED: 24

                    GILES
          Aha. Yes. Good work?

                    BUFFY
          My work?

                    GILES
          Yes. This is most illuminating: it   *
          seems that Rodney's killer might be   *
          the mummy.

                    WILLOW
          Where's it say that?

Giles points to more pictograms.

                    GILES
          Here. It implies that the mummy is   *
          capable of feeding off the life force   *
          of a person. Effectively freeze-   *
          drying them, you might say.   ^
          Extraordinary.   *

                    BUFFY
          So then, we just have to stop the
          mummy. Which leaves the question:
          How do we a: find and b: stop the
          mummy?

                                        CONTINUED

24 CONTINUED: (2)   24

                    GILES
              (re: seal fragment)
          That answer is still locked somewhere
          in here. Or in the rest of the seal.

                                        CUT TO:

25 EXT. FOOTBALL BLEACHERS - SAME TIME - DAY   25

    CLOSE UP: A CURVED KNIFE BLADE

                    PERU MAN (O.C.)
          Give me the seal!

    The blade SWIPES DOWN between Xander and Ampata. The knife
    blade lodges into the bench. Peru Man screams at Xander.

                    PERU MAN
          You stole the seal. Where is it?

    Xander struggles with Peru Man as Ampata shrieks. Peru Man
    glances at her. A startled beat of recognition.

                    PERU MAN (cont'd)
          It is you...

    XANDER kicks Peru Man. He falls through the bleachers.
    Xander grabs Ampata's hand.

                    XANDER
          Come on!

    Xander and Ampata escape.

                                        CUT TO:

26 INT. LIBRARY - MOMENTS LATER - DAY   26

    Xander comforts a distraught Ampata at the table.

                    XANDER
          Are you okay?

                    AMPATA
          You protect me. Make me safe.

                                                              *

                    BUFFY   *
          So, our bodyguard strikes again. Why   *
          is he so into us? What's he want?   *

                                        CONTINUED

26 CONTINUED: 26

>   XANDER   *
>   He said "give me the seal."   *

                                              CONTINUED

BUFFY THE VAMPIRE SLAYER "Inca Mummy Girl" (PINK) 8/8/97   29.

26 CONTINUED: (2)   26

                              GILES
                    Apparently, this seal fragment is
                    even more popular than we realized.
                    I'm just not sure what we should do
                    with it.

                              AMPATA (O.C.)
                    Destroy it.

They turn to look at her.

                              AMPATA
                    If you do not, someone could die.

                              GILES
                    I'm afraid someone already has.

                              AMPATA
                    You mean the man with the knife
                    killed someone?

                              BUFFY
                    Well, no, not exactly...   *

                              AMPATA
                    You are not telling me everything.

Xander takes her hands.

                              XANDER
                    You're right, Ampata. And it's time
                    we do. We're not in Archaeology
                    Club. We're in--

The others look at him, horrified.

                              XANDER (cont'd)
                    --Crime Club. It's like Chess Club.
                    Only... with crime. And no chess.

                              AMPATA
                    Please, understand me. That seal
                    nearly got us killed. It must be
                    destroyed!

She runs off.

                              XANDER
                    Ampata!

Xander goes after her.

                                        CUT TO:

27 INT. HALL - SECONDS LATER - DAY   27

Xander runs up to a shaken Ampata.

                    XANDER
            Ampata, listen to me. Nobody's going
            to hurt you. I won't let them.

                    AMPATA
            Your investigation is dangerous. I
            don't want that. Just normal life.

Xander watches as Ampata goes to a drinking fountain and
splashes water on her face. Willow appears behind Xander.

                    WILLOW
            Is she okay?

                    XANDER
            Wigged. I wanna convince her that
            our lives aren't just danger and
            peril here.

                    WILLOW
            You should take her to the dance.

                    XANDER
            Yeah, that'll be fun. We can all...

                    WILLOW
            I mean just you.

                    XANDER
            But you were all psyched... your
            costume...

                    WILLOW
            I'll see you there.

A moment, as he smiles.

                    XANDER
            Thanks. You know what, Willow?
            You're my best friend.

Willow watches Xander return to Ampata.

                    WILLOW
                (to herself)
            I know.

                                        CUT TO:

28 INT. LIBRARY - SAME TIME - DAY   28

     Giles and Buffy look at the seal fragment.

                    BUFFY
          Why would the Bodyguard have such a
          jones for a broken piece of rock?

                    GILES
          He probably needs this to put with
          the other pieces--

                    BUFFY
          At the museum.

                    GILES
          Precisely. We'll go to the museum
          and use this fragment as bait to lure
          in the Bodyguard.

                    BUFFY
          And he'll lead us to mummy dearest.
               (smiling)
          Hey, look at us. We came up with a
          plan. A good plan.

                    GILES
          We can meet there tonight after the
          museum is closed.

                    BUFFY
          No! Bad plan! I have other plans.
          Dance plans.
               (off his look;
                solemnly)
          Cancel plans.

                                        CUT TO:

29 INT. HALL - A SHORT TIME LATER - DAY   29

     The halls are nearly empty as Xander and Ampata walk along.

                    XANDER
          Okay. I have something to tell you.
          It's kind of a secret. And a little
          bit scary.

     She looks at him, suddenly anxious.

                    XANDER (cont'd)
          I like you. A lot. And I want you
          to go with me to the dance.

                                        CONTINUED

29 CONTINUED: 29

She giggles, relieved.

                    AMPATA
          Why was that so scary?

                    XANDER
          Well, because you never know if the
          girl is going to say yes, or if she's
          going to laugh in your face, pull out
          your still-beating heart, and crush
          it into the ground with her heel.

                    AMPATA
          Then you are very courageous.
                    (then)
          Can I tell you a secret?

Xander listens carefully.

                    AMPATA (cont'd)
          I like you, too.

                    XANDER
          Really?

                    AMPATA
          Really.

                    XANDER
          That's great! Really?

                    AMPATA
          Really.

                    XANDER
          That's great!
                    (then)
          You're not a preying mantis, are you?
                    (off her)
          Sorry. Someone else.

Ampata looks at him. She coyly smiles and starts away.

                    AMPATA
          I will return to you.

                    XANDER
          Where are you going?

                    AMPATA
          Where you can not follow.

                                                                    *

                                                          CONTINUED

29 CONTINUED: (2)   29

                         XANDER   *
          Hey, I'll follow you anywhere you   *
          go -   *
                    (sees WOMEN'S   *
                    RESTROOM sign)   *
          -except for not in there. I'll wait   *
          outside.   *

She heads inside. The door closes.   *

                                             CUT TO:

30 INT. WOMEN'S RESTROOM - CONTINUOUS - DAY   30

Ampata looks in the mirror. Combing her hair. The happy
look of a girl in love. She flips her hair and sees:

Peru Man in the mirror. He walks forward, knife at his side.

                         AMPATA
          I beg you.... do not kill me.

                         PERU MAN
          You are already dead. For 500 years.

                         AMPATA
          It was unfair. I was innocent.

                         PERU MAN
          The people that you kill now so that
          you may live -- they are innocent.

                         AMPATA.
          Please. I am in love.

He backs her against a wall.

                         PERU MAN
          You are the Chosen One. You must
          die. You have no choice.

Peru Man's arm WHIZZES by her, but Ampata coolly catches it.
Twists it, grabs the knife and twists his arm painfully. We
hear it start to CRACK. His eyes go wide.

                         AMPATA
          Yes I do.

She grabs him by the jaw. KISSES him. His face shrivels.

                                             CUT TO:

31 INT. HALL - LATER - DAY   31

Xander glances at his watch, anxious. The door opens.
Ampata steps out. She looks gorgeous. Refreshed.

                    AMPATA
          I have thought.

Xander looks at her expectantly.

                    AMPATA (cont'd)
          The dance. I will go with you.   *
          Gladly.   *

Xander smiles. Takes her hand. And they walk off.

                              BLACK OUT.

          END OF ACT TWO

ACT THREE

32 INT. BUFFY'S BEDROOM - NIGHT   32

Buffy brings a trunk in, places it by a second one by her bed.

                    AMPATA (O.S.)
          Buffy, I cannot find lipstick.

                    BUFFY
          Should be on the dresser.

Ampata enters from the bathroom. She's dressed as the Incan
princess. She's beautiful. Radiates confidence. Until she
sees the trunk.

                    AMPATA
          What is that?

                    BUFFY
          They sent your stuff from the station.

                    AMPATA
          Of course! I forgot all about it.
          I will unpack it later.

                    BUFFY
          I can do it.

                    AMPATA
          But you must get ready for the dance.

                    BUFFY
          I'm not going.

                    AMPATA
          Why not?

                    BUFFY
          I've got work to do. I mean, crime   *
          club work. It's nothing for you to   *
          worry about.   *

                    AMPATA
          I am not worried. Thanks to Xander.

                    BUFFY
          He seems very happy around you.

                    AMPATA
          I am happy, too. He has a way of...
          making the milk come out of my nose.

                                              CONTINUED

32 CONTINUED: 32

                        BUFFY
            And that's good?   *

                        AMPATA
            From making me laugh.

        Buffy smiles. Ampata searches Buffy's dresser top.

                        AMPATA (cont'd)
            It is not here.

                                            CONTINUED

BUFFY THE VAMPIRE SLAYER "Inca Mummy Girl" (BLUE) 8/7/97   36.

32 CONTINUED: (2)   32

                          BUFFY
            I'll help you look.

Buffy walks to the TWO TRUNKS from the bus station. Ampata's
still turned away, searching the dresser.

                          AMPATA
            Thank you. You are always thinking
            of others before yourself. You
            remind me of someone from very long
            ago. The Inca princess.

                          BUFFY
            A princess? Cool.

Buffy opens one of the trunks. She pulls out a pair of BOY'S
PANTS. Looks at them, curiously. Ampata opens Buffy's
drawer, then turns to Buffy.

                          AMPATA
            They told her she was the only one,
            that only she could defend her people
            from the netherworld.

Buffy looks up as Ampata's words register.

                          AMPATA (cont'd)
            Out of all the girls in her
            generation, she was--

                          BUFFY
            --chosen.

Buffy sees the open dresser drawer, filled with a Crucifix,
stakes, Slayer things. Buffy quickly crosses over.

                          AMPATA
            You know the story?

                          BUFFY
            It's fairly familiar.

Buffy surreptitiously closes the drawer and spies the
lipstick on the dresser. She hands it to Ampata.

                          AMPATA
            She was sixteen. Like us. She was
            offered as a sacrifice and went to
            her death. Who knows what she gave
            up to fulfill her duty to others.
            What chance at love?

Ampata picks up a picture of Xander. Smiles at it.

                                                        CONTINUED

32 CONTINUED: (3)   32

                         BUFFY
              Who knows?

This thought lingers for a beat.

                                                                          *

                         BUFFY (cont'd)
              Let me unpack the rest of your stuff.

Buffy opens the OTHER TRUNK LID, revealing

33 CLOSE UP: THE BODY OF THE EXCHANGE STUDENT -- MUMMIFIED 33

But just as she is about to peer in, THE DOORBELL RINGS.
Buffy looks up at Ampata, now standing above her.

                         BUFFY
              Xander and Willow. I'll get it.

Buffy walks out. Ampata puts her hands on the trunk lid

                                                                          *

34 CLOSE UP: 34

as the lid shuts over the mummified student.

                                                                          *

                                              CONTINUED

34 CONTINUED: 34

She locks the trunk.

                                        CUT TO:

35 INT. BUFFY'S HOUSE - A MOMENT LATER - NIGHT   35

Buffy, in sweats, opens the door. Xander stands there,
wearing a poncho and squinting with a little cigar clenched   *
between his teeth. He looks more than a little bit like   *
Clint Eastwood.

                    XANDER
          I have come for the dance.

                    BUFFY
          What culture are you?

                    XANDER
          I am from the country of Leone. It's
          in Italy, pretending to be Montana.
                    (then, re: her sweats)
          And what are you? From the country
          of white trash?

                    BUFFY
          New line-up. You and Willow are
          taking Ampata, Giles and I are
          hunting mummies.
                    (then)
          Where's you and Willow?

                    XANDER
          She's not coming. With us.

                    BUFFY
          Oh. On a date. Romance. Lips.

Ampata enters. Stunning. Xander can't take his eyes off her.

                    AMPATA
          Hello, Xander.

Xander manages a few sporadic noises.

                    XANDER
          Uh, ngh... bff...

                    BUFFY
          I can translate America Salivating
          Boy-talk. He said you're beautiful.

                                        CONTINUED

35 CONTINUED: 35

                         XANDER
                        (to Buffy)
              Cch... krl...

                         BUFFY
              You're welcome.

Joyce comes in.

                         JOYCE
              Ampata, don't you look wonderful. I
              wish you could talk my daughter into
              going with you.

                         AMPATA
              I tried. She's very stubborn.

                         JOYCE
              I'm glad someone else sees that.

Ampata moves to the door. She and Xander turn to Buffy.

                         AMPATA
              Well, good-bye, then.

                         XANDER
              Be careful.

                         BUFFY
              I will.
                        (then)
              And Xander? You look good.

He smiles. Joyce and Buffy watch as they head out.

                         JOYCE
              Look at that. Only two days in
              America, and Ampata already seems
              like she belongs here. She's really
              fitting in.

Buffy watches after them, wistfully.

                         BUFFY
              Yeah. How about that?

                                             CUT TO:

36 EXT. BRONZE - NIGHT   36

    Establishing. Music plays.

                                            CUT TO:

37 INT. BRONZE - NIGHT   37

    THE BAND plays wildly on stage. Devon plays the bass and
    sings, thrashing about the stage. Oz plays ripping guitar
    with the quiet concentration of someone knitting.

    The place is full of KIDS dressed in the style of various
    cultures. A parade of BEAUTIFUL GIRLS enter, each costume
    more provocative than the previous one. Last to come in is
    Cordelia, who wears a Hawaiian grass skirt with a coconut
    shell top. She approaches Willow, who is dressed as an   *
    Eskimo. Puffy, furry, hooded parka. A harpoon at her side.   *

                    CORDELIA
            Ooh, what a near faux-pas. I almost
            wore the same thing.   *

    Cordelia walks away. Constrained by her outfit, Willow has
    to turn her entire body to watch her go. Cordelia approaches
    some Cordettes, including GWEN.   *

                    GWEN   *
            Where's Sven?

                    CORDELIA
            I keep trying to ditch him, but he's
            like one of those dogs you leave at
            the Grand Canyon on vacation, it
            follows you back across four states.

    Sven enters, dressed like a Viking. He finds Cordelia and   *
    stands silently next to her.

                    CORDELIA (cont'd)
            See? My own speechless, human
            boomerang.

                    GWEN   *
            He's kind of cute. Maybe it's nice,
            skipping the small talk.

                                            CONTINUED

37 CONTINUED: 37

                    CORDELIA
          Small talk? Try simple instructions.
               (gestures to Sven)
          Get punch-y? You? Fruit drinky?

Sven remains motionless. Gwen pulls his hand.   *

                    GWEN   *
          He can follow me.

38 ANGLE: XANDER AND AMPATA   38

as they enter. They're gorgeous together.

Willow watches as they move through the crowd. She bends   *
down to look down at her own costume.   *

                    WILLOW
          I guess I should have worn something   *
          sexy.

Ampata takes in the scene, like Cinderella at the Ball --
it's too good to be true. They approach Willow, who peers *
out of her hood.   *

                    WILLOW (cont'd)
          Wow. You guys look great.

                    AMPATA   *
          I love your costume. It's very   *
          authentic.   *

                    WILLOW
          Thanks.   *

                    XANDER
          Yeah. You look... snug.   *

                    WILLOW
          That's what I was going for.

                                                           *

                    WILLOW (cont'd)
                                                           *
               (tries to look around)
          Where's Buffy?

                              CUT TO:

39 OMITTED   39

                                              CUT TO:

40 INT. BUFFY'S HOUSE - A MOMENT LATER - NIGHT   40

Buffy opens the door. Giles is there.

                        GILES
            Thank heavens. You're home.

                        BUFFY
            Yep. Not at the dance. Not with my
            friends. Not with a life.
                    (then)
            What are you doing here? I thought
            we were going to meet at the museum
            to find the bodyguard?

                        GILES
            I'm afraid he's already been found.
            In a school restroom. Mummified.

                        BUFFY
            I don't get it. Why would the mummy
            kill her own bodyguard?

                        GILES
            Well I've cross-referenced and now   *
            I've looked at the pictograms anew.   *
            The man was a guard alright, but his   *
            task was to insure the mummy didn't   *
            awaken and escape.   *

                                                      *

                                                      *

                        BUFFY
            So Ampata translated wrong?

                                              CONTINUED

40 CONTINUED: 40

                    GILES
          Perhaps.   *

                    BUFFY
          Well, wait... She was wiggy about the
          seal from minute one.

                    GILES
          Yes, I guess she was.

                    BUFFY
                 (thinking)
          Her trunks.

                    GILES
          What about them?

                                        CUT TO:

A41 INT. BUFFY'S BEDROOM   NIGHT   A41

     As Buffy pulls at the lock of one, Giles goes through the
     clothes in the other.

                    GILES
          These are definitely boys clothes.
          Why would a girl pack these?

     Buffy breaks the lock, opens the other trunk. After reacting.

                    BUFFY
          How about this one? What kind girl
          travels with a mummified corpse...

41 ANGLE: IN THE TRUNK   41

     we see the corpse of the real Ampata.

                    BUFFY (cont'd)
          ...and doesn't even pack lipstick.

                                        CUT TO:

42 INT. BRONZE - NIGHT   42

     The band starts playing a slow-danceable song. Xander and
     Ampata are standing near the dance floor.

                    XANDER
          Do you want, uh... would you like to,
          you know...

                                                    CONTINUED

42 CONTINUED: 42

> AMPATA
> I would love to dance.

Xander takes Ampata's hand and leads her to the dance floor.
The crowd magically parts as the two make their way to the
center. All eyes are on the couple.

Willow stands alone off to one side.

Ampata dances slowly with Xander, full of quiet joy. It's a
true Cinderella moment.

43 ANGLE: THE BAND   43

as they continue to play an instrumental portion of a song.
Oz is looking into the crowd, uncharacteristically riveted.
He moves to Devon.

> OZ
> Who is that?

> DEVON
> She's an exchange student. From
> South America.

CONTINUED

43 CONTINUED: 43

                          OZ
              No. The Eskimo.

We FOLLOW HIS GAZE to Willow, who is swaying (or, more
accurately, weeble-ing) to the music.

                                        CUT TO:

44 INT. GILES' CAR - NIGHT   44   *

                          BUFFY   *
              Come on... Can't you put your foot   *
              down?   *

                          GILES   *
              It is down.   *

                          BUFFY   *
              One of these days you have to get a   *
              grown up car.   *

WRENCHING of gears.   *

                                        CUT TO:

45 INT. BRONZE - NIGHT   45

Xander and Ampata are slow dancing. Staring deeply. She
clasps her hands behind his head. He leans in for a kiss.

46 ANGLE: AMPATA'S FINGERTIPS   46

suddenly whither and freeze-dry. Horrified, she pulls away.
Hides her hands behind her back. Smiles, scared. Xander,
hesitant, smiles back.

She runs into the crowd. Xander's bewildered.

                          XANDER
              Okay. At least I can rule out,
              'Something I said.'

                                        CONTINUED

46 CONTINUED: 46

Ampata struggles through the crowd, past Willow, searching
desperately for her next victim. She looks at her fingers.
They whither to the knuckle.

A LONE MALE STUDENT, JONATHAN, looks around. Nods his head
to the music. Ampata heads toward him.

                                            CUT TO:

47 INT. GILES' CAR - NIGHT   47

The car speeds along.

                    BUFFY
          I should've guessed. Remember?
          Ampata wanted us to hide the seal.

                    GILES
          And then she wanted us to destroy it,
          because --
                    (realizing)
          Wait.

A long beat as Giles thinks something through.

                    BUFFY
          Waiting.

                    GILES
          We already know that the seal was
          used to contain the mummy.

                    BUFFY
          What? You mean that, if breaking the
          seal freed her--

                    GILES
          --reassembling it will trap her.

The car SCREECHES to a stop. Giles takes the seal.

                    GILES (cont'd)
          I'll go to the museum. Piece
          together the fragments there.

                    BUFFY
          I'll get Xander. Before he gets   *
          smootchie with Mummy Dearest.   *

She opens the car door and starts to get out.

                                            CONTINUED

47 CONTINUED: 47

                         GILES
                   Be careful.   *

                         BUFFY
                   I will. Besides, I've got the   *
                   element of surprise. Ampata still
                   doesn't know <u>my</u> secret identity.

Buffy slams the door as Giles shifts his car into gear.

                                        CUT TO:

48 INT. BRONZE - NIGHT   48

Xander runs up to Willow.

                         XANDER
                   You seen Ampata?

Willow tries lifting her arms to shrug. Bulky costume.

                         XANDER (cont'd)
                   What was that?

                         WILLOW
                   I shrugged.

                         XANDER
                   Next time you should probably say,
                   'shrug.'

He runs off. Willow stands there.

                         WILLOW
                   Sigh.

49 OMITTED   49   *
AND   AND
50   50

A51   ANGLE: GWEN   A51   *

        listening, enraptured, to Sven, as he now chats away.   *

                            SVEN
                I thought this exchange student thing
                would be a great deal. But look what
                I got stuck with. 'Momento'?
                'Punchy fruity drinky?' Is Cordelia
                even from this country?

                                        CUT TO:

51   INT. BACKSTAGE - NIGHT   51

        Ampata strokes Jonathan's hair. He's nervous.

                            JONATHAN
                Your hands feel kind of... rough.

        Ampata's gnarled hands grab the hair on the back of his head.

                            JONATHAN (cont'd)
                Aren't you with Xander?

                            AMPATA
                Do I look like I am with Xander?

        She closes in for the kiss.

                            XANDER (O.S.)
                Ampata! Ampata!

                            JONATHAN
                Whoa! That's my cue to leave.

        He bails. Ampata breathes heavily in frustration. Xander
        rounds a corner.

                            XANDER
                There you are.
                        (going to her)
                Why did you run away?

                            AMPATA
                Because I... I do not deserve you.

                                        CONTINUED

51 CONTINUED: 51

     Xander gasps, can barely contain his disbelief.

                         XANDER
               Ha! Wh-- You think you don't...
                    (pointing back and
                     forth)
               ...that I would think...
                    (then, laughing)
               Man, I love you!

     Xander stops, mortified at what he said. Ampata pulls away.

                         XANDER (cont'd)
               Uh, I mean...well, I guess...
                    (then)
               Yeah.

     Ampata looks up at him. She's crying.

                         XANDER (cont'd)
               Are those tears of joy? Pain?
               Revulsion?

                         AMPATA
               I am very happy. And very sad.

     Xander pulls back a bit, confused.

                         XANDER
               Then talk to me. Tell me what's
               wrong.

                         AMPATA
               I can't!

     Ampata buries her sobbing face on his shoulder.

                                             CUT TO:

52 OMITTED   52   *

53 INT. BACKSTAGE - NIGHT   53

     Ampata hugs Xander tightly.

                                             CONTINUED

53 CONTINUED: 53

                         XANDER
             I know why you can't tell me. It's
             a secret, right?

Ampata looks up sadly from his shoulder. Nods yes. Xander
smiles. Tries to ease the tension.

                         XANDER (cont'd)
             And if you told me, you'd have to
             kill me?

She starts crying again.

                         XANDER (cont'd)
             Okay. Bad joke. Delivery was off,
             too. I'm sorry, I--

They look at each other. Xander's lips move closer.

54 CLOSE: THEIR LIPS MILLIMETERS APART.   54

Ampata's swept away in the moment. Their lips touch. And
they KISS. Lightly. Then, more passionately. Until Ampata
grabs Xander's head, holding him.

55 CLOSE UP: XANDER'S EYES OPEN WIDE WITH SHOCK.   55

                                        BLACK OUT.

                         END OF ACT THREE

ACT FOUR

56   INT. BACKSTAGE - NIGHT   56

Ampata is still kissing Xander as he fights for air. Ampata
opens her eyes. Breaks away from the kiss, sobbing.

Xander drops to his knees. Face drawn. Reeling, like half
his life's been sucked out.

                                        CUT TO:

57   INT. NATURAL HISTORY MUSEUM - BURIAL CHAMBER - NIGHT   57

Giles kneels on top of the step pyramid. Arranges the many
seal fragments. Reads from the text book.

                    GILES
          'Inca cosmology unites the bird head
          with its paler twin.'
              (studying the Seal)
          Ah, yes... the paler twin.

He starts to fit together the seal fragments.

                                        CUT TO:

58   INT. BACKSTAGE - SAME TIME   58

Ampata is kneeling next to Xander, holding him in her arms.

                    AMPATA
          Xander, I am sorry.

Suddenly, she's jolted. She looks at her arms. The freeze-
drying crackles up to her elbows. She lets go of Xander.

                    AMPATA (cont'd)
              (in pain)
          The seal!

She gets up and runs out the back door.

                    XANDER
              (dazed)
          Ampata...

                                        CUT TO:

59 INT. BRONZE - NIGHT   59

Buffy enters, goes to Willow.   *

                    BUFFY   *
          Where's Xander?   *

                    WILLOW   *
          He was looking for Ampata.   *

                    BUFFY   *
          We've got to find them. Ampata is the   *
          mummy.   *

                    WILLOW   *
          Oh.   *
                    (smiles)   *
          Good.   *
                    (stops smiling)   *
          Xander!   *

                    BUFFY   *
          Where'd they go?   *

                    WILLOW   *
          Backstage, I think.   *

They race backstage, REVEALING Oz, who was just about to tap   *
Willow on the shoulder. He watches his little Eskimo
disappear.

                    OZ
          Who **is** that girl?

                                             CUT TO:

60 INT. BACKSTAGE - NIGHT   60

The door from the dance floor bursts open. Buffy and Willow
race toward Xander. Sit him up.

                    BUFFY
          Are you all right?

Xander shakes his head, focusing. Takes deep breaths.

                    XANDER
          I think so.
                    (touching his jaw)
          That was some kiss.

                    BUFFY
          Where's Ampata?

                                             CONTINUED

BUFFY THE VAMPIRE SLAYER "Inca Mummy Girl" (PINK) 8/8/97   51A.

60 CONTINUED: 60

                    XANDER
          She said something about the seal.

                    BUFFY
          The seal. Giles. Come on!   *

                    XANDER
          What's going on?

Willow looks at him.

                    WILLOW
          He doesn't know.

                    BUFFY
          We'll tell him on the way.

Buffy and Willow pull Xander with them out the back door.

                              CUT TO:

61 INT. NATURAL HISTORY MUSEUM - NIGHT   61

Giles sweats over the seal. Hears a noise. Looks up. The
room is empty. Shadows flicker. Giles returns to his text.

                    GILES
          'The Condor soars... But the prey is
          in his talons.' That's it!

Giles glues two pieces together. Smiles triumphantly.

62 ANGLE: AMPATA   62

in the shadows, grimaces painfully. The skin on her arms is
now mummified up to her bare shoulders. She fights the urge
to scream. She moves into the light. Face still beautiful.

                                        CUT TO:

63 EXT. NATURAL HISTORY MUSEUM - NIGHT   63

Buffy, Xander, and Willow run into view. Willow has ditched   *
the outfit (parka and mittens) except for the pants. Xander   *
has most of his strength back.

                    XANDER
          No. Giles must've... researched
          wrong.

                    WILLOW
               (softly)
          Xander, he didn't.

                    XANDER
          But I know Ampata. This can't be.
          She told me... she said...

His voice trails off. Buffy looks at him sadly.

                    BUFFY
          I know.

Buffy points up at an open, third-story window.

                    BUFFY (cont'd)
          Listen, you two get to the fire   *
          escape. I'll take a short cut.   *

Buffy starts climbing toward the window.   *

                                        CUT TO:

64   INT. NATURAL HISTORY MUSEUM - NIGHT   64

                    GILES
          'The spondylus shell evokes
          Mamacocha, mother of all the water.'

Giles glues in the penultimate fragment. Excited.

                    GILES (cont'd)
          Just one more piece.

65   CLOSE: HIS FINGERS INSERT THE LAST PIECE   65

when suddenly Ampata's gnarled hand rips away the seal and
hurls it down, SHATTERING it beyond repair. She grabs Giles
by the throat, squeezes him unconscious. Pulls his face in
for the kiss.

                    BUFFY (O.C.)
          I'll say one thing for you Incan
          mummies--

Ampata turns to see Buffy on the museum floor.

                    BUFFY
          --You don't kiss and tell.

Buffy does a forward HANDSPRING up the step pyramid, landing
in front of a startled Ampata.

                    AMPATA
          Looks like you've been keeping some
          secrets from me.

Ampata drops Giles' unconscious body into the sarcophagus
hole, as she and Buffy square off against each other.

                    AMPATA (cont'd)
          You're not a normal girl.

She LUNGES for Buffy's throat with her two mummified arms.
Buffy looks at them, repulsed.

                    BUFFY
          Oh, and you are?

They struggle, rolling toward the open sarcophagus. Ampata's
face gets closer for the kiss. Buffy headbutts Ampata.
Ampata staggers backwards.

Buffy charges. Ampata uses Buffy's momentum to hurl Buffy
into the sarcophagus.

                    AMPATA
          I shared your life--

66   BUFFY'S POV: THE SARCOPHAGUS LID   66

Slides shut overhead. Blackness.

                    AMPATA
          --Now you'll share my death.

Ampata desperately grabs her neck, as the mummification
advances. She races down the steps, running smack into:

Willow. Petrified. Ampata clasps her hand around Willow's
throat.

67   POV: AMPATA'S FACE   67

                    AMPATA
          This won't hurt.

                    XANDER (O.S.)
          Let her go.

Ampata looks around. Xander is there.

                    XANDER
          If you're going to kiss anybody, it
          should be me.

Ampata looks at Xander for a beat, then back at Willow.

                              CUT TO:

68   INT. THE SARCOPHAGUS - CONTINUOUS - NIGHT   68

Pitch black. We hear a stone slab being moved. A SHAFT OF
LIGHT comes in through a crack, and we see Buffy in the
sarcophagus, straining to move the stone lid aside.

                              CUT TO:

69   INT. NATURAL HISTORY MUSEUM -BURIAL CHAMBER- CONTINUOUS   69

Xander approaches Ampata. Tears well up in her eyes.

                    AMPATA
          Xander, we can be together. Just let
          me have this one.

Xander looks at her still-beautiful face.

                    XANDER
          That's never gonna happen.

                                            CONTINUED

69 CONTINUED: 69

                              AMPATA
                    I must do this, now, or it is the
                    end. For me and for us.

She moves in for Willow.

                              XANDER
                    No!

Xander steps between them, pushing Willow back to safety.

                              XANDER (cont'd)
                    You want life, you're gonna have to
                    take mine. Can you do that?

There is fear and confusion in her face -- and then it is
gone. Replaced by something colder.

                              AMPATA
                    Yes.

She lunges at him.

70 ANGLE: THE SARCOPHAGUS LID   70

    as it is tossed aside. Buffy pops out, then hurls herself
    from the top of the pyramid;

Xander struggles to hold Mummy Ampata away as Buffy appears.

Buffy KICKS Mummy Ampata. She FLIES through the air and
SLAMS onto the stone pyramid steps.

The mummy SHATTERS on impact. Nothing but dust.

Silence.

Willow goes to Xander. He looks up at her; tries to smile.
She smiles back, starts to help him to his feet. Buffy helps
Giles out of the sarcophagus. The two of them head over to
join the others.

PULL BACK AND AWAY as the four of them walk out together.

                                        CUT TO:

71 EXT. SCHOOL COURTYARD - THE NEXT DAY   71

Buffy and Xander walk together, Buffy sipping a soda. They
are quiet for a while. She offers him a sip, he shakes his
head.

                                        CONTINUED

71 CONTINUED: 71

> XANDER
> I'm really the fun talking guy today,
> huh? Sorry.

> BUFFY
> We don't have to talk.

> XANDER
> I just... Present company excluded,
> I have the worst taste in women Of
> anyone. In the world. Ever.

> BUFFY
> Ampata wasn't evil. At least not to
> start with. And I do think she cared
> for you.

> XANDER
> Yeah, but I think the whole sucking-
> the-life-out-of-people thing would
> have been a strain on the
> relationship.

> BUFFY
> She was gypped. She was just a girl
> and she had her life taken from her.
> I remember when I heard the prophesy
> that I was going to die. I wasn't
> exactly obsessed with doing the right
> thing.

> XANDER
> But you did. You gave up your life.

> BUFFY
> I had you to bring me back.

They smile at each other, then settle back into a comfortable
silence.

                                        BLACK OUT.

                        THE END

BUFFY THE VAMPIRE SLAYER

"Reptile Boy"

Written and Directed By

David Greenwalt

SHOOTING SCRIPT

August 13, 1997
August 18, 1997 (Full Blue Script)
August 20, 1997 (Full Pink Script)
August 21, 1997 (Yellow Pages)
August 22, 1997 (Green Pages)

BUFFY THE VAMPIRE SLAYER

"Reptile Boy"

CAST LIST

BUFFY SUMMERS......................... Sarah Michelle Gellar
XANDER HARRIS......................... Nicholas Brendon
RUPERT GILES.......................... Anthony S. Head
WILLOW ROSENBERG...................... Alyson Hannigan
CORDELIA CHASE........................ Charisma Carpenter
ANGEL................................. David Boreanaz

CALLIE................................*Jordana Spiro
RICHARD/HOODED FIGURE.................*Greg Vaughan
TOM...................................*Todd Babcock
YOUNG MAN.............................*Coby Bell
TACKLE................................*Christopher Dalhberg
MACHIDA...............................*Robin Atkin Downes
*FRESHMAN (JONATHON)..................*Danny Strong
*LINEBACKER...........................*Jason Posey

BUFFY THE VAMPIRE SLAYER

"Reptile Boy"

SET LIST

INTERIORS

SUNNYDALE HIGH SCHOOL
    LIBRARY
    HALL
    HALL OUTSIDE LIBRARY
    CLASSROOM
    LOUNGE

BUFFY'S HOUSE
    BUFFY'S BEDROOM

FRAT HOUSE
    BASEMENT
    FRAT BEDROOM
    UPSTAIRS
    FOYER
    SECOND FLOOR HALLWAY

THE BRONZE

EXTERIORS

SUNNYDALE HIGH SCHOOL
    FRONT OF SCHOOL

BUFFY'S HOUSE

WOODS

FRAT HOUSE
    FRONT PORCH
    FRONT PATIO

GRAVEYARD

BUFFY THE VAMPIRE SLAYER

"Reptile Boy"

TEASER

1 EXT. BUFFY'S HOUSE - NIGHT   1

After a beat we HEAR a STRANGE, HIGH PITCHED WAILING --

                                        CUT TO:

2 INT. BUFFY'S BEDROOM - NIGHT   2

CLOSE ON XANDER - Concerned

                    XANDER
          Is she dying?

BUFFY AND WILLOW

Flank him on the couch. Slumped down in high teen boredom,
sodas and junk food pilfered from Buffy's kitchen scattered
about, watching T.V. --

                    BUFFY
          She's singing.

3 ANGLE - THE T.V.   3

An EAST INDIAN soap opera on an obscure cable channel: an
INDIAN WOMAN sings (in a foreign language) something very
heartfelt into a telephone.

4 BUFFY, WILLOW & XANDER   4

                    XANDER
          To a telephone, in Hindi... now   *
          that's entertainment. Why is she
          singing?

                    WILLOW
          She's sad because her lover gave her
          a dozen gold coins but then the
          wizard cut open the bag of salt and
          the dancing minions had no place to
          put their big Maypole...
               (gestures)
          ...fish thing.

                    XANDER
          Uh huh. And why is she singing?

                                        CONTINUED

4 CONTINUED: 4

> BUFFY
> Her lover? I thought he was her
> chiropractor.

> WILLOW
> Because of that thing he did with her
> feet? No, that was personal.

They stare at the screen for a beat. The PIERCING SINGING
continues under:

> XANDER
> And we thought just 'cause we didn't
> have any money or anywhere to go
> this'd be a lackluster evening.

> WILLOW
> Hey, I know -- we could go to the
> Bronze, sneak in our own tea bags and
> ask for... hot water.

> XANDER
> Hop off that outlaw train, Will,
> before you land us all in jail.

> BUFFY
> I for one am giddy and up. There's a
> kind of hush all over Sunnydale, no
> vampires or demons to slay, I'm here
> with my friends and --
>   (re: T.V.)
> -- where does the water buffalo fit
> in again?

                                        CUT TO:

5 EXT. HOUSE - NIGHT   5

PUSHING IN on the quiet, affluent house and then --

AN UPSTAIRS WINDOW IS SHATTERED

And a PRETTY GIRL (17) bursts through the glass, hits the
ground and runs for her life.

A moment later, several dark figures in hooded robes emerge
from other windows and doors like malevolent ghosts and give
chase.

                                                    CONTINUED

5 CONTINUED: 5

She bolts into the woods. She's fast.

They're faster.

6 EXT. WOODS - NIGHT   6

She tears through running for all she's worth.

The hooded figures close the gap behind her.

She scales a tall stone wall.

A7 EXT. GRAVEYARD - NIGHT   A7

She scrambles over the wall and runs. Three hooded figures
scramble over the wall after her.

As she passes a crypt, a HOODED FIGURE coolly steps out and
qrabs her. She SCREAMS, he purrs:

                    HOODED FIGURE
          Callie... Where are you going?

The girl, her eyes wild with fear, claws at him, pulling his
hood off revealing the face of a handsome twenty year old
sadist. He deflects her blows and grabs her wrists, puts his
face close to hers.

                    FIGURE
          The party ain't even started yet.

And, not without charm, the Figure smiles at Callie. Then
nods at the brethren. Several of them hustle Callie back
towards the house.

                    CALLIE
          No! no!

The Figure takes a deep breath of the bracing night air and
walks out of frame.

                              BLACK OUT.

                    END OF TEASER

ACT ONE

7 INT. SCHOOL HALL - DAY - A COUPLE   7   *

SMOOCH in f.g., part, revealing CORDELIA, laughing in a   *
HIGHLY AMUSED if somewhat forced manner. She's with a
Cordette. KIDS are arriving for school.

                    CORDELIA
          Ha ha ha ha ha.

Cordelia shows the Cordette a magazine (TEEN TIME). Pretty
girl on the cover holding a fishing rod and big lure;
headline: HOW TO LAND HIM AND KEEP HIM.

                    CORDELIA (cont'd)
          Doctor Debbi says when a man is
          speaking you make serious eye contact
          and really, really listen. And you
          laugh at everything he says... ha ha
          ha ha...

8 ANOTHER ANGLE - BUFFY AND WILLOW   8

Heading downstairs.   *

                    WILLOW
          You dreamed about Angel again?

                    BUFFY
          Third night in a row.

                    WILLOW
          What did he do in the dream?

                    BUFFY
          Stuff.

                    WILLOW
          Ooh, stuff. Was it one of those
          vivid dreams where you could feel his
          lips and smell his hair?

                    BUFFY
               (nods)
          It had surround sound. I'm just
          thinking about him so much lately.

                    WILLOW
          Well you guys are so right for each
          other, except for the, uh...

                                                    CONTINUED

                        BUFFY
          Vampire thing?

CONTINUED

> WILLOW
> That doesn't make him a bad person.
> Necessarily.

> BUFFY
> I'm brainsick, I can't have a
> relationship with him.

> WILLOW
> Well maybe not in the day time... but
> you could ask him for coffee some
> night.
>   (off Buffy's look)
> It's the non-relationship drink of
> choice. It's not a date, it's a
> caffeinated beverage -- okay it's hot
> and bitter, like a relationship that
> way but --

Xander slides into step with them.

> XANDER
> What's like a relationship?

> BUFFY
> Nothing I have.
>   (mulling, to Willow)
> Coffee.

> XANDER
> Huh?

As they pass Cordelia and the Cordette.

> CORDELIA
> There's really no comparison between
> college men and high school boys --
>   (re: Xander)
> -- I mean look at that.

> XANDER
> Cor, you datin' a college guy now?

> CORDELIA
> Not that it's any of your business,
> but I happen to be seeing a Delta
> Zeta Kappa.

> XANDER
> Oh, an extra-terrestrial, so that's
> how you get a date once you've
> exhausted all the human guys.

CONTINUED

8 CONTINUED: (3)   8

                    CORDELIA
          You'll go to college some day,
          Xander, I just know your pizza
          delivery career will take you so many
          exciting places. Ha ha ha ha.

Buffy, Xander and Willow move off as a bell RINGS O.S.

                    BUFFY
          Ooops, I told Giles I'd meet him in
          the library ten minutes ago --
                    (moving off)
          -- there hasn't been much paranormal
          activity lately, he won't be upset.

                                        CUT TO:

9 INT. LIBRARY - DAY - GILES IS UPSET   9

Faces Buffy, circles her as.

                    GILES
          Just because the paranormal has been
          more normal and less... para lately,
          that is no excuse for tardiness or
          letting your guard down.

                    BUFFY
          I haven't let my guard down.

                    GILES
          Oh really? You yawned your way
          through weapons training last week,
          you skipped hand to hand entirely --
          I suppose you're prepared if some
          demon springs up behind you and does
          this!

Without warning, Giles swings at her from behind. Without
turning, Buffy's hand shoots backwards, grabs Giles' wrist.
Buffy pivots and whips Giles' hand around behind his back, in
a painful arm lock.

                    GILES (cont'd)
          Yes, well, I'm no demon...
                    (beat)
          ...which is why you should let go now.

She does. He massages his wrist.

                                        CONTINUED

> GILES (cont'd)
> When you live atop a mystical
> convergence it's only a matter of
> time before a fresh hell breaks
> loose. Now is the time to train more
> strictly, hunt and patrol more
> keenly, hone your skills day and
> night --

> BUFFY
> And the little scrap of my life that
> still belongs to me -- say from seven
> to seven oh five in the morning --
> can I do what I want to then?

> GILES
>   (beat)
> Buffy, you think I don't know what
> it's like to be sixteen?

> BUFFY
> I think you don't know what it's like   *
> to be sixteen and a girl and a Slayer.

> GILES
> Well, I don't.   *

> BUFFY
> Or what it's like to stake vampires   *
> while you're having fuzzy feelings
> towards one.

> GILES
> Ohh... ahh...   *

> BUFFY
> And "eee"... digging on the undead   *
> doesn't exactly do wonders for your   *
> social life.

> GILES
> But you see that's just where being   *
> different comes in handy.   *

> BUFFY   *
> Who needs a social life when they've   *
> got their very own hellmouth?   *

> GILES
> Yes! You have a duty, a purpose, you
> have a life long commitment. How many
> people your age do you think can say
> that?

CONTINUED

9 CONTINUED: (2)   9

                         BUFFY
              We talkin' foreign or domestic -- how
              'bout <u>none</u>.

Giles sighs, he tried.

                         GILES
              Well here's a hard fact of life: we
              all have to do things we don't like.
              You have hand to hand this afternoon
              and patrol tonight. You'd best come
              right here after sixth period and get
              your homework done. Don't dawdle with
              your friends.

Buffy just stands there pouting.

                         GILES (cont'd)
              And don't think standing there
              pouting is going to get to me. It
              doesn't.

She pouts. He lies:

                         GILES (cont'd)
              Not getting to me.

                                             CUT TO:

10 EXT. SUNNYDALE HIGH - DAY   10

     After school. Cars pulling up, KIDS taking off. Buffy dawdles
     on a wall near the street. Xander and Willow move up.

                         XANDER
              Wow, what a long day.

                         WILLOW
              You cut three periods.

                         XANDER
              Yeah, and of course <u>they</u> flew by.
              Buffy!

                         WILLOW
              Aren't you s'posed to be doing your
              homework in the library --

                         BUFFY
              I'm dawdling. With my friends.

                                             CONTINUED

10 CONTINUED: 10

Buffy tips forward on the wall like she's going to fall --
catches herself by draping her arms over Xander's shoulders.

                    XANDER
          Works for me.

11 ANOTHER ANGLE - FRONT OF THE SCHOOL - CORDELIA   11

Looking luscious, waits expectantly as a sleek, dark BMW
(tinted windows, we can't see who's inside) pulls to the curb.

She moves to the car. The dark window rolls down revealing
RICHARD (the twenty year old sadist from the teaser) in
expensive slacks and sport coat. As are the other two DELTA
ZETAS in back.

In the passenger seat is TOM, also 20, but dressed casually.
Tom is rich, too, but he's not a prick, he's a low key,
decent guy.

                    RICHARD
          Cordelia.

                    CORDELIA
          Hi Richard. Nice car.

As instructed by her teen magazine, Cordelia never takes her
eyes of Richard.

We PUSH PAST Richard to Tom, totally engaged by:

12 TOM'S POV - BUFFY   12

Dawdling with Xander and Willow.

                    BUFFY
          Dawdle, dawdle, dawdle... I'm a rebel
          and I'll never ever be any good...

13 TOM   13

Takes a breath. Something about Buffy...

14 RICHARD   14

                    RICHARD
          So we're having a little get together
          at the house tomorrow night...

Richard sees the look on Tom's face, follows it to Buffy,
never skipping a beat with Cordelia

                                                CONTINUED

14 CONTINUED: 14

                         RICHARD (cont'd)
               ...it's going to be a really special
               evening...

                         CORDELIA
               Ha ha ha ha.

                         RICHARD
               Excuse me.

                         CORDELIA
                    (recovering)
               Oh I'd love to --

                         RICHARD
               Who's your friend?

Cordelia turns, sees Buffy behind her on the wall clowning
with Xander and Willow.

                         CORDELIA
               Her? She's not my friend.

                         TOM
               She's amazing.

                         CORDELIA
               She's more like a sister, really.
               We're that close.

                         RICHARD
               Why don't you introduce us?

15 BUFFY, XANDER AND WILLOW   15

                         XANDER
               Okay so tonight, Channel fifty nine,
               Indian T.V. -- sex, lies and
               incomprehensible story lines --I'll
               bring the beetle nuts.

Cordelia walks up, grabs Buffy.

                         CORDELIA
               Come on, Richard and his fraternity
               brothers want to meet you.

                         BUFFY
               I don't really want to meet any
               fraternity --

                                                        CONTINUED

                         CORDELIA
             And if there was a God, don'tcha'
             think He'd keep it that way?

Buffy is dragged away.

                         XANDER
             Hey, I believe we were hanging here...

16 ANGLE   16

Cordelia drags Buffy to Richard who has now gotten out of his car. Confident, cool, he flashes his perfect smile at Buffy.

                    RICHARD
          Hi, sweet thing. I'm Richard. And
          you are?

                    BUFFY
          So not interested.

                    CORDELIA
          She's such a little comedienne!

Cordelia hits Buffy who is about to turn away when Tom appears behind Richard.

                    RICHARD
          What, is she playing hard to get?

                    TOM
          No Richard, I think you're playing
          easy to resist.
                    (to Buffy)
          Feel free to ignore him. I do all
          the time.

Buffy hesitates, this guy seems okay.

                    TOM (cont'd)
          I'm Tom Warner. I'm a Senior at   *
          Crestwood College and I feel like a
          complete dolt meeting you this way --
          so here I stand in all my
          doltishess...

17 XANDER AND WILLOW   17

                    XANDER
          She's gonna walk away... now.
                    (snaps fingers)
          Okay boots, start walkin'...

18 BUFFY AND TOM   18

                    BUFFY
          I'm Buffy Summers.

                    TOM
          Nice to meet you. Are you a Senior?

                    BUFFY
          Junior.

                                                    CONTINUED

18 CONTINUED: 18

> TOM
> Me too, except I'm a Senior, and in
> college.
> (beat)
> So, we have that in common.
> (beat)
> I major in History.

> BUFFY
> History stumps me. I have a hard
> enough time remembering what happened
> last week.

> TOM
> Nothing happened last week, don't
> worry, I was there.

Buffy smiles, not smitten but charmed. Behind them, Richard,
with other frat guys looking on, says something to Cordelia.
We HEAR her "Ha ha ha ha".

19 XANDER AND WILLOW   19

Xander shakes his head, disgusted.

> XANDER
> I hate these guys. Whatever they want
> just falls into their laps. Don't you
> hate these guys?

> WILLOW
> Yeah, with their charmed lives and
> their movie star good looks and more
> money than you can count...
> (off his look)
> I'm hating.

20 BUFFY AND TOM   20

> TOM
> (re: Richard and
> Cordelia)
> So my friend asked your friend to
> this party we're having tomorrow
> night...
> (lowers voice)
> ...actually he's not really my
> friend -- I only joined the
> fraternity 'cause my father and
> grampa were in it before me. It meant
> a lot to them. I know, I talk too
> much.
> (more)

                                                               CONTINUED

20 CONTINUED: 20

                    TOM (cont'd)
          Anyway, they're really dull parties
          full of really dull people so, uh,
          how would you like to come and save
          me from a really dull fate?

                    BUFFY
               (beat)
          I wish I could but... I'm sort of
          seeing someone.

                    TOM
          Oh. Sure, of course you are. Well,
          thanks for letting me ramble...

                    BUFFY
          People underestimate the value of a
          good ramble.

Tom smiles.

                    GILES (O.S.)
          Buffy!

Buffy turns, sees Giles near the front door of school,
pointing to his watch.

                    BUFFY
          I gotta... nice to meet you.

                    TOM
          Same here.

Buffy takes off. Tom watches her, intrigued.

                                        CUT TO:

21 INT. LIBRARY - NIGHT   21

Buffy practices her hand to hand with Giles (who wears much
protective gear). There's a certain not-so-sub-text here:
they're pissed at each other.

                    GILES
          I'm going to attack you. Word of
          caution: for your own good, I won't
          be pulling any punches.

                    BUFFY
          Please don't.

                                        CONTINUED

21 CONTINUED: 21

    He comes at her with the short sword -- she kicks it out of
    his hand. He immediately counters with a wooden rod -- she
    chops it in half.

    He lunges. She sidesteps. He slides past her on the table   *
    top.   *

                        GILES
              Good. So you're on patrol and I'll
              see you in the morning.

                                                                      *

                                CUT TO:

22 EXT. GRAVEYARD - NIGHT   22

    Dark, empty, dangerous.

    Buffy moves through the dark shadows, her hand instinctively
    checking the stakes in her belt.

23 ANGLE - A LARGE TREE   23

    As Buffy moves past. Something moves in the dark -- a FIGURE,
    watching Buffy.

24 THE FIGURE'S POV   24

    Buffy moves through the graves. The Figure follows.

25 BUFFY   25

    Stops, sees something glinting in the leaves at her feet. She
    kneels down.

26 INSERT - BUFFY'S HAND   26

    Picks up a BROKEN SILVER PIECE of an I.D. bracelet. Three
    letters, E, N and T, can be seen, inscribed in the delicate
    bracelet.

27 BUFFY   27

    Studies the bracelet, then:

                        ANGEL (O.S.)
              There's blood on it.

                                                          CONTINUED

Startled, Buffy jumps to her feet, sees ANGEL.

                    BUFFY
          Oh... hi. Nice to... blood?
               (studies bracelet)

                    ANGEL
          I can smell it.

                    BUFFY
               (beat)
          It's pretty thin, probably belonged
          to a girl.

Angel glances around the woods.

                    ANGEL
          Probably.

Buffy laughs. He looks back.

                    BUFFY
          I was just thinking, wouldn't it be   *
          funny to see each other some time
          when it wasn't a blood thang?

Nothing from Angel.

                    BUFFY (cont'd)
          Not funny ha ha.

                    ANGEL
          What are you saying, you want to have
          a date?

                    BUFFY
          No --

                    ANGEL
          You don't want to have a date.

                    BUFFY
          Who said date? I never said date.

                    ANGEL
          Right, you just want to have coffee
          or something.

                    BUFFY
          Coffee?

Buffy makes a "that's ridiculous" sound.

                                              CONTINUED

            ANGEL
I knew this would happen.

            BUFFY
Really? And what do you think is
happening?

            ANGEL
You're sixteen years old, I'm two
hundred and forty-one.

            BUFFY
I've done the math.

            ANGEL
You don't know what you're doing, you
don't know what you want.

            BUFFY
Oh I think I do: I want out of this
conversation.

She turns to walk away. He grabs her.

            ANGEL
Listen. If we date you and I both
know one thing's going to lead to
another.   *

            BUFFY
One thing's already lead to another.   *
It's a little late to be reading me   *
the warning label.   *

            ANGEL   *
I'm just trying to protect you. This   *
could get out of control.   *

            BUFFY   *
Isn't that the way it's supposed to   *
be?   *

And he pulls her closer. Roughly. There could be a kiss   *
pending -- or an attack. She looks up at him, half scared,   *
half attracted.   *

            ANGEL   *
This isn't some Fairy Tale: when I
kiss you you don't wake up from a
deep sleep and live happily ever
after.

                                                         CONTINUED

27 CONTINUED: (3)   27

                          BUFFY
              No. When you kiss me I want to die.

        She holds his gaze -- then she walks out of frame.

                                                    CUT TO:

28 INT. CLASSROOM - DAY   28

        Buffy is gathering her stuff as students head out.

                                                    CONTINUED

28 CONTINUED: 28

                    CORDELIA (O.S.)
          Buffy!

Cordelia moves up.

                    CORDELIA
          Did you lose weight? And your hair...
                (Buffy ignores her)
          All right, I respect you too much to
          be dishonest, the hair's...
                (makes a face)
          ...well that's not the point here, is
          it. The Zeta Kappas have to have a
          certain balance at their party --
          Richard explained it all to me but I
          was so busy REALLY LISTENING to him
          that I didn't hear much -- anyway,
          the deal is they need you to go. And
          if you don't go...
                (her eyes moisten)
          ...I can't! I'm talking about Richard
          Anderson, okay? As in Anderson Farms,
          Anderson Aeronautics...   *
                (she can no longer
                 hold back the tears)
          ...and Anderson Cosmetics! Do you
          have a hankie?

Buffy shakes her head.

                    CORDELIA (cont'd)
          Well you can see why I have to go.
          These men are rich, Buffy, and I'm
          not being shallow -- think of the
          poor people I could help with all my
          money.

                    BUFFY
          I'll go.

                    CORDELIA
          I'm not going to beg you -- please,
          oh please -- you'll go? Great! We'll
          take my car. Oh Buffy, we're just
          like sisters... with really different
          hair.

And Cordelia happily moves off. Off Buffy's expression, pre-
lap:

                                                    CONTINUED

BUFFY THE VAMPIRE SLAYER "Reptile Boy" (PINK) 8/20/97 18.

28 CONTINUED: (2)   28

>   RICHARD (O.S.)
>   I pledge my life... and my death.

                                            CUT TO:

29 OMITTED   29

30 INT. FRAT HOUSE - BASEMENT - DAY   30

SHOOTING HIGH ABOVE AN ALTER that's built up around a dark
circle, like a well -- an apparently bottomless pit.

ANOTHER ANGLE - Richard and other frat minions, in robes (no
Tom) are gathered before the alter which has eyes, fangs,
diamond shape carvings -- an abstract but frightening
representation of some horrible *thing* they worship. Possibly
a thing that lives in the bottomless pit.

The basement is cut into the bed rock -- cave-like out
croppings of stone add an ancient touch to the decor.

A YOUNG MAN is naked from the waist up and Richard holds the
sword to his chest, carving a large diamond shaped SCAR into
his flesh. (Yes, we'll be tasteful.)

>   YOUNG MAN
>   I pledge my life and my death...

>   RICHARD
>   To the Delta Zeta Kappas and to
>   Machida whom we serve.

>   YOUNG MAN
>   To the Delta Zeta Kappas and to
>   Machida whom we serve.

>   RICHARD
>   In blood I was baptized, in blood I
>   shall reign, in His Name!

>   YOUNG MAN
>   In blood I was baptized, in blood I
>   shall reign, in His Name!

Richard finishes carving the diamond shape.

                                            CONTINUED

30 CONTINUED: 30

                              RICHARD
                    You are now one of us.

                              YOUNG MAN
                    In His Name!

The others reply: "In His Name!"

                              RICHARD
                    Brewski time!

Someone opens a cooler -- beers are flung about. Someone
turns on a boom box. Suddenly it's a bunch of college guys in
robes guzzling beer and listening to loud music.

The various brethren congratulate the Young Man. Richard sees
something O.S., moves to:

31 CALLIE   31

The girl from the teaser. Chained to the rock wall.

                              RICHARD
                    So what's a girl like you doing in a
                    place like this?

                              CALLIE
                    Please, let me go.

                              RICHARD
                    Let you go. Okay, let me think --
                    uhhh, no.

She cries. He laughs.

                              RICHARD (cont'd)
                    Gawd I love high school girls.

Richard sips his beer, tapping his head to the music, digging
his world.

                         END OF ACT ONE

ACT TWO

32 EXT. SUNNYDALE HIGH - ESTABLISHING   32

                    WILLOW (O.S.)
            You're going to the fraternity party?

33 INT. SCHOOL - LOUNGE - DAY   33   *

    Buffy and Willow talk, gathering up study books. Xander reads   *
    a SKATEBOARD magazine, lounging on the couch.   *

                    WILLOW
            What made you change your mind?

                    BUFFY
            Angel.

                    WILLOW
            He's going with you?
                (to Xander)
            She's got a date with Angel. Isn't
            that exciting?

                    XANDER
            I'm elated.

                    BUFFY
            I'm not going with Angel. I'm going
            with... yee gods, Cordelia.

                    WILLOW
                (a little jealous)
            Cordelia? Did I sound a little
            jealous just then? Cause I'm not
            really... Cordelia?

                    XANDER
            Cordelia's much better for you than
            Angel.

    They exit the upper part of the lounge and head DOWN THE HALL.   *

                    WILLOW
            What happened with Angel?

                    BUFFY
            Nothing. As usual. A whole lot of
            nothing with Angel.

                    XANDER
                (hot diggity)
            Bummer.

                                                CONTINUED

33 CONTINUED: 33

> WILLOW
> I don't understand. He likes you.
> More than likes.

> BUFFY
> The guy hardly ever says two words to
> me...

> XANDER
> Don't you hate that.

> BUFFY
> ...and he treats me like a child.

> XANDER
> That bastard!

> BUFFY
> At least Tom can carry on a
> conversation.

> XANDER
> Yeah, Tom -- who's Tom?

> WILLOW
> The frat guy.

> XANDER
> Oh, I don't think so, Buffy, frying
> pan and the fire, know what I'm
> saying?

They wheel into:

34   INT. LIBRARY - DAY   34

Giles, his back to the doors, short sword in hand, deals with
an unseen opponent.

> GILES
> What if a vampire came up behind you
> and did that!

Giles swings the sword to the left while ducking and jumping
to the right.

TRACK WITH Buffy, Xander and Willow as they move into the
room and see there is no opponent, Giles is refining the move
he tried on Buffy yesterday.

> GILES (cont'd)
> Or this!

                                                                        CONTINUED

34 CONTINUED: 34

Giles twists, cuts high, then low --

                    GILES (cont'd)
          Hah!

-- then sees the three of them, quickly straightens up with
as much dignity as he can muster.

                    GILES (cont'd)
          Oh, didn't see you three...
                 (under his breath)
          ...sneaking up like that.

He puts the sword down, turns to Buffy.

                    GILES (cont'd)
          All went well last night?

Buffy nods, pulling out the piece of the bracelet she found.

                    BUFFY
          I found this.

INSERT BRACELET -- as she holds it out.

Willow looks at it as Giles takes it.

                    GILES
               (reads letters on it)
          "E" "n", "t"...

                    WILLOW
          I've seen something like that
          somewhere...

                    BUFFY
          It's broken in two, I don't know what
          the other letters might have
          spelled... and there's blood on it.

                    GILES
          I don't see --

                    BUFFY
          Angel showed up. Said he could smell
          it.

                    XANDER
          The blood.
               (Buffy nods)
          There's a guy you want to party with.

                                              CONTINUED

                         GILES
          Blood...

                         WILLOW
          Yeah, in Sunnydale, what a surprise.

                         XANDER
                    (re: Buffy)
          She should probably make the rounds
          again tonight while we try and figure
          out who that bracelet belongs to.

                         GILES
                    (nods)
          Good idea. She'll patrol, we'll
          reconvene after school --

                         BUFFY
          Hello, "she's" standing right here.
          And she's not available tonight.

                         GILES
          Why not?

                         XANDER
          Buff, this is a little more important
          than --

                         BUFFY
                    (shut up, Xander)
          -- I've got a mountain of homework,
          my mom's sick and she needs me to
          take care of her, and I'm starting to
          feel a little woozy myself.

     Buffy touches her forehead. Willow and Xander exchange a look.

                         GILES
          Oh, if you're not feeling...

                         BUFFY
          I'll make a quick pass early this
          evening, and another one later on,
          but for the bulk of the evening...

                         GILES
          You need to be home with your mother.

     Buffy nods.

                                        CUT TO:

35 INT. HALL OUTSIDE LIBRARY - DAY   35

       As Xander, Buffy and Willow exit. They walk in silence for a
       beat.

                         BUFFY
              Well, say it.

                         XANDER
              I'm not going to say it 'cause --

                         WILLOW
              You lied to Giles.

                         XANDER
                    (re: Willow)
              -- she will.

                         BUFFY
              I wasn't lying. I was protecting him.
              From information he wouldn't be able
              to... digest properly.

                         XANDER
              Like a corn dog.

                         WILLOW
              Like you don't have a sick mother but
              you'd rather go to a Fraternity party
              where there'll be drinking and older
              boys and probably an orgy?

                         XANDER
              Enh! Rewind, when did they start
              having orgies and how come I'm not on
              the mailing list?

                         BUFFY
              There's no orgy.

                         WILLOW
              I've heard some really wild things go
              on at the D.Z.K. parties.

                         BUFFY
              Look, six days a week I'm busy saving
              the world. Once in a great while I
              want to have some fun. And that's
              what I'm going to have tonight... fun.

                                        CUT TO:

36 INT. SCHOOL LOUNGE - DAY - CORDELIA   36

Lectures Buffy.

> CORDELIA
> This isn't about fun tonight, it's
> about duty: you're duty to help me
> achieve permanent prosperity. Okay,
> do's and don'ts. Don't wear black,
> silk, chiffon, or spandex -- these
> are my trademarks -- don't do that
> weird thing to your hair.

> BUFFY
> What weird...?

> CORDELIA
> Don't interrupt. Do be interested if
> someone should speak to you -- may or
> may not happen -- do be polite, do
> laugh at appropriate intervals -- ha
> ha ha ha -- and do lie to your mother
> about where we're going: it's a
> fraternity, there'll be drinking.

Willow and Xander pass by.   *

> XANDER
> So Cor, are you printing up business
> cards with your pager number and
> hours of operation or just going with
> the halter top tonight?

> CORDELIA
> Ahh, are we a little envious? Don't
> be, you could join a fraternity of
> rich, powerful men... in the Bizarro
> world.

> BUFFY
> You guys want to...
>   (gestures: join us?)

> XANDER
> Nah, I gotta digest and all.

Xander and Willow move off. Cordelia studies Buffy, tapping
her fingers, thinking hard.

> CORDELIA
> Make-up, make-up... well, just give
> it your all and keep to the shadows.
> We are going to have a blast!

37   ANGLE - WILLOW AND XANDER   37

     As they sit some distance away.

                         WILLOW
               I can't believe she lied to Giles. My
               world is all askew.

                         XANDER
               Buffy lying? Buffy going to frat
               parties? That's not askew, that's
               cockeyed!

                         WILLOW
               Askew means cockeyed.

                         XANDER
               Oh.

                         WILLOW
               Well there's nothing we can do about
               it. We'll help Giles --

                         XANDER
               I'm going to the party.

                         WILLOW
               What?

                         XANDER
               I want to keep an eye on Buffy, those
               frat guys creep me.

                         WILLOW
               You want to protect her.
                    (he nods)
               And you want to prove you're as good
               as those rich, snotty guys.
                    (he nods)
               And maybe catch an orgy.

                         XANDER
               If it's on early.

                                        CUT TO:

38   EXT. FRAT HOUSE - NIGHT   38

     Lots of cars, young folks arriving, MUSIC blasting. Those
     little white lights strung in trees and along the roof line.

     A CAR ROARS UP to CAMERA. We read the personalized license
     plate: QUEEN C.

                                             CONTINUED

38   CONTINUED: 38

Cordelia squeezes her car into a parking place (smashing the car behind and in front if we can afford). Cordelia and Buffy get out. Oh yeah, they look fantastic.

                    CORDELIA
          Why do they park so darn close to you?
                    (to Buffy)
          You up for this?

                    BUFFY
          I don't know... maybe it isn't such
          a good idea --

                    CORDELIA
          Me too, let's do it!

Cordelia charges ahead. Buffy reluctantly follows.

39   INT. FRAT HOUSE - NIGHT   39

This ain't Animal House. This is a well furnished, wealthy home. But still being partied in by a gaggle of rich young snobs. The men wear coats and ties. The women are sexy but not cheap. WAITERS (actually pathetic guys, some in their underwear, some with fruit hats, all with a big sign PLEDGE hung around their necks) serve drinks and hors d'oeuvres.

THE TACKLE DRINKS A HUGE STEIN OF BEER   *

Standing next to the Linebacker.   *

                    TACKLE   *
          Beaucoup babes.   *

                    LINEBACKER   *
          Yahh!   *

CORDELIA AND BUFFY

In a far corner of the room. Standing alone, perhaps a little awkwardly.

                    CORDELIA
          You know what's so cool about
          college? The diversity. You've got
          rich people and you've got... all the
          other people. Richard!

Richard approaches, hands them each a drink.

                    RICHARD
          Welcome, ladies.

                                                       CONTINUED

39 CONTINUED: 39

                         CORDELIA
              Thank you.

     Richard toasts, drinks. Cordelia follows suit.

                         BUFFY
                      (re: drink)
              Is there alcohol in this?

                                                    CONTINUED

39 CONTINUED: (2)   39

                    RICHARD
          Just a smidge.

                    CORDELIA
          C'mon Buffy, it's just a smidge.

                    BUFFY
          I'll just...
               (setting drink down)

                    RICHARD
          I understand. When I was your age I
          wasn't into grown-up things, either.

Buffy gives him a look. He turns to Cordelia.

                    RICHARD (cont'd)
          Have you seen our multi-media room?

                    CORDELIA
          The one with the cherry walnut
          paneling and the two forty-eight inch
          televisions on satellite feed? No,
          why don't you show me?

As they head off:

                    RICHARD
               (re: Buffy)
          What about -- ?

                    CORDELIA
          She's happiest by herself.

40 BUFFY   40

Watches them go. Looks around for a friendly face. Doesn't
find one. Turns her back, looks out window.

41 OMITTED   41   *
AND   AND
42   42

A43 INT. FRAT HOUSE - NIGHT - ISOLATED WINDOW   A43   *

We PUSH past a couple of partiers and discover Xander peering   *
in the window. He slides the window up and lithely slips in.   *
falling into step with a PLEDGE WAITER, grabbing a drink off   *
his tray.   *

                    XANDER   *
          Cheers.   *

43 XANDER MOVES THROUGH THE PARTY   43

Unaware of Buffy, still standing off by herself (she doesn't
see him, either). Buffy looks down at that drink. Picks it
up. Puts it back. Clasps her hands awkwardly together. Looks
around for a friendly face. Sees:

A COOL GUY across the way. He toast her with his glass. Buffy
picks her glass up, toasts back, not wanting to appear
unsophisticated, takes a polite sip -- it's strong. Then she
sees the BIG TACKLE, hammered, heading her way.

                    TACKLE
          New girl. Dance. Ahhhyeeahh.

Buffy looks left and right for an avenue of escape as the
Tackle lumbers in for a landing. Just as he's upon her, Tom
steps between them, takes Buffy's hand --

                    TOM
          Could I have this dance?

-- and pulls her to the dance floor. Perhaps we hear a crash
of plates O.S.

44 INT. FRAT HOUSE - NIGHT   44

BUFFY AND TOM

Dance to a cool slow song.

                                        CONTINUED

                         BUFFY
                   (re: tackle)
               Thanks for...

                         TOM
               We're not all a bunch of drunken
               louts. Some of us are sober louts.
                   (Buffy smiles)
               I'm really glad you decided to come.
                   (nothing from Buffy)
               And you're not.

                         BUFFY
               No. It's just... I shouldn't be here.

                         TOM
               Because you're seeing someone.

                         BUFFY
               No.

                         TOM
               You're not seeing someone.

                         BUFFY
               Someone's not seeing me.

                         TOM
               So why shouldn't you be here?

                         BUFFY
               I have obligations, people I'm
               responsible to... or for... or with,
               it's complex.

                         TOM
               You're big on responsibility. I like
               that. But there's such a thing as too
               mature. You should relax and enjoy
               yourself once in a while.

                         BUFFY
               You think I'm too mature.

                         TOM
               I talk too much. Have you picked up
               on that yet? Anyway the Hulk is gone
               so you don't have to dance with me
               any --

He starts to step back -- she doesn't let him go.

                                                     CONTINUED

44 CONTINUED: (2)   44

                          BUFFY
                He might come back.

He smiles. And she puts her head on his shoulder. And they
dance for a couple of beats.

45 ANGLE: XANDER CHATS WITH TWO CO-EDS   45

He swipes the air with a couple of crab claws.

                          XANDER
                Godzilla is attacking downtown Tokyo!
                Argh! Argh!

The co-eds laugh.

46 ANOTHER ANGLE - THE TACKLE, RICHARD AND THE LINEBACKER   46   *

Watch him.

                          TACKLE
                Who's this dork?   *

                          RICHARD
                Never saw him before in my life.   *

                          LINEBACKER   *
                We got us a crasher.   *

Richard smiles unpleasantly. Moves off towards Xander. As do   *
the Linebacker and the Tackle.   *

47 XANDER AND CO-EDS   47

                          XANDER
                So have either of you seen a pair of
                girls here? One is about so high --

Richard, the Tackle and the Linebacker suddenly surround him.

                          XANDER (cont'd)
                Hey guys.

The Tackle grabs one shoulder, the Linebacker the other.

                          RICHARD
                New Pledge!

                          TACKLE
                New Pledge!

                                                       CONTINUED

47 CONTINUED: 47

And they drag him away from the co-eds, other Delta Zetas
gathering around, chanting "new pledge!", blotting poor
Xander out of sight.

48 EXT. FRAT HOUSE - FRONT PATIO - NIGHT   48

Buffy wanders out to get some air. We see the party through
the large windows or French doors behind her. She looks off
into the woods beyond the back fence. Something CRUNCHES
beneath her feet. She bends down.

49 INSERT - BUFFY'S HAND   49

Picks up some broken glass.

50 BACK TO SCENE   50

Buffy straightens up and looks up at the second story. We see
the broken and partially patched window the girl burst out of
in the teaser.

Buffy looks off to the woods where she found the bracelet: is
there some connection here?

She turns back towards the house, startled to find:

                    TOM
          You okay?

                    BUFFY
          Yeah. I was just... thinking.

From inside we hear the party and the music crank up. Richard
hurries out, tipsy, thrusts a drink in each of their hands.
Clinks their glasses with his own.

                    RICHARD
          To my Argentinian junk bonds which
          just matured in double digits!

He holds up his glass and drinks merrily. Tom looks at Buffy,
embarrassed by Richard.

                    TOM
          To... maturity.

Tom clinks her glass.

                    BUFFY
               (re: drink)
          Ahhh, what the hell.

                                                        CONTINUED

50 CONTINUED: 50

      She downs the whole drink. Tom's a little surprised.

                        BUFFY (cont'd)
            I'm tired of being mature.

      Tom smiles.

                                              CUT TO:

51 INT. LIBRARY - NIGHT   51

      CLOSE on the bracelet fragment, the letters "N", "T".

      Willow is typing a list of possibilities on the computer.
      Giles stands behind her, helping.

                        WILLOW
            Bent.

                        GILES
            Sent.

                        WILLOW
            Rent.

                        GILES
            Lent.

                        WILLOW
            Kent -- Kent, that's it!

                        GILES
            Her boyfriend's name is Kent.

                        WILLOW
                  (typing)
            No. Kent Preparatory School. Just
            outside town. That's where I've seen
            those bracelets.

                        GILES
            What are you doing?

                        WILLOW
            Pulling up their school newsletter
            for the last few months, to see if
            there's anything about...

      She stops speaking. Giles sees it on the computer:

                        GILES
            A missing girl...

52 INSERT COMPUTER   52

    KENT SCHOOL NEWS -- a picture of a pretty girl, the girl from
    the teaser. Headline: CALLIE, OUR HEARTS AND PRAYERS ARE WITH
    YOU.

                                      CUT TO:

53 INT. FRAT HOUSE - NIGHT   53

    We see two lines of people facing one another. Dancing down
    the middle of the gauntlet (all hope of escape barred by the
    Tackle and the Linebacker) is:

    XANDER

    A hideous wig of long dark curls parked on his head; an
    (extremely) large bra strapped over his shirt; a painful
    party smile plastered on his face. Some of the guys swat him
    with paddles.

                    XANDER
          Okay, big fun... who's next?

    He tries to walk away. The big Tackle shoves him back.

                  TACKLE
          Dance, stranger.

    Xander dances.

54 BUFFY   54

    comes out of a bathroom looking a little wobbly. She touches
    her head.

55 BUFFY-CAM   55

    Her pov of the party. Distorted, a macabre Mardi Gras.

                  BUFFY
             (looking around)
        Tom?

56 BUFFY WEAVES HER WAY   56

    To the stairs, moves up.

57 OMITTED   57   *
AND   AND
58   58

59 INT. FRAT BEDROOM - NIGHT   59

    Buffy stumbles in. A big bed. Looks so inviting.

                    BUFFY
          Okay. Just need to stop spinning for
          a...

    Buffy collapses on the bed. Out cold. A figure appears
    silhouetted in the doorway. Moves to her. Rolls her over.
    It's Richard. He admires her unconscious form for a beat then
    reaches for her blouse. Undoes the top button. Reaches for
    the next button when

60 A HAND   60

    Grabs his hand. Spins him around. It's Tom.

                    TOM
          Get away from her.

    And Tom hits Richard, hard. Richard is flung back against the
    wall.

                    RICHARD
          I wasn't doing anything.

                    TOM
          I saw what you were doing.

                    RICHARD
          I just wanted to have a little fun.

                    TOM
          She's not here for your fun you
          pervert!

    PUSH IN on Tom.

                    TOM (cont'd)
          She's here for the pleasure of the
          one we serve.

                    RICHARD
              (obediently)
          In His Name.

                    TOM
          And that goes for the other one, too.

                                            CONTINUED

60 CONTINUED: 60

We now see Cordelia, passed out in a dark corner of the floor. Off Tom's eyes, the eyes of the zealot and true believer,

                        END OF ACT TWO

ACT THREE

61   INT. LIBRARY - NIGHT   61

Willow types at the computer. Giles reads a print-out of the Kent School News.

                    GILES
          Callie Megan Anderson... missing for
          over a week. No one's seen her, no
          one knows what happened to her...

                    WILLOW
          This being Sunnydale and all, I guess
          we can rule out something good.

                    GILES
                (nods, grabs phone)
          I'm calling Buffy.

                    WILLOW
          No!

                    GILES
          Why not?

                    WILLOW
          Because Buffy... and her mother...

                    GILES
          Are sick. You're right, we shouldn't
          disturb them until we know more.

                    WILLOW
                (re: computer,
                 alarmed)
          You mean like if there are others...?

Giles follows Willow's gaze to her computer.

                    WILLOW (cont'd)
          Brittany Oswald, Junior at St.
          Michael's, disappeared a year ago...
          so did Kelly Percell, sophomore at
          Grant...

                    GILES
          A year ago...

                    WILLOW
          Almost to the day.

                                              CONTINUED

61 CONTINUED: 61

                          GILES
                    (piecing it together)
               An anniversary... or some other event
               that has significance for the killer.

                          WILLOW
               Killer? Now there's a killer? We
               don't know there's a...

                          GILES
               No. But this being Sunnydale and
               all...

                          WILLOW
               Gulp.

                          GILES
               We need to know where Buffy found
               that bracelet -- and begin a search
               from there.

          Giles again reaches for the phone.   *

                          WILLOW
               Good idea, call Angel.   *

          Giles looks at her.   *

                          WILLOW (cont'd)
               He was there when Buffy found it --   *
               we're gonna need all the help we can
               get.

          Giles nods, reaches for the phone.   *

                                             CUT TO:

62 EXT. FRAT HOUSE - FRONT PORCH - NIGHT   62

          We see the last few partiers stumble out, then Xander, still
          in wig and bra, is hurled out by the Tackle and Linebacker.

          They shut the door, Xander stops it with his hand.

                          XANDER
               A friend of mine was here --

                          TACKLE
               Party's over, jerkwater. You know, in
               that light, with the wig and all,
               you're still butt ugly.

                                             CONTINUED

62 CONTINUED: 62

The Tackle slams the door in his face. Xander stands there
steaming, HEARING their laughter from inside. He rips off wig
and big bra, storms off the porch.

CONTINUED

62 CONTINUED: 62

                                                                    *

                                                                    *

                                                                    *

                                                                    *

63 INT. FRAT HOUSE - BASEMENT - NIGHT   63

    Tom, stripped to the waist, kneels before the alter which
    surrounds the dark pit.

    Several ROBED BRETHREN keep a respectful distance from Tom
    whose arms and chest sport a dozen or more of the sword-
    carved diamond shapes. Tom is pretty much the high priest
    around here.

    He finishes whatever silent prayer he was offering, picks up
    the long sword, holds it over the pit as a form of blessing,
    then hands it to a brethren.

    The brethren begins carving yet another diamond on Tom as we
    (discreetly) PAN AWAY to:

64 CORDELIA - COMING TO   64

    Chained to a rock wall. Her hair is mussed and as she takes
    in her surroundings, her eyes fill with fear. She looks to

65 BUFFY   65

    Chained next to her. Buffy is already awake and alert, gazing
    around the basement, taking everything in. From this angle
    she can only see Tom from the back (i.e. she doesn't know
    it's Tom.)

                            CORDELIA
                  Buffy... where are we?

                                                    CONTINUED

65 CONTINUED: 65

                          BUFFY
          In the basement, far as I can tell.

                          CORDELIA
          What's happening? What did they...?

                          BUFFY
          They drugged us.

                          CORDELIA
          Why? What are they gonna do?

                          BUFFY
          I don't know...

                          CORDELIA
                  (really scared)
          I want to go home.

                          CALLIE (O.S.)
          No one's going home.

They turn and see Callie as she leans out of the shadows: a
once pretty girl who's been chained in a basement for a week.

                          CALLIE
          Ever.

Callie stares at them with the look of the condemned.

                          CALLIE (cont'd)
          One of them's different from the
          others, nicer...

                          BUFFY
          Tom.

And Tom turns around on the alter. His eyes meet Buffy's. He
slips into a robe held by two brethren.

                          CALLIE
          He's the one to watch out for.

Callie leans back into the shadows. Tom gazes at Buffy for a
long, creepy beat.

                          TOM
          She's last.

                          CORDELIA
          Last for what? Who's first?

                                                        CONTINUED

65 CONTINUED: (2)   65

Tom turns back to his priestly duties. He picks up three round stones, holds them over the pit in a ritual blessing.

CONTINUED

65 CONTINUED: (3)   65

                         BUFFY
          Three stones... three of us.

                         CORDELIA
          Buffy...

                         BUFFY
          Stay calm. We'll get out of this.

                         CORDELIA
          Why'd I ever let you talk me into
          coming here!

                                             CUT TO:

66 INT. LIBRARY - NIGHT - ANGEL   66

    Moves INTO FRAME, the glass window of Giles' office behind
    him.

                         ANGEL
          She found the bracelet in the   *
          cemetery, near the South Wall.   *

67 REVERSE - WILLOW AND GILES   67

    Willow leans forward, staring hard at something behind Angel.

                         GILES
          South Wall...?   *
               (to Willow)
          -- what are you doing?

                         WILLOW
          Oh. Sorry. The reflection thing, that
          you don't have, Angel, how do you
          shave? -- South Wall, that's out by   *
          the college, right near ...   *
               (realizing)
          ...the fraternity house.

                         GILES
          A fraternity?

    Willow nods, unable to speak.

                         ANGEL
          Could they be taking these girls?

    Willow nods again, petrified.

                                             CONTINUED

67 CONTINUED: 67

                    ANGEL (cont'd)
          Let's get out there.

Willow finally blurts out:

                    WILLOW
          Buffy --!

                    GILES
          We don't know this is concrete, let's
          not disturb her until --

                    WILLOW
          -- is there. With Cordelia. They went
          to a party at the Zeta Kappa house!

                    GILES
          She... lied to me?

                    WILLOW
          Well...

                    ANGEL
          Did she... have a date?

                    WILLOW
          Well...

Losing it, she turns on them both in a sudden Willow-fury.

                    WILLOW (cont'd)
               (to Angel)
          Why do you think she went to that
          party? Because you gave her the brush
          off...
               (to Giles)
          ...and you never let her do anything,
          except work and patrol and -- I know
          she's the Chosen One but you're
          killing her with the pressure, she's
          sixteen going on forty --
               (to Angel)
          -- and you, I mean you're gonna live
          forever, you don't have time for a
          cup of coffee?

Willow takes a breath, no less surprised by her outburst than
they are.

                    WILLOW (cont'd)
          Okay. I don't feel better now and we
          gotta help Buffy.

                                                      CONTINUED

67 CONTINUED: (2)   67

     Willow runs for the door. They follow.

                                                       CUT TO:

68 INT. FRAT HOUSE - BASEMENT - NIGHT   68

     Buffy, Cordelia and Callie watch as the brethren (including
     Richard) gather around the alter.

                         TOM
                 Machida...

     The others murmur "Machida" (pronounced Ma-Kee-Da).

                         TOM (cont'd)
                 We who serve you, we who receive all
                 that you bestow, call upon you in
                 this holy hour.

     Again the others murmur "Machida".

                         TOM (cont'd)
                 We have no wealth, no possession,
                 except that which you give us. We
                 have no power, no place in the world,
                 except that which you give us.

                         OTHERS
                 Except that which you give us.

69 BUFFY AND CORDELIA   69

                         CORDELIA
                 What are they, some kind of cult?

                         BUFFY
                 A psycho-cult.

                         CORDELIA
                 You gotta do something.

     Buffy tests her chains (secured to metal eyes sunk in the
     wall). They hold her fast.

70 TOM AND THE BRETHREN   70

                         TOM
                 It has been a year since our last
                 offerings... a year in which our
                 bounty overflowed... We come before
                 you with fresh offerings... we hope
                 you find them worthy.

71 BUFFY AND CORDELIA   71

                    CORDELIA
          Offerings... he's talking about us?

Callie peers out of the shadows.

                    CALLIE
          You see anyone else chained up in
          here?

72 TOM AND THE BRETHREN   72

                    TOM
          Accept our offering, dark lord, bless
          us with your power, Machida!!

                    OTHERS
          Machida!

Tom drops the stones into the pit. A long silent beat,
followed by the sound of the stones PLOPPING into water far,
far below.

73 BUFFY AND CORDELIA   73

                    CORDELIA
          What... what's down there?

74 TOM AND BRETHREN   74

                    TOM
          Come forth, let your terrible
          countenance look upon your servants
          and their humble offerings! We call
          you, Machida!

                    OTHERS
          In his name! Machida!

A substantial RUMBLING is heard far below, gathering power
and speed. It fills the chamber, growing ever nearer.

75 BUFFY AND CORDELIA   75

Cordelia is terrified.

                    CORDELIA
          There's something down there.
                    (Buffy nods)
          And they're gonna throw us down there
          with it!

                    BUFFY
          I don't think so.

                                                    CONTINUED

75 CONTINUED: 75

> CORDELIA
> (grasping at straws)
> No? Well that's good, that's...

> BUFFY
> I don't think we go to it, I think <u>it</u>
> <u>comes to us</u>...

76 AT THE ALTER   76

The rumbling grows louder and more fierce. The brethren are
all glassy-eyed, murmuring "Machida" feverishly. And
suddenly, with a great explosion, the HORRIBLE THING bursts
out of the big black pit.

MACHIDA is half man, half snake. He has a muscular body (from
the waist up) and the enlarged and frightening head of a man
with the fangs and horrible eyes of a snake. His skin has the
diamond pattern of a snake -- thus the diamond carvings on
his "people". From the waist down he is all snake -- and a
big 'un, too, his snake body trails behind him into the
depths of the pit: God knows how long this guy is.

Machida towers over the brethren and stretches his glistening
body so he can look down on Buffy, Cordelia and Callie.

Off Buffy, looking up at the hideous Delta Zeta deity, and
Cordelia screaming for all she's worth,

                        END OF ACT THREE

ACT FOUR

77   INT. FRAT HOUSE - BASEMENT - NIGHT   77

As before. Machida hovers over the girls.

> TOM
> For he shall rise from the depths and
> we shall tremble before him. He who
> is the source of all we inherit and
> all we possess. MACHIDA!

> OTHERS
> Machida!

> TOM
> And if he is pleased with our
> offerings, then our fortunes shall
> increase.

> OTHERS
> Machida, let our fortunes increase.

> TOM
> And on the tenth day of the tenth
> month he shall be enhungered and we
> shall feed him.

Richard and a brethren start to unlock Cordelia's chains.

> CORDELIA
> Feed him. FEED HIM?!

Buffy pulls like hell at her own chains. They hold fast.
Richard and brethren drag Cordelia, whimpering now, before
Machida. Cordelia looks like she's about to lose her mind.
Buffy struggles with her chains.

Machida rises up, ready to dive for Cordelia.

> BUFFY
> Hey, Reptile Boy!

Machida turns his gaze to Buffy.

> TOM
> No woman speaks to him!

> BUFFY
> You don't want her. She's all skin
> and bones. Half hour later you'll be
> hungry again. Why don't you try me --

                                                      CONTINUED

77 CONTINUED: 77

And Tom backhands her viciously, nearly knocking her out.
Brandishes the sword.

                         TOM
          Speak again and I'll cut your throat.

                                        CUT TO:

78 EXT.   FRAT HOUSE - NIGHT   78

Angel, Willow and Giles exit the Giles-mobile and head for
the darkened frat house.

                         WILLOW
          Looks like everyone's gone.

As they approach, a robed figure steps out of the shadows
behind them. Angel senses the intruder, slows his pace and
suddenly leaps on him.

           ANGEL   XANDER
     Hey!   Hey!

It's Xander, in one of the D.Z. robes. He pulls the hood
back. There's a tear in the front of the robe.

                         XANDER
          What are you doing here?

                         WILLOW
          There's a bunch of girls missing, the
          Zeta Kappas may be involved and
          Buffy -- are you wearing make-up?

                         XANDER
              (rubs at his face)
          No. I think Buffy's still inside
          somewhere with Cordelia.
              (points to car)
          That's her car.

                         GILES
          Why are you wearing that...?

                         XANDER
          I found it in their trash.
              (re: house)
          I saw them through the windows,
          wearing robes, going down to the
          basement. I was going to use it to
          sneak in.

                                              CONTINUED

78 CONTINUED: 78

>   GILES
> They may be involved in some kind of
> ritual.

>   WILLOW
> With the missing girls.

>   ANGEL
> With Buffy.

Angel looks to the house, his anger mounting, and DOES NOT   *
MORPH, but rather changes into a vampire with a fierce growl.   *
Willow and the others take a step back.

>   XANDER
> Okay, that is the guy you want to
> party with.

>   CUT TO:

79 INT. FRAT HOUSE - NIGHT   79

The Tackle and the Linebacker keep a watch in the darkened
rooms. They hear someone KNOCKING, move to one of the doors
in back, see a dark figure in a robe outside.

>   XANDER
>   (in robe)
> Got locked out dumping the trash. Let
> me in, I don't want to miss the "you
> know what..."

The Tackle peers hard at the robed figure, unlatches the
door. The minute he does, Xander hits him as hard as he can   *
in the face.   *
                                                                  *
The Tackle staggers back.   *

>   XANDER (cont'd)
>   (to Tackle)
> Where are they?!

Xander doubles over, grabbing his fist in pain as the   *
Linebacker charges him. Angel decks the Linebacker as Willow   *
and Giles charge in behind him.   *

80 INT. FRAT BASEMENT - SAME TIME   80

Tom stands behind Cordelia, beneath Machida.

>   TOM
> Receive our offering!

80 CONTINUED: 80

They hear fighting and bodies crashing to the floor above.

> TOM (cont'd)
> Go!

Richard charges upstairs with several of the brethren.

Machida rises to his full height.

> TOM (cont'd)
> Feed.

Cordelia cowers beneath him.

Machida dives.

DIVING POV - WE SWOOP DOWN TOWARDS CORDELIA

Who screams bloody murder.

Buffy uses all her strength and rips her chain and eye-hooks right out of the wall.

Buffy whips the chain and hits Machida with it. He rears back, screaming.

The two brethren release Cordelia who scampers to relative safety, and they head for --

Buffy, who finds one of them behind her, one of them in front. She takes out the guy behind without even looking, whipping the chain into his head behind her. Then she spin kicks and takes out the guy in front.

Tom picks up the sword and charges Buffy who ducks and backs away as he attacks, nearly taking her head off.

81 INT. FRAT HOUSE - UPSTAIRS - NIGHT 81 *

Angel throws a robed guy to the floor. Willow jumps over the guy's body, heads for the cellar door, disappears inside. Xander is on the Tackle, piggy back, hitting him on the head from behind.

> XANDER
> That's for the wig, and that's for
> the bra...

Giles ducks a punch from Richard, trips him, looks mildly pleased with himself and moves after Willow.

A82   INT. FRAT CELLAR STEPS - NIGHT   A82

    Willow runs down two steps. Her eyes go wide. She turns
    around and runs back up.

B82   INT. FRAT HOUSE - UPSTAIRS - NIGHT   B82

Willow appears as another robed guy flies through frame.

                    WILLOW
          Some guy's attacking Buffy with a
          sword!
                    (beat, realizes:)
          Also, there's a really big snake.

                    XANDER
          ...that's for the make-up and that's
          for the last sixteen and a half years!

Xander gives him one last good wallop and leaps off. The
tackle falls forward, out of frame, we HEAR him crash. Angel
decks two more guys.

                    WILLOW
          Guys, Buffy, snake, basement, now!

They all charge toward the basement door.

82   INT. FRAT HOUSE - BASEMENT - NIGHT   82

Buffy scrambles away from Tom and his attacking sword.

                    TOM
          You... bitch. I'll serve you to him
          in pieces!

He swings hard. Buffy ducks and counters with the chain,
wraps it around Tom's neck. His eyes go wide with surprise
and pain.

                    BUFFY
          Tom... you talk too much.

Buffy yanks him over her shoulder and into the wall. Down and   *
out.

Angel, Xander, Willow and Giles tear downstairs as Machida
gathers Cordelia in his arms.

                    CORDELIA
          Hellllppppp!!!

Buffy suddenly looms up with the sword.

                                        CONTINUED

82 CONTINUED: 82

                         BUFFY
                Back off, wormy!

Machida ROARS at her. Buffy raises the sword and brings it
down hard and fast on the middle of Machida's snake body,
cutting him in half.

83 XANDER, GILES, WILLOW   83

And Angel react.

84 OMITTED   84

85 THE PIT   85

    As what's left of the severed snake jiggles and lies still a
    couple of feet from the upper torso.

86 BUFFY   86

    Helps Cordelia up. Willow and Xander un-chain a <u>very freaked
    out</u> Callie.

                       CORDELIA
                You did it, you saved us.

Cordelia walks right past Buffy and hurls herself into
Angel's arms. (He is now not a vamp.)

                     CORDELIA (cont'd)
                I've never been so happy to see
                anyone in my whole...
                       (fights the tears)
                You guys, I just really... hate you
                guys, the weirdest things always
                happen around you!

Tom comes to near the alter. And, unbeknownst to any of our
heroes, the snake body begins slowly moving. Until it joins
up with the torso. A squooshy sound of flesh and protoplasm
meeting and the two halves re-join!

                     CORDELIA (cont'd)
                       (to Tom)
                You're going to jail for about
                fifteen thousand years. Oh god, it's
                over... it's really...

That's when Machida, re-joined, suddenly pops up again.

Angel takes a threatening step forward next to Buffy, growls.

                                                        CONTINUED

86 CONTINUED: 86

Machida towers over Tom:

                    MACHIDA
          For a hundred years I have given your
          forbears wealth and power. And this
          is how you repay me. From this day
          forth you are alone in the world.

Machida slides back down. Cordelia is afraid to breathe. With
good reason. Machida pops back up, grabs Tom.

                    MACHIDA (cont'd)
          Lil' somethin' for the road.

Machida disappears into the pit with Tom. We hear Tom's
screams, a quick couple of chomps and then silence.

Willow and Xander help Callie toward the stairs.

Buffy moves to Giles.

                    BUFFY
          I told one lie, I had one drink...

                    GILES
          And you nearly got devoured by a
          giant demon-snake. I think the words
          "let that be a lesson" are a tad
          redundant at this juncture.

                    BUFFY
          Sorry, Giles.

                    GILES
          I am, too. I drive you too hard,
          because I know what you have to
          face... from now on no more pushing,
          no more prodding...

Buffy smiles.

                    GILES (cont'd)
          Just... an extraordinary amount of
          nudging.

Off them,

                                        DISSOLVE TO:

87 INT. BRONZE - NIGHT   87

A high school freshman (JONATHON), a real young looking one,   *
stands at the coffee bar. Says to bartender: *

                    JONATHON   *
          C'mon, c'mon. Hurry up.   *

He gets a cappuccino, moves to Cordelia, hands her the coffee   *
and a muffin. He looks up at her (being so much shorter and
all) adoringly.

                    CORDELIA
          Thank you, Jonathon. Did we forget   *
          something?   *

                    JONATHON   *
          Cinnamon, chocolate, half-calf, non-   *
          fat -- Extra Foam!   *

He grabs the coffee and hurries out of frame. Cordelia turns
to

88 BUFFY, WILLOW, XANDER   88

Sitting at a nearby table. Xander studies a newspaper.

                    CORDELIA
          Young men. The only way to go.

CLOSE ON NEWSPAPER - We see a picture of the Delta Zeta house
and the headline: FRATERNITY ARRESTED.

                    XANDER
          Says here they'll all get consecutive
          life sentences: investigators found
          bones of the missing girls in a huge
          cavern beneath the frat house... and
          other bones dating back fifty years...

                    WILLOW
          They didn't find the snake?
                    (Xander shakes his
                    head)
          Which means we probably will some
          day. Oh goody.

                    XANDER
                    (reads)
          "A surprising number of corporations
          whose Chairmen and Founders are
          former Delta Zeta Kappas are
          suffering falling profits, I.R.S.
                    (more)

                                          CONTINUED

88 CONTINUED: 88

                    XANDER (cont'd)
          raids and suicides in the board
          room..."
                    (to Buffy and Willow)
          Starve a snake, lose a fortune. Boy,
          the rich really are different.

                    WILLOW
                    (to Buffy)
          Have you heard from Angel?

She shakes her head.

                                                    CONTINUED

> WILLOW (cont'd)
> When he got so mad about you being in
> danger and changed into...
>   (makes a face)
> ...grrrr... it was the most amazing
> thing I ever saw. I mean how many
> guys can --

> XANDER
> Angel, Angel, Angel. Does every
> conversation always have to come
> around to that freak?

Xander notices Angel standing right next to him. Doesn't skip
a beat.

> XANDER (cont'd)
> Hey man, how ya' doin'?

> ANGEL
> Buffy.

Beat.

> BUFFY
> Angel.

Beat.

> XANDER
> Xander...

> ANGEL
> I hear this place serves coffee.
> Thought maybe you and I should get
> some...
>   (nothing from Buffy)
> ...sometime.
>   (nothing from Buffy)
> If you want.

Buffy considers him for a long moment, then:

> BUFFY
> Yeah.

Angel brightens.

> BUFFY (cont'd)
> Sometime. I'll let you know.

CONTINUED

88 CONTINUED: (2)   88

   And she gets up and goes. Xander, Willow, Angel stare at her
   departing back. Xander kind of respects what she just did. So
   does Angel.

   ANGLE - BUFFY - WALKING AWAY

   Tracking backwards with her. Letting her grow into a tight
   close up. So we can see how pleased she is. Then she walks
   out of frame and we --

                                          FADE OUT:

                    END OF ACT FOUR

BUFFY THE VAMPIRE SLAYER

"Halloween"

Written By

Carl Ellsworth

Directed By

Bruce Seth Green

SHOOTING SCRIPT

August 28, 1997
September 12, 1997(Blue Pages)

BUFFY THE VAMPIRE SLAYER

"Halloween"

CAST LIST

BUFFY SUMMERS......................... Sarah Michelle Gellar
XANDER HARRIS......................... Nicholas Brendon
RUPERT GILES.......................... Anthony S. Head
WILLOW ROSENBERG...................... Alyson Hannigan
CORDELIA CHASE........................ Charisma Carpenter
ANGEL................................. David Boreanaz

MR. SNYDER.........................*Armin Shimerman
SPIKE..............................*James Marsters
DRUSILLA...........................*Juliet Landau
ETHAN RAYNE........................*Robin Sachs
LARRY..............................*Larry Bagby, III
MRS. PARKER........................*Marjorie Lovett
OZ.................................*Seth Green
GIRL...............................*Abigail Gershman

BUFFY THE VAMPIRE SLAYER

"Halloween"

SET LIST

INTERIORS

SUNNYDALE HIGH SCHOOL
      HALL
      LIBRARY
      LOUNGE
      WOMEN'S RESTROOM
BUFFY'S HOUSE
      BUFFY'S BEDROOM
      FOYER
      KITCHEN
      DINING ROOM
THE BRONZE
THE FACTORY
ETHAN'S COSTUME SHOP
      BACK ROOM
WAREHOUSE
OZ'S VAN

EXTERIORS

SUNNYDALE HIGH SCHOOL
      COURTYARD
PUMPKIN PATCH
NEIGHBORHOOD BLOCK
      ANOTHER PART OF NEIGHBORHOOD
      STREET
MRS. PARKER'S HOUSE
      SIDEWALK
      PORCH
      YARD
ALLEY
INDUSTRIAL AREA
OZ'S VAN

BUFFY THE VAMPIRE SLAYER

"Halloween"

TEASER

FADE IN:

1 EXT. PUMPKIN PATCH - NIGHT   1

We move through a pick-em yourself patch to a wooden sign on
a post: POP'S PUMPKIN PATCH - ONLY 2 DAYS TILL HALLOWEEN! (5,
4 & 3 DAYS ARE ALREADY CROSSED OUT.)

We TILT DOWN to reveal a jack-o'-lantern, its candle
flickering when:

SLAM! A body falls on the jack-o'-lantern, CRUSHING it. A
beat. Then the fallen person moves and we see that it's
BUFFY, covered in jack-o-muck. She's breathing hard in
battle mode. She rolls, grabs a baby pumpkin - HURLS it at
the VAMPIRE descending on her. The pumpkin hits the vamp in
the face, momentarily throwing him off his game.

CLOSE ON VAMP

Who starts to recover when - BAM! Another baby pumpkin gets
him square between the eyes. He stumbles back.

BUFFY

Whips out a stake and FIRES it at the vamp, who manages to
sidestep and CATCH IT. Buffy notes this with interest, if
not dire concern.

                    BUFFY
          Hmmn.

The vamp SNAPS the stake in half and moves in. Buffy takes
a defensive posture as the vamp performs a few moves on her.
Two SIDEARM BLOWS and LOWER KICK send Buffy to the ground.

VIDEO CAMERA P.O.V. - THE FIGHT

Through the VIEWFINDER of a HOME VIDEO CAMERA -- we see the
fight in progress.

BACK ON PUMPKIN PATCH

A man we can't quite make out is lurking. VIDEOTAPING Buffy
and the vamp from behind the cashier's booth a safe distance
away.

                                              CONTINUED

VIDEO CAMERA P.O.V. - THE FIGHT

We see Buffy getting a few more hits in. Two hard UPPERCUTS
and a JUMPING KICK that catches the vamp in the jaw.

The LOW BATTERY indicator flashes in the corner of the
viewfinder. We hear a frustrated GRUNT.

The IMAGE SHAKES, refocuses on BUFFY, who's now gained the
upper hand. A vicious HEAD BUTT and a swift KICK to the
vamp's CHEST send him headlong into a pile of pumpkins.

Buffy BREAKS THE WOODEN SIGN that advertises the pumpkin
patch at the base, then uses the jagged end of the post as a
STAKE. She drives it deep into the VAMP'S HEART. VAMP DUST.

There is a FLASH of STATIC on the video image. Buffy gets to
her feet. Walks away.

The VIDEO IMAGE goes to SNOW

BACK ON PUMPKIN PATCH

The man who was lurking steps out of the shadows, still
holding the video camera to his eye.

The RED RECORD LIGHT goes out.

The man comes forward and lowers the video camera to reveal:
the face of a VAMPIRE. He smiles, pleased with his efforts
as he watches Buffy walk away.

Then he too disappears into the night.

                                        BLACK OUT.

                        END OF TEASER

ACT ONE

2 INT.   THE BRONZE - NIGHT   2

Another night at the Bronze. We move through the crowd until
we land on ANGEL, sitting at a table alone. Looking a little
bored, impatient. A voice snaps him out of his brooding.

                    CORDELIA (O.C.)
          I know. Is the Bronze not-happening,
          or what?

Angel looks up to see CORDELIA standing over him. Looking
amazing, as usual. And knowing it, as usual.

                    ANGEL
          Um, hi. I'm waiting for Buffy.

                    CORDELIA
          Great.

Cordy sits down. Makes herself comfortable..

                    CORDELIA (cont'd)
          I'm supposed to be meeting Devon, but
          he's nowhere to be seen. It's like
          he thinks being in a band gives him
          an obligation to be a flake. Well,
          his loss is your incredible gain...

She drones on. Angel isn't thrilled, smiles thinly.

ON BUFFY

Who enters, looking a little sheepish. She's worked from the
pumpkin patch episode. Runs her fingers through her hair,
pulling seeds and bits of pumpkin muck from it. She sees-

ANGEL & CORDELIA

At the table. Cordelia says something. Laughs. Angel
shakes his head - finally laughs, too. Maybe at her. Maybe
not. Cordelia looks radiant - in full flirt mode.

ON BUFFY

Who looks at herself. At the mess that is Buffy. She
hesitates. Then starts to turn away.

ON ANGEL

Who sees her. Gets up despite the fact that Cordelia is
chattering away-

                                                        CONTINUED

2 CONTINUED:

> CORDELIA (cont'd)
> ...So then I told Devon - you call
> that a leather interior? My Barbie
> Dream Car had nicer seats-

> ANGEL
> Buffy?

He gets up. Leaves a befuddled Cordy mid-rant. He moves to

BUFFY

Who, caught, tries to put on her game face.

> BUFFY
> Oh. Hi. I'm...

> ANGEL
> Late.

> BUFFY
> Rough day at the office.

Angel smiles - notices something in her hair. He pulls a
piece of straw from her locks. Hands it to her.

> ANGEL
> So I see.

> BUFFY
> (humiliated)
> Hey. It's a look. A... seasonal...
> look.

Cordelia passes. Smirks to Buffy.

> CORDELIA
> Buffy. Love your hair. It just
> screams street urchin.

That's it. Buffy gives.

> BUFFY
> You know what? I need to go... put
> a bag over my head.

> ANGEL
> Don't listen to her. You look fine.

> BUFFY
> You're sweet.
> (then)
> A terrible liar. But sweet.

CONTINUED

2 CONTINUED: (2)   2

She turns to go. Angel stops her.

                   ANGEL
     I thought we had... you know.

Buffy turns back - vents.

                   BUFFY
     A date? So did I. But who am I
     kidding? Dates are things normal
     girls have. Girls who have time to
     think about nail polish and facials
     and stuff. You know what I think
     about? Ambush tactics. Beheading.
          (then)
     Not exactly the stuff dreams are made
     of.

She goes. Angel is at a loss. Cordelia glides up with two
coffee cups in hand, triumphant.

                 CORDELIA
        (to Angel)
     Cappuccino?

3 INT. SUNNYDALE HIGH/HALL - DAY   3

The hall, decorated for Halloween, is buzzing with students
moving to and from class. A long table has been set up with
signs that announce "VOLUNTEERS ARE WINNERS" and "SAFE AND
SANE HALLOWEEN" A few kids sit behind the table with sign up
sheets.

CLOSE ON PRINCIPAL SNYDER

Who grabs an unsuspecting young girl.

                 GIRL
     Hey!

                 MR. SNYDER
     You're volunteering.

                 GIRL
     But I have to get to class --

He steers the reluctant kid to the sign-up table.

ON BUFFY, WILLOW & XANDER

Who wander past, curious.

CONTINUED

                         WILLOW
          Snyder must be in charge of the
          volunteer safety program for
          Halloween this year.

                         XANDER
          Note his interesting take on the
          "volunteer" concept.

                         BUFFY
          What's the deal?

                         XANDER
          A bunch of little kids need people to
          take them trick-or-treating. Sign up
          and you get your very own pack of
          sugar-hyped runts for the night-

                         BUFFY
          Yikes. I'll stick to vampires-

A hand falls on her shoulder. Snyder.

                         MR. SNYDER
          Ms. Summers. Just the juvenile
          delinquent I've been looking for.

                         BUFFY
          Principal Snyder-

                         MR. SNYDER
          Halloween must be a big night for
          you, huh? Tossing eggs. Keying
          cars. Bobbing for apples. One
          pathetic cry for help after another.
          Well. Not this year, missy.

He walks her to the table. Willow and Xander follow.

                         BUFFY
          Gosh, I'd love to volunteer, but I
          recently developed... carpal tunnel
          syndrome and, tragically, I can no
          longer hold a flash light-

Snyder hands her a pen.

                         MR. SNYDER
          The program starts at four and the
          children have to be home by six
          thirty.

                                              CONTINUED

3 CONTINUED: (2)   3

   Now Snyder turns his attention to Xander and Willow. Hands
   THEM both pens.

4 INT. SCHOOL LOUNGE - DAY   4

   Buffy, Willow, & Xander enter. Looking dejected.

                    XANDER
          I can't believe this. We have to
          dress up and the whole deal?

                    WILLOW
          Snyder said costumes were "mandatory."

                    BUFFY
          Great. I was going to stay in and
          veg. It's the one night a year that
          things are supposed to be quiet for
          me.

                    XANDER
          Halloween quiet? I figured it would
          be a big old vamp "scare-a-palooza".

                    BUFFY
          Not according to Giles. He swears
          that tomorrow night is, like, dead
          for the un-dead. They stay in.

                    XANDER
          Those wacky vampires. That's what I
          love about 'em. They just keep you
          guessing.

   Buffy and Willow move ahead as Xander stops at the drinks
   machine. He puts in change, but nothing comes out. Xander
   is approached by LARRY, a large, ill-tempered jock. He slams
   a MEATY HAND on him.

                    LARRY
          Harris.

                    XANDER
          Larry. Looking very cro mag, as
          usual. What can I do for you?

   Larry glances at BUFFY and WILLOW, who are sitting and
   talking on one of the couches, oblivious to them. Then-

                    LARRY
          You and Buffy - you're just friends,
          right?

                                                      CONTINUED

4 CONTINUED: 4

                         XANDER
          I like to think of it less as a
          friendship and more as a solid
          foundation for future bliss-

Larry is getting impatient.

                         LARRY
          So she's not your girlfriend?

                         XANDER
          Alas, no.

                         LARRY
          You think she'd go out with me?

                         XANDER
          Well, Lar, that's a hard question
          to... no. Not a chance.

                         LARRY
          Why not? I heard some guys say she
          was fast.

Xander suddenly loses his sense of humor.

                         XANDER
          I hope you mean in the "like the
          wind" sense.

                         LARRY
                    (leering)
          You know what I mean.

That's it. Xander grabs Larry by the lapels. Furious.

                         XANDER
          That's my friend you're talking about.

Larry is simultaneously amused and pumped up by Xander's
outburst. He pulls himself up to his full hugeness.

                         LARRY
          Oh yeah? What are you going to do
          about it?

                         XANDER
          I'm going to do what any man would do
          about it. Something... damn manly.

Xander tries to SHOVE Larry into the soda machine, but Larry
barely budges. Larry draws his fist back - about to PUMMEL
our friend. Xander grimaces but is ready to take it.

CONTINUED

4 CONTINUED: (2)   4

CLOSE ON LARRY'S HAND

As another hand grabs his FIST, snapping it back from
Xander's face.

ON BUFFY

Who holds LARRY'S FIST.

In a flash, she SPINS him around, PINS his ARMS behind his
back and SLAMS him into the SODA MACHINE. Naturally, the
impact causes the machine to dispense a free drink.

                    BUFFY
                (to Larry)
          Get gone.

Larry doesn't wait to be asked twice. He scurries.

Without missing a beat, Buffy takes the fallen soda from the
machine - pleased.

                    BUFFY (cont'd)
          Ooh. Diet.

Xander just stands there. Aghast.

                    XANDER
          Do you know what you just did?

                    BUFFY
          Saved a dollar?

                    XANDER
          Larry was about to pummel me.

Buffy waves off what she thinks is gratitude.

                    BUFFY
          Oh, that. Forget about it.

                    XANDER
                (fuming)
          I will. Maybe fifteen, twenty years
          from now. When my rep for being a
          sissy-man finally fades.

                    BUFFY
          Xander-

                                                    CONTINUED

4 CONTINUED: (3)   4

                         XANDER
              A black eye heals, Buffy. But
              cowardice has a nearly unlimited
              shelf-life.
                         (then)
              But thanks. Thanks for your help.

He stomps off. Willow and Buffy share a look.

                         BUFFY
              I think I just violated the guy code.
              Big time.

                         WILLOW
              Poor Xander. Boys are so fragile.

They move back to the couches. Sit.

                         WILLOW (cont'd)
              Speaking of - how was your date last
              night?

                         BUFFY
              Misfire. I was late due to
              unscheduled slayage. Showed up
              looking trashed.

                         WILLOW
              Was he mad?

                         BUFFY
              Actually, he seemed pretty un-mad.
              Which may have had to do with the
              fact that Cordelia was drooling in
              his cappuccino.

                         WILLOW
              Buffy, Angel would never fall for her
              act.

                         BUFFY
              You mean that "actually showing up,   *
              wearing a stunning outfit, embracing   *
              personal hygiene" act?   *

                         WILLOW
              You know what I mean. She's not his
              type.

                                                  CONTINUED

4 CONTINUED: (4)   4

                    BUFFY
          Are you sure? I mean, I don't really   *
          know what his type is. I don't know   *
          his "turn-ons and turn-offs" or his   *
          "idea of the perfect evening." I've   *
          known him less than a year and he's   *
          not one to over-share.   *

                    WILLOW
                (innocent)
          True. It's too bad we can't sneak a
          look at the watcher diaries and read
          up on Angel. I'm sure it's full of
          fun facts to know and tell.

     Buffy looks at her, as a plan begins to form.   *

                    BUFFY
          Yeah, it's too bad. That stuff is   *
          private.

                    WILLOW
          Also, Giles keeps them in his office.   *
          In his personal files.   *

                    BUFFY
          Most importantly, it would be wrong.

5 INT. LIBRARY - DAY   5

     Buffy enters the library, Willow staying by the door (which
     remains open). Buffy creeps toward the office, not noticing
     Giles emerging from the book cage behind her.

                    GILES
          Buffy. Excellent.

                    BUFFY
                (spinning)
          Nothing! Hi.

                    GILES
          I wanted to talk to you about
          tomorrow night. As it should be
          calm, I thought we might work on new
          battle techniques-

                    BUFFY
          You know, Giles, you're scaring me
          now. You need to have some fun.

                                              CONTINUED

She deliberately moves to the table so that his back is to his office -- and motions for Willow to enter the office. Willow gives a WHO ME? look and then starts a-creepin'.

> BUFFY (cont'd)
> There's this amazing place you can go and sit down in the dark - and there are these moving pictures. And the pictures tell a <u>story</u>-

> GILES
> Ha, ha. Very droll. I'll have you know I have many relaxing hobbies.

> BUFFY
> Such as?

Giles is struggling to come up with something.

> GILES
> Well. I'm very fond of cross-referencing.

Buffy just shakes her head.

> BUFFY
> Do you stuff your own shirts or do you send them out?

Giles closes his book and moves to go to the office. Willow freezes.

> BUFFY (cont'd)
> (turning him back)
> So, how come Halloween is such a yawner? Do the demons just hate how commercial it's become?

> GILES
> Well, it's interesting --

Willow nears the office --

> GILES (cont'd)
> But not, I suspect, to you. What is it you're after?

Willow stops. Are they busted?

> BUFFY
> Well, of course it's of interest!
> I'm the Slayer!
> (more)

CONTINUED

5 CONTINUED: (2)   5

                         BUFFY (cont'd)
          I need to know this stuff! You can't
          keep me in the dark anymore!
                    (as he almost turns
                     to the office)
          Look at me when I talk to you!

                         GILES
          Buffy, I don't have time to play
          games --

                         BUFFY
          Ms. Calendar said you were a babe!

This stops him. He does face her, intrigued and a little
thrown. Behind him, Willow makes a "shame on you that's so
low" face.

                         GILES
          She said what?

Willow slips into the office, starts getting the diaries.

                         BUFFY
          She said, you know, that you were
          hot. A hunka hunka burning...
          something or other. So. What do you
          think of that?

                         GILES
          I, well, um, I don't -- a burning
          hunk of what?

                         BUFFY
          You know, gross as it is for me to
          contemplate you grown-ups having
          smootchies, I think you should go for
          it.

Willow slips out with the diaries, moves silently to the door.

                         GILES
          Buffy, I appreciate your interest,
          but --

                         BUFFY
          I've overstepped my bounds! It's
          none of my business. My God, what
          was I thinking? Shame. **SHAME.** Gotta
          go.

And she's gone. Giles looks after her, brows furrowed.
After a beat...

                                                      CONTINUED

5 CONTINUED: (3)   5

                    GILES
          A babe?
               (smiles)
          I can live with that.

6 INT.   WOMEN'S RESTROOM - DAY   6

Buffy and Willow sit on the bathroom floor, pouring over the
watcher diaries. Buffy sees something in the book.

                    BUFFY
          Man - look at her.

CLOSE ON BOOK

There is a detailed DRAWING of a beautiful woman with long,
dark hair. She wears a flowing 18th century gown.

ON BUFFY & WILLOW

                    WILLOW
          Who is she?

                    BUFFY
          It doesn't say. But the entry is
          dated 1775.

                    WILLOW
          Angel was 18. And still human.

                    BUFFY
          So this was the kind of girl he hung
          around. She's pretty... coifed.

                    WILLOW
          She looks like a noblewoman or
          something, which means being
          beautiful was sort of her job.

                    BUFFY
          And, clearly, this girl was a
          workaholic. Willow - I'll never be
          like this...

                    WILLOW
               (at a loss)
          Come on. She's not that pretty.
          She's got a funny... waist. See how
          tiny it is?

                    BUFFY
          Now I feel better. Thanks.

                                                   CONTINUED

6 CONTINUED: 6

                    WILLOW
No really. She's like a freak. A
circus freak. Yuck.

                    BUFFY
          (ignoring her)
It must have been wonderful. To put
on some fantabulous gown and go to a
ball, like a princess... have
servants and horses and yet more
gowns...

                    WILLOW
Yeah.
         (then)
Still, I think I prefer being able to
vote... Or I will, when I can...

The bathroom door opens and CORDELIA steps in. She goes to
the mirror. Checks her look.

                  CORDELIA
So, Buffy, you ran off and left poor
Angel by his lonesome last night. I
did everything I could to comfort him.

                    BUFFY
I bet.

                  CORDELIA
What's his story, anyway? I mean, I
never see him around.

                    WILLOW
Not during the day, anyway.

                  CORDELIA
Please don't tell me he still lives
at home. Like he has to wait until
his dad gets home to take the car?

                    BUFFY
I think his parents have been dead
for, um, a couple hundred years.

                  CORDELIA
Oh, good. I mean-
         (then)
What?

                    BUFFY
He's a vampire, Cordelia. I thought
you knew.

                                CONTINUED

6 CONTINUED: (2)   6

A beat as Cordy takes this in. Then she smiles.

                    CORDELIA
          Oh. He's a vampire. Of course. But
          the cuddly kind. Like a Care Bear
          with fangs.

                    WILLOW
          It's true.

                    CORDELIA
          You know what I think? You're trying
          to scare me off because you're afraid
          of the competition.
                    (then)
          Look Buffy, you may be hot-stuff when
          it comes to demonology or whatever,
          but when it comes to dating - I'm the
          Slayer.

Cordelia closes her purse. Flounces off. Buffy watches her
leave - stinging a little.

7 INT.   ETHAN'S COSTUME SHOP - DAY   7

A musty, run-down shop, stocked with every kind of costume
imaginable. The place is packed with kids.

Buffy moves through the store - searching unenthusiastically
for something to dress up as. Willow approaches.

                    BUFFY
          What did you find?

                    WILLOW
          A time honored classic.

Willow pulls a costume out of her bag.

CLOSE ON COSTUME

The package shows a person covered with a large white GHOST
sheet - complete with eye holes, a ghostly smile and the word
BOO stenciled on it.

ON BUFFY AND WILLOW

                    BUFFY
          Willow. Can I give you a little
          friendly advice?

                                                    CONTINUED

                         WILLOW
          It's not spooky enough?

                         BUFFY
          It's just, you're never going to get
          noticed if you keep hiding. You're
          missing the whole point of Halloween.

                         WILLOW
          Free candy?

                         BUFFY
          It's come as you aren't night. The
          perfect chance for a girl to get sexy
          and wild with no repercussions.

                         WILLOW
          I don't get wild. Wild on me equals
          "spaz."

                         BUFFY
          You've got it in you, Will. You're
          just scared-

Xander walks over, still a little sore at Buffy. Willow
seizes the opportunity to change the subject.

                         WILLOW
          Hey Xander. What did you get?

He opens his shopping bag - pulls out a cheesy orange PLASTIC
MACHINE GUN.

                         BUFFY
          That's not a costume.

                         XANDER
          I've got some fatigues from the Army
          surplus at home. Call me the two
          dollar costume king, baby.

                         BUFFY
          Hey, Xander, about this morning. I'm
          really sorry-

                         XANDER
          Do you mind, Buffy? I'm trying to
          repress.

                         BUFFY
          I promise I'll let you get pummeled
          from now on.

                                              CONTINUED

A beat. Xander can't stay mad. No way.

                    XANDER
          Thank you. Okay. Actually, I think
          I could have-

He stops - noticing that Buffy's attention has completely
wandered.

                    XANDER (cont'd)
          Hello? That was our touching
          reconciliation you just left..

                    BUFFY
          Sorry... It's just, look at that.

They all turn their attention to what Buffy is looking at-

AN 18TH CENTURY GOWN

draped over a mannequin in the back of the store. It looks
almost exactly like the one in the picture from the watcher
diaries.

BUFFY

Moves to it, mesmerized. Willow and Xander follow.

                    WILLOW
          It's... amazing.

                    XANDER
          Too bulky. I prefer my women in
          spandex.

Buffy is about to touch it when ETHAN RAYNE, the shop owner,
approaches. He has a devilish glint in his eye and speaks
with just a hint of a British accent.

                    ETHAN
          Please. Let me.

                    BUFFY
          It's-

                    ETHAN
          Magnificent. I know.

He takes it off the mannequin. Holds it up to her.

                    ETHAN (cont'd)
          My. Meet the hidden princess.

                                        CONTINUED

7 CONTINUED: (3)   7

ON BUFFY IN THE MIRROR

With the dress in front of her - she is indeed transformed.

ON ETHAN

                    ETHAN (cont'd)
          I think we've made a match, don't you?

                    BUFFY
          I'm sorry. There's no way I can
          afford this.

                    ETHAN
          Nonsense. I feel quite... moved...
          to make you a deal you can't refuse.

                    BUFFY
          Really?

Buffy turns back to her image in the mirror a goner Ethan
smiles.

8 INT.   THE FACTORY - NIGHT   8

Moving through the dark hallway, we hear voices.

                    SPIKE (O.C.)
          Here it comes-

9 INT. FACTORY - NIGHT   9

The room is awash in BLUE LIGHT that emits from a bank of
televisions lining one wall. SPIKE and the VAMP VIDEOGRAPHER
are watching as an image flickers to life on the screens.
It's BUFFY'S FIGHT IN THE PUMPKIN PATCH.

Spike watches the tape with single minded concentration.

ON THE TELEVISION

Buffy falls on the pumpkin. Then gets up and BEANS her
attacker with a baby pumpkin.

ON SPIKE

                    SPIKE
          Rewind that. I want to see it again.

Spike paces, wired.

                                                    CONTINUED

9 CONTINUED: 9

                        SPIKE (cont'd)
           She's tricky. Baby likes to play.

           The video plays again. This time Spike points to the part
           where she BREAKS THE SIGN AND STAKES THE VAMP WITH IT.

                        SPIKE (cont'd)
                           (intense)
           See that? Where she stakes him with
           that thing? That's what you call
           resourceful.
                           (then)
           Rewind it again.

                        DRUSILLA (O.C.)
           Miss Edith needs her tea.

           Spike turns to see Drusilla, who has wandered in with one of
           her dolls. She is pouty, dreamy as usual. Spike welcomes
           her - but his attention stays on the video of Buffy.

                        SPIKE
           Come here, poodle.

           She wafts to him. He puts his arms around her.

                        DRUSILLA
           Do you love my insides? The parts
           you can't see?

                        SPIKE
           Eyeballs to entrails, my sweet.
           That's why I have to study this
           slayer. Once I know her, I can kill
           her. And once I kill her, you can
           have your run of Sunnyhell and get
           strong again.

                        DRUSILLA
           Don't worry. Everything's switching.
           Outside to inside. It makes her weak.

           This gets his attention.

                        SPIKE
           Really. Did my pet have a vision?

                        DRUSILLA
           Do you know what I miss? Leeches.

                        SPIKE
           Talk to daddy. This thing that makes
           the slayer weak. When is it?

                                                        CONTINUED

9 CONTINUED: (2)   9

                        DRUSILLA
            Tomorrow.

                        SPIKE
            But tomorrow is Halloween. Nothing
            happens on Halloween.

                        DRUSILLA
            Someone's come to change it all.
            Someone new.

10 INT. ETHAN'S COSTUME SHOP - NIGHT   10

    We move through the shop until we see a figure moving into a
    back room wearing a HOODED BLACK ROBE.

11 INT. ETHAN'S BACK ROOM - NIGHT   11

    CLOSE ON

    A HAND as it lights a number of BLACK CANDLES that circle
    some sort of altar. We WIDEN to see-

    ETHAN

    In the black robe. Before him, in the center of the circle
    there is a STATUE of a woman. Her features are placid,
    beautiful.

    Kneeling before it, Ethan speaks as he squeezes his hands
    tightly closed. He reopens them, revealing bleeding
    STIGMATA-like wounds in each palm.

                        ETHAN
            The world that denies thee, thou
            inhabit. The peace that ignores
            thee, thou corrupt.

    Ethan dabs his blood on his eyelids. Crosses it on his
    forehead.

                        ETHAN (cont'd)
            Chaos. As ever, I am your faithful,
            degenerate son.

                                                    CONTINUED

11 CONTINUED:

CLOSE ON STATUE

As the camera comes around it, revealing on the back a
HIDEOUS, MALE VISAGE. A mask of pure EVIL.

                                        BLACK OUT.

                    END OF ACT ONE

ACT TWO

12 INT. BUFFY'S ROOM - DAY   12

Buffy stands in front of her mirror in her costume - the gown
from Ethan's costume shop. She also has a brunette wig on,
the hair elegantly piled up. She looks absolutely stunning.
Then we hear Willow call from the bathroom-

                    WILLOW (O.C.)
          Where are you meeting Angel?

                    BUFFY
          Here. After trick-or-treating.
          Mom's gonna be out.

                    WILLOW (O.C.)
          Does he know about your costume?

                    BUFFY
          Nope. Call it a blast from his past.
          I'll show him I can coif with the
          best of em'.
                    (then)
          Come on out, Will. You can't stay in
          there all night.

                    WILLOW (O.C.)
          Okay. But don't laugh.

Buffy turns around.

                    BUFFY
          I won't-

She stops dead when she sees WILLOW, who emerges from the
bathroom in the costume Buffy picked out for her. Total
rocker babe - black halter top, leather mini-skirt, boots.
She looks drop dead gorgeous - and totally uncomfortable.

                    BUFFY (cont'd)
          Wow.

Willow grabs her GHOST SHEET and immediately turns back for
the bathroom - but Buffy stops her.

                    BUFFY (cont'd)
          Will. You're a dish! I mean, really-

                    WILLOW
          But this just isn't me.

CONTINUED

12 CONTINUED: 12

                         BUFFY
             That's the point! Halloween is the
             night that <u>not</u> you, is you, but not
             <u>you</u>, you know?

Willow is trying to find a response when The DOORBELL RINGS.

                         BUFFY (cont'd)
             That's Xander. You ready?

                         WILLOW
             Yeah. Okay.

Willow smiles. But her eyes tell another story. A deer
caught in the headlights. Terror supreme.

                         BUFFY
             Cool! I can't wait to watch the boys
             go non-verbal when they see you.

13 INT. FOYER - MOMENTS LATER - DAY   13

Buffy opens the door.

XANDER enters, dressed in a low-rent army costume. Ripped
camouflage pants and jacket, a tank tee, aviator sunglasses
and his plastic gun. He salutes.

                         XANDER
             Private Harris. Reporting for-

He stops. Stunned by her. He drops to one knee.

                         XANDER (cont'd)
             Buffy. My Lady of Buffdom. The
             duchess of Buffonia. I am in awe.
             I completely renounce spandex.

                         BUFFY
             Thank you, kind sir. But wait till
             you see --

                         WILLOW (O.C.)
             Hi...

Xander and Buffy turn at her voice, expectant.

WILLOW is once again covered in her GHOST SHEET.

                         BUFFY
             -- Casper.

                                                        CONTINUED

13 CONTINUED: 13

                         XANDER
                Hey, Will. That's-
                     (re: "BOO" on sheet)
                -a fine "BOO" you have there.

Buffy looks at her, disappointed. Willow just hangs her
head.

14 EXT. SUNNYDALE HIGH SCHOOL - COURTYARD - AFTERNOON   14

Kids are being dropped off, heading inside in their costumes.

15 INT. SCHOOL - CONTINUOUS - AFTERNOON   15

Kids everywhere -- lots of little DEMONS & GOBLINS running
around with trick-or-treat bags.

ON XANDER

As LARRY descends on him. Larry is dressed as a PIRATE - and
his costume is even less imaginative than Xander's. A
t-shirt, pair of baggy shorts, an eye patch. He brandishes
a plastic sword as he approaches.

                         LARRY
                Where's your bodyguard, Harris?
                Curling her hair?

Xander glares at him. Larry makes a sudden jerking move at
Xander, who flinches. Laughing, Larry moves off.

Xander takes aim at him with his plastic machine gun - almost
"fires" - but stops himself. A plastic pacifist.

ON BUFFY AND SNYDER

As Snyder leads a couple of children over to her. One of
them is dressed like a VAMPIRE, of course.

                         MR. SNYDER
                Here's your group, Summers. No need
                to speak to them - the last thing
                they need is your influence. Just
                bring them back in one piece and I
                won't expel you.

Off Buffy's reaction.

16 ANGLE ON: OZ   16

standing at his locker, his guitar with him. He is accosted
by Cordelia, who wears a typical cat outfit -- tightfitting
leotard, ears and drawn on whiskers.

                    CORDELIA
          Oz. Oz.

He turns, assesses her.

                    OZ
          Cordelia. You're like a great big
          cat.

                    CORDELIA
          That's my costume. Are you guys
          playing tonight?

                    OZ
          At the shelter club.

                    CORDELIA
          Is mister "I'm the lead singer I'm so
          great I don't have to show up for a
          date or even call" gonna be there?

                    OZ
          Yeah. You know, he's just going by
          "Devon" now.

                    CORDELIA
          Well, you can tell him that I don't
          care, and that I didn't even mention
          it and I didn't even see you so
          that's just fine.

                    OZ
          So what do I tell him?

                    CORDELIA
          NOTHING! Jeez, get with the program.

She stalks off. Oz watches her a moment, unimpressed and
unperturbed.

                    OZ
          Why can't I meet a nice girl like
          that?

He turns and bumps into WILLOW, still in her sheet. Takes a
moment untangling himself.

                    OZ (cont'd)
          Sorry.

                                              CONTINUED

16 CONTINUED: 16

                         WILLOW
               Sorry.

                          OZ
               Sorry.

She moves on. He watches her a moment, then heads out.

ON XANDER

Who has a group of three little costumed munchkins.

                        XANDER
               Okay. On sleazing extra candy.
               Tears are key. Tears'll usually get
               you a double-bagger. You can also
               try the old "you missed me"
               routine - but it's risky. Only go
               there for chocolate. Understood?

The kids all nod.

                     XANDER (cont'd)
               Good. Troops... Let's move out.

                                          FADE TO:

17 EXT. NEIGHBORHOOD BLOCK - NIGHT   17

Excited Trick-or-treaters race from house to house.

ON BUFFY AND HER GROUP

Her kids return from a house, looking really dejected.

                        BUFFY
               What'd Mrs. Davis give you?

The kids all open their hands, revealing BRAND NEW
TOOTHBRUSHES. Buffy feels for them.

                     BUFFY (cont'd)
               She must be stopped.
                    (brightly)
               Let's hit one more house. We still
               have a few minutes before we've got
               to get back.

The kids perk up. Run off.

18   INT. ETHAN'S BACK ROOM - CONTINUOUS - NIGHT   18

BLACK CANDLES are lit. ETHAN RAYNE kneels before the statue,
hood covering his face, as he speaks his LATIN PRAYER-

                    ETHAN
                  (in Latin)
          **<Janus, hear my plea. Take this
          night as your own. Come forth and
          show us your truth.>**

19   EXT. MRS. PARKER'S PORCH - CONTINUOUS - NIGHT   19

CLOSE ON

A front door as it opens, revealing the smiling FACE of MRS.
PARKER, a kind lady in her 50's. Before her stands Willow's
group, Willow waiting behind near the sidewalk.

                    KIDS
          Trick or treat!

                    MRS. PARKER
          Oh my goodness. Aren't you adorable!

20   INT. ETHAN'S BACK ROOM - CONTINUOUS - NIGHT   20

Ethan picks up the statue, his hands making BLOODY prints-

                    ETHAN
                  (in Latin)
          **<The mask is made flesh. The heart
          is curdled by your holy presence.
          Janus, this night is <u>yours</u>!>**

21   EXT. NEIGHBORHOOD BLOCK - CONTINUOUS - NIGHT   21

BUFFY ushers her kids down the block. A gust of WIND sends
a CHILL down her back. She stops, sensing something not
quite right.

22   EXT. MRS. PARKER'S PORCH - CONTINUOUS - NIGHT   22

Mrs. Parker looks in the plastic pumpkin she holds - a look
of concern crossing her features.

                    MRS. PARKER
          Oh, dear. Am I all out? I could
          have sworn I had some candy left-

23 INT. ETHAN'S BACK ROOM - CONTINUOUS - NIGHT   23

All the candles SUDDENLY BLOW OUT. The only light now issues
from the statue which GLOWS sickly GREEN.

CLOSE ON ETHAN

Who lowers his hood, showing his face as A SATISFIED GRIN
spreads across it.

                    ETHAN
          Show time.

24 EXT. MRS. PARKER'S PORCH - CONTINUOUS - NIGHT   24

MRS. PARKER leans to the unmoving GARGOYLE - apologetic.

                    MRS. PARKER
          I'm sorry, Mr. Monster. Maybe I-

CLOSE ON MRS. PARKER

As her words are SILENCED by the DEATH GRIP of a HORRIBLE
SLIMY GREEN HAND.

In a FLASH, the hand PULLS MRS. PARKER FORWARD, revealing
that it is attached to A REAL AND HIDEOUS GARGOYLE, who has
suddenly taken the place of the costumed TIM.

ON WILLOW

                    WILLOW
          Let her go!

Willow MOVES TO HELP. But she is BLOCKED by another member
of her trick-or-treat group - who has now turned into a
DEMONIC HORNED CREATURE.

Now the DEMON turns and ATTACKS the GARGOYLE. A vicious
FIGHT ENSUES, giving MRS. PARKER a chance to SCRAMBLE to the
safety of her house. She SLAMS the door.

ON WILLOW

Who can't believe her eyes. She backs off the porch.

                    WILLOW (cont'd)
          What- What's-

She stumbles. GASPING FOR BREATH. Eyes wide and full of
terror. Suddenly falls to the ground. Then - no more breath
at all. Her body goes limp, LIFELESS.

25   EXT. ANOTHER PART OF THE NEIGHBORHOOD - CONT. - NIGHT   25

The SOUNDS OF CHAOS have begun.   SCREAMS.   CAR ALARMS.

CLOSE ON XANDER

Who reacts as panicked KIDS AND ADULTS run for cover.
Instinctively, he de-shoulders his plastic machine gun, moves
it OUT OF FRAME.   Then something hits him -- he looks dizzy
for a moment.   Then he clears.   His posture becoming ramrod
straight.

He raises the gun back up - and IT'S A FULLY FUNCTIONAL M-16
MACHINE GUN.   We'd expect this to surprise him - but he's got
the demeanor of a career military man now.

26   EXT. SIDEWALK IN FRONT OF MRS.PARKER'S HOUSE-CONT.-NIGHT 26

ON WILLOW'S SHEET-CLAD FORM

As the "ghost" Willow, dressed in her rocker babe outfit,
sits up - emerging from her "dead" body, which remains
unmoving on the ground.

> WILLOW
> Oh.   Oh my God...

She stands, sees her BOOTS submerged in the sheet.

> WILLOW (cont'd)
> I'm a... I'm a real ghost --

THE SOUND OF MACHINE GUN FIRE turns her head and she sees-

XANDER

Backing across the street, looking around him in silent panic.

> WILLOW (cont'd)
> Xander!

She RUNS -

27   EXT. ACROSS THE STREET - CONTINUOUS - NIGHT   27

Overjoyed to see him.   But she stops when he WHIPS AROUND and
points the GUN RIGHT AT HER.

> WILLOW
> Xander, it's me.   Willow!

Seeing her, Xander cautiously LOWERS THE GUN a little.

CONTINUED

> XANDER
> I don't know any Willow.

> WILLOW
> Quit messing around, Xander. This is
> no time for jokes.

> XANDER
> What the Hell is going on here?

> WILLOW
> You don't know me?

> XANDER
> Lady, I suggest you find cover.

He starts to move past her. She --

> WILLOW
> No, wait!

-- steps in front of him. But instead of stopping him - he
PASSES RIGHT THROUGH HER.

CLOSE ON WILLOW

Emerging on the other side of Xander. Some kind of
PLEASURABLE PHYSICAL RUSH moving though her. She shudders.

> WILLOW (cont'd)
> Oooh.

XANDER

Spins, freaking. Raises the gun on her again.

> XANDER
> What are you?!

Willow snaps out of her reverie.

> WILLOW
> Xander. Listen to me. I'm on your
> side, I swear. Something crazy is
> happening. I was dressed as a ghost
> for Halloween and now I am a ghost.
> You were supposed to be a solider,
> and now, I guess, you're a real
> solider-

> XANDER
> And you expect me to believe that?

CONTINUED

27 CONTINUED: (2)   27

A little vampire emerges from the bushes, growling. Xander
aims at it.

                    WILLOW
            No! No guns. That's still a little
            kid in there-

                    XANDER
            But-

                    WILLOW
            No GUNS. That's an order. Let's
            just get --

Willow stops. Seeing something down the street.

                    WILLOW (cont'd)
            Buffy!

WHAT WILLOW SEES

Buffy, in her gown, stumbling unsteadily toward them.

WILLOW

Races to Buffy. Xander follows.

                    WILLOW (cont'd)
            Buffy, are you okay?

As they approach her, they hear another roar. The vampire
has been joined by a grown-up sized demon, and they head for
our bunch.

28 ANGLE: OUR THREE   28

Buffy stands between the two and a bit behind as they turn to
face the new menace.

                    XANDER
            This could be a situation.

                    WILLOW
            Buffy, what do we do?

In answer, Buffy FAINTS right out of frame.

                    BLACK OUT.

                    END OF ACT TWO

ACT THREE

29 EXT. STREET - NIGHT   29

Xander hoists his rifle and fires above the demons' heads.
They take off. He turns to Buffy as Willow kneels before her.

Buffy is just waking up.

                    WILLOW
          Buffy! Are you all right?

                    BUFFY
          What?

                    XANDER
          Are you hurt?

                    WILLOW
          Buffy, are you **hurt**?

                    BUFFY
          Buffy?

                    WILLOW
                (to Xander, fears
                 confirmed).
          She's not Buffy.

                    XANDER
          Who's Buffy?

                    WILLOW
          Oh, this is fun.
                (to Buffy)
          What year is this?

                    BUFFY
          Seventeen seventy five... I
          believe... I don't understand. Who
          are you?

They help her up.

                    WILLOW
          We're friends.

                    BUFFY
          Friends of whom? Your dress is...
          everything is strange...
                (panic rising)
          How did I come to be here?

                                              CONTINUED

29 CONTINUED: 29

                         WILLOW
                Okay, breathe, okay? You're gonna
                faint again.
                         (to Xander)
                How are we supposed to get through
                this without the Slayer?

                         XANDER
                What's a Slayer?

A Demon jumps Buffy from behind. She screams and bats at it.
It pulls her wig -- which is now her real hair, coming loose
about her head.

Xander butts the demon with his rifle and it runs off.

                         XANDER (cont'd)
                I suggest we get inside before we run
                into any other - -

30 CLOSE ON: BUFFY   30

screaming!

                         BUFFY
                Demon! A demon!

The others spin to see:

31 ANGLE: A CAR   31

Driving toward them.

Buffy shrinks into Xander's arms, hides her face.

                         WILLOW
                It's not a demon. It's a car.

                         BUFFY
                What does it want?

                         XANDER
                         (to Willow)
                Is this woman insane?

                         WILLOW
                She's never seen a car.

                         XANDER
                She's never seen a car.

                         WILLOW
                She's from the past.

CONTINUED

31 CONTINUED: 31

                    XANDER
          And you're a ghost.

                    WILLOW
          Yes. Now let's get inside.

                    XANDER
          I just want you to know I'm taking a
          lot on faith here. Where do we go?

                    WILLOW
               (thinks)
          Where's the closest -- Uh, we can go
          to a friend's house.

32 INT. BUFFY'S KITCHEN/DINING ROOM/FOYER - NIGHT   32

     The back door opens and the girls are rushed in, Xander
     following. He shuts the door and looks out the window.

     Buffy is entirely confused by the kitchen and its appliances.

                    XANDER
          I think we're clear.

                    WILLOW
               (calls out)
          Hello! Mrs. Summers?
               (no response)
          Good. She's gone.

                    BUFFY
          Where are we?

                    WILLOW
          Your place. Now we just need to --

     A violent POUNDING on the front door startles them all.
     Xander starts for the front, Willow right behind and Buffy
     trailing last.

                    WILLOW (cont'd)
          Don't open it!

                    XANDER
          It could be a civilian.

                    WILLOW
          Or a mini-demon.

     The pounding stops. They wait, Xander looking out the windows.

33 ANGLE: BUFFY   33

has stayed in the dining room as the other two approached the
door. Her attention is caught by something. She approaches
the mantle to see:

A PICTURE

of her. She picks it up, deeply puzzled. Willow approaches
her.

                    BUFFY
          This... this could be me...

                    WILLOW
          It is you. Buffy, can't you remember
          at all?

                    BUFFY
          No, I... I don't understand any of
          this, and I...
                    (re: picture)
          this is some other girl, I would
          never wear this... this low apparel
          and I don't like this place and I
          don't like you and I just want to go
          home!

                    WILLOW
          You **are** home!

The POUNDING starts again. Buffy, who has begun to cry,
shrieks.

                    WILLOW (cont'd)
          You couldn't have dressed up like
          Xena..

Xander looks out the window in the door again -- and a
demonic hand SMASHES through, grabbing at him. He jumps back.

                    WILLOW (cont'd)
          Not a civilian.

                    XANDER
          Affirmative.

He sticks his gun out the window --

                    WILLOW
          Hey! What'd we say?

He fires up, a short burst. We HEAR the demon scamper away.

                                              CONTINUED

33 CONTINUED: 33

                         XANDER
               Big noise scare monster. Remember?

                         WILLOW
               Got it.

From far off, a SCREAM. Xander looks out the window again.

                         XANDER
               Dammit.

Xander exits. Buffy comes abreast of Willow, eyes on the
door, worried.

                         BUFFY
               Surely he'll not desert us?

                         WILLOW
                    (just had enough)
               Whatever...

34 EXT. BUFFY'S STREET - CONTINUOUS   34

The scream was Cordelia's. She runs down the street, her
costume torn, her hair a mess. Scratches on her face.
Several yards behind her lopes something hairy.

Xander heads across the street toward her. There is a car
sitting diagonally in the middle of the road, the door open
and the driver long gone. Figures run by in the distance --
still chaosville.

Xander intercepts her, grabbing her shoulders. She screams!
Then realizes --

                         CORDELIA
               Xander?

                         XANDER
               Come inside.

He rushes her toward the house.

35 INT. BUFFY'S HOUSE - CONTINUOUS   35

Xander brings Cordelia in, slamming the door behind them.

                         WILLOW
               Cordelia!

                         CORDELIA
               What's going on?

                                                            CONTINUED

                    WILLOW
          Okay -- your name is Cordelia, you're
          not a cat, you're in high school,
          we're your friends -- well, sort of --

                    CORDELIA
          That's nice, Willow, and you went
          mental **when**?

                    WILLOW
          You know us?

                    CORDELIA
          Yeah, lucky me. What's with the name
          game?

                    WILLOW
          A lot's going on.

                    CORDELIA
          No kidding. I was just attacked by
          Jo-Jo the dogfaced boy. Look at my
          costume! Think Party-Town's gonna
          give me my deposit back? Not on the
          likely.

She notices a particularly big rip up the side. Xander
notices too, and takes off his jacket, puts it around her.
Over the following, both Willow and Cordy notice Xander's
pumped, tattoo covered biceps.

                    XANDER
          Here.

                    CORDELIA
          Thanks.

                    WILLOW
          Okay. You three stay here while I
          get help. If something tries to get
          in, just fight it off.

                    BUFFY
          It's not our place to fight. Surely
          some men will come and protect us?

                    CORDELIA
          What's **that** riff?

                    WILLOW
          It's like amnesia, okay? They don't
          know who they are. Just sit tight.

                                        CONTINUED

35 CONTINUED: (2)   35

    She takes off. She passes Cordelia, who remarks to the
    others --

                    CORDELIA
          Who died and made her the boss?

    -- just as Willow PASSES THROUGH THE WALL behind her.

36 EXT. STREET - NIGHT   36

    A couple of little demons run by SPIKE. His eyes wide - a
    child on Christmas morning.

                    SPIKE
          Well, this is just... neat.

37 INT. BUFFY'S HOUSE - NIGHT   37

    Xander is pushing the table against the window. He checks
    the smaller ones, making sure they're locked. Buffy follows
    him around, not wanting to be alone.

                    BUFFY
          Surely there's somewhere we can go?
          Some safe haven?

                    XANDER
          The lady said stay put.
                    (to Cordy)
          Check upstairs. Make sure
          everything's locked.

                    BUFFY
                    (to Xander, genuinely
                     confused)
          You would take orders from a woman?
          Are you feeble in some way?

                    XANDER
          Ma'am, in the army we have a saying.
          Sit down and shut the -- whoah.

    He has happened on a picture as well. Picks it up.

38 ANGLE ON: THE PICTURE   38

    This one is all three of them: Xander, Willow, and Buffy.

                    XANDER
          She must be right. We must have some
          kind of amnesia.

                                                   CONTINUED

                         BUFFY
          I don't know what that is but I'm
          sure I don't have it. I bathe quite
          often.

                         XANDER
                    (re: picture)
          How do you explain this?

                         BUFFY
          I don't! I was brought up as a
          proper lady. I'm not meant to
          understand things. I'm just meant to
          look good and then someone nice will
          marry me. Possibly a baron.

                         XANDER
          This isn't a tea party, princess.
          Sooner or later, you're going to have
          to fight.

                         BUFFY
          Fight? These low creatures? I'd
          sooner die.

                         XANDER
          Then you'll die.

                         ANGEL (O.C.)
          Oh, good. You guys are all right.

     They turn to see Angel entering from the kitchen.

                         ANGEL
          It's total chaos out there.

                         BUFFY/XANDER
          Who are you?

38 INT. LIBRARY - NIGHT   39

     Giles is working on the book catalog. Cross-referencing, no
     doubt. He hears something, gets up. Was it a growl?

     He gets up, starts slowly for the door.

     WILLOW

     COMES RUNNING THROUGH THE WALL.

                         GILES
               GNYEHAHH!

                                              CONTINUED

39 CONTINUED: 39

He jumps, books flying. Willow stops. Holds up her hand.

                    WILLOW
              Hi.

40 INT. BUFFY'S HOUSE - NIGHT   40

                    ANGEL
              Okay, does somebody want to fill me
              in?

                    XANDER
              Do you live here?

                    ANGEL
              No! You know that. Buffy... I'm
              lost here. You...
                    (suddenly peering)
              What's up with your hair?

                    CORDELIA
                    (entering)
              They don't know who they are,
              everyone's become a monster, it's a
              whole big thing. How are you?

There is suddenly pounding all around them -- and THE LIGHTS
GO OUT. Buffy shrieks and grabs Cordelia.

                    CORDELIA (cont'd)
              Do you mind?

                    XANDER
                    (to Angel)
              Take the princess here and secure the
              kitchen. Catwoman, you're with me.

Cordelia hands Buffy over to Angel and follows Xander into
the living room (which we do not see).

                    BUFFY
              But, I don't want to go with you --
              I like the man with the musket.

                    ANGEL
              Come on.

                    BUFFY
              Do you have a musket?

They enter the kitchen. The back door is open.

                                        CONTINUED

40 CONTINUED: 40.

> ANGEL
> I didn't leave that open.

He moves cautiously toward the door. Buffy watches,
frightened. She is standing right next to the door to the
cellar. Silently, it opens behind her and and a full-sized
VAMPIRE starts moving from the shadows toward her.

Angel shuts the door. Turns.

> ANGEL (cont'd)
> Look out!

Buffy spins -- the vampire grabs at her -- and she actually
does something useful: she grabs the door and slams it on its
arms.

But the vamp is much more powerful than she. It flings the
door wide, sending her sprawling on the floor. Angel
dive-tackles it, taking it out of Buffy's view and into the
dining room.

Buffy gets up, looks about her for a weapon. She grabs a big
knife, peers timidly into the room and sees

41 ANGLE: ANGEL   41

On top of the vamp, his back to her. Struggling to hold it
down.

> ANGEL
> A stake!

> BUFFY
> What?

He turns --

> ANGEL
> Get me a stake!

And she sees his VAMPIRE FACE.

She screams. Turns and runs out the back.

> ANGEL (cont'd)
> Buffy, no!

But the vamp takes the moment to throw him off, coming around
on top of him.

42 INT. LIBRARY - NIGHT   42

    Giles and Willow are surrounded by books, looking for
    something - anything. Willow looks up, frustrated.

                    WILLOW
          I don't even know what to look for.
          Plus I can't turn the page.

                    GILES
          Right. Okay, then, let's review. At
          sundown, everyone became whatever
          they were masquerading as-

                    WILLOW
          Right. Xander was a solider and
          Buffy was an 18th century girl.

    Giles stares at her outfit. A non-sexual stare. Of course.

                    GILES
          And - your costume?

                    WILLOW
          I'm a ghost.

                    GILES
          Yes, but a ghost of what, exactly?

                    WILLOW
                (embarrassed)
          This is nothing. You should have
          seen what Cordelia was wearing. A
          unitard. And those little cat
          things. Ears and stuff.

                    GILES
          Good heavens. Cordelia became an
          actual feline?

                    WILLOW
                (realizing)
          No. She was still the same old
          Cordelia, just in a cat costume.

                    GILES
          She didn't change.

                    WILLOW
          No. Hold on... Party Town. She told
          us she got her outfit from Party Town-

                    GILES
          And everybody who changed, where did
          they acquire their costumes?

                                                  CONTINUED

42 CONTINUED: 42

                              WILLOW
               We all got ours at this new place.
               Ethan's.

Off their realization.

43 EXT. STREET - NIGHT   43

Xander, Cordy and the human-looking Angel come out of the
shrubs.

                              XANDER
               You're sure she came this way?

                              ANGEL
               No.

                              CORDELIA
               She'll be okay.

                              ANGEL
               BUFFY would be okay. Whoever she is
               now, she's helpless. Come on.

They take off and as we pan with them we pick up SPIKE,
standing in the shadows. A small demon and a small vampire
clustered by him.

                              SPIKE
               Do you hear that, my friends?
               Somewhere out here is the tenderest
               meat you've ever tasted. And all we
               have to do...

44 EXT. STREET - NIGHT   44

Buffy wanders, lost, alone, terrified.

                              SPIKE (V.O.)
               ... is find her first.

                                        BLACK OUT.

                         END OF ACT THREE

ACT FOUR

45 EXT. INDUSTRIAL AREA - NIGHT   45

BUFFY enters in her 18th Century SHOES, ripped stockings,
TORN and MUDDIED GOWN. She looks around her, terrified.
Keeps walking -- and bumps into:

LARRY

Once a bully and pseudo-PIRATE. Now the real thing. He
smiles. A lascivious, BLACK-TOOTHED grin.

46 INT. ETHAN'S COSTUME SHOP - NIGHT   46

Giles and Willow enter, step inside.

                    GILES
          Hollo? Is anyone in?

The move through the room and into-

47 INT. ETHAN'S BACK ROOM - CONTINUOUS - NIGHT   47

Where Willow sees ETHAN'S ALTAR WITH THE GOLDEN STATUE.

                    WILLOW
          Giles.

Giles turns. Sees the statue.

                    GILES
          That's Janus, a Roman mythical God.

                    WILLOW
          What does it mean?

                    GILES
          Primarily, it represents the division
          of self. Male and female. Light and
          dark-

                    ETHAN (O.C.)
          Chunky and creamy style. No, sorry.
          That's peanut butter.

ETHAN

Steps from a shadow, smiling at Giles. As Giles makes him
out, his SHOCK is obvious. He steps in front of Willow,
never taking his eyes off Ethan.

CONTINUED

47 CONTINUED: 47

> GILES
> Willow. Get out of here. Now.

> WILLOW
> But-

> GILES
> NOW, Willow.

Willow knows this tone from Giles can only mean business.
She BOLTS. Ethan and Giles face off.

> GILES (cont'd)
> Hello, Ethan.

> ETHAN
> Hello, Ripper.

48 EXT. INDUSTRIAL AREA - NIGHT   48

ON BUFFY

As she HITS THE GROUND, whimpering. She moves to crawl away
but LARRY lifts her to her feet again.

> BUFFY
> (weakly)
> No... No...

He GRABS BUFFY'S FACE, HARD. Opens his mouth and runs his
TONGUE ALONG BLACK TEETH. He moves in for a KISS when

XANDER

Comes out of nowhere - gives the PIRATE a FLYING TACKLE.
Buffy scrambles away as Xander and Larry go at it.

BUFFY

Runs right into Cordelia.

> CORDELIA
> Buffy? Are you okay?

Buffy throws herself into Cordy's arms. Trembling. Cordelia
isn't quite sure what to do with this.

XANDER AND LARRY

Do battle. The pirate is strong, but in this incarnation,
XANDER IS STRONGER. Larry tries to reach for his sword, but
Xander knocks it away.

CONTINUED

48 CONTINUED:

ANGEL arrives on the scene. Buffy SCREAMS and grips Cordelia even tighter.

                    CORDELIA (cont'd)
                 (to Buffy)
          What is your deal? Take a pill!

                    BUFFY
                 (re: Angel)
          He's... he's a vampire!

Cordelia rolls her eyes - looks to Angel like, "what a ditz".

                    CORDELIA
                 (to Angel)
          She's got this thing where she
          thinks - ah, forget it.
                 (humoring her)
          It's okay. Angel is... a good
          vampire. He'd never hurt you.

                    BUFFY
          He - really?

                    CORDELIA
          Absolutely. Angel is our friend.

Buffy looks timidly at Angel, who crosses to Xander.

XANDER

Finishes LARRY off with a HEADBUTT and a couple of SWIFT
PUNCHES. The pirate goes DOWN - out cold.

                    XANDER
                 (to Angel)
          It's strange, but... beating up that
          pirate gave me a weird sense of
          closure.

Willow arrives at a dead (I'm so funny) run.

                    WILLOW
          Guys!

                    ANGEL
          Willow!

                    WILLOW
          You guys gotta get inside.

She points. They turn. They see:

49 ANGLE: SPIKE   49

Walking towards them, flanked by four child-sized and two
grown-up sized monsters.

                    XANDER
          We need to triage.

                    ANGEL
          This way. Find an open warehouse.

                    XANDER
          Ladies... we're on the move.

They BOLT, but Buffy is having trouble keeping up. Angel
SWEEPS her into his arms, carries her.

ON BUFFY

Afraid - but giving into his protection.

50 INT. ETHAN'S BACK ROOM - NIGHT   50

Ethan and Giles are squared off. Ethan's manner is
light. He clearly gets off on pathos.

                    ETHAN
          What, no hug? Aren't you happy to
          see your old mate?

                    GILES
          I'm surprised I didn't guess it was
          you. This Halloween stunt stinks of
          Ethan Rayne.

                    ETHAN
                (proud)
          It does, doesn't it? Not to blow my
          own horn, but - it's genius. The
          very embodiment of "be careful what
          you wish for."

                    GILES
          It's sick. And brutal. It harms the
          innocent-

                    ETHAN
                (wry)
          Oh, and we all know that you are the
          champion of innocence and all things
          pure and good, Rupert.
                (then)
          This is quite an act you've got going
          here, old man.

                                              CONTINUED

50 CONTINUED: 50

                    GILES
          It's no act. It's who I am.

                    ETHAN
          It's who you are? The Watcher?
          Sniveling tweed-clad guardian of the
          Slayer and her kin? I think not. I
          know who you are. And I know what
          you're capable of.
               (then/realizing)
          But they don't, do they? They have
          no idea where you come from.

Giles is clearly threatened by Ethan's attack - but responds
with a POWERFUL ANGER instead of bluster. This, indeed, is
a Giles we don't know.

                    GILES
          Break the spell, Ethan. Then leave
          this place and never come back.

                    ETHAN
          Why should I? What do I get in the
          bargain?

                    GILES
          You get to live.

                    ETHAN
          Ooooh. You're scaring-

But before he can finish, GILES DROPS Ethan with a VICIOUS
PUNCH.

51 EXT. ALLEY - NIGHT 51

Xander, Cordelia and Angel, still with Buffy in his arms,
round the corner.

Angel leads them to a warehouse door.

                    ANGEL
          Over here!

They SLIDE the door open and dash inside, just as SPIKE and
his minions appear. They manage to SHUT the door with only
seconds to spare.

52   INT. WAREHOUSE - CONTINUOUS - NIGHT   52

There are some old crates and furniture against one wall.
Xander immediately starts moving the stuff against the door
so it won't slide, calls to ANGEL.

                    XANDER
          Check and see if there are any other
          ways in!

Angel tries to put Buffy down.

                    ANGEL
          Just stay here-

He hands her off to CORDELIA as he moves off. Buffy FALLS
into Cordelia's arms again. Cordelia rolls her eyes.

                    CORDELIA
          Faboo. More clinging.

XANDER

Starts as SOMETHING JERKS the WAREHOUSE DOOR. DEMONIC hands
start to PUNCH through it, TEAR IT APART.

The door jerks again and then starts to SLIDE OPEN, sending
the barricade everywhere.

Xander and Angel step back, retreating as the WAREHOUSE DOOR
SLIDES COMPLETELY OPEN and SPIKE steps inside, followed by
his LOYAL MINIONS.

53   INT. ETHAN'S BACK ROOM - CONTINUOUS - NIGHT   53

CLOSE ON ETHAN

Face plastered to the floor and badly bloodied. BUT SMILING.

                    ETHAN
          And you said "Rupert the Ripper" was
          long gone...

GILES stands over him.

                    GILES
          How do I stop the spell?

                    ETHAN
          Say pretty ple-

GILES KICKS HIM. Not holding back.

                                        CONTINUED

53 CONTINUED:

                          ETHAN (cont'd)
                 Janus. Break the statue.

Giles grabs the statue. THROWS IT AGAINST THE WALL.

CLOSE ON STATUE

SLO MO as the statue HITS AND SHATTERS.

ON GILES

Who turns to ETHAN, but Ethan is gone. Disappeared.

Off Giles' reaction.

54 INT. WAREHOUSE - CONTINUOUS - NIGHT   54

ANGEL & XANDER are pinned or held at bay by the minions, who
keep them from

SPIKE

Who moves to BUFFY, speaking to her softly, kindly.

                          SPIKE
                 Look at you. Shaking, terrified.
                 Alone. Lost little lamb.

Buffy fights her tears. Totally petrified. Spike smiles.
SLAPS HER HARD ACROSS THE FACE.

                          SPIKE (cont'd)
                 I love it.

                          ANGEL
                 Buffy!

ANGEL

Tries to break free of his guards, but to no avail.

ON SPIKE

As he GRIPS BUFFY'S HAIR with one hand and her arm with the
other. Starts to LEAN IN.

Xander breaks free, grabs his rifle and stands. WILLOW comes
up to Xander, watching Spike.

                          WILLOW
                 Now THAT guy, you can shoot.

                                                    CONTINUED

54 CONTINUED: 54

XANDER

Raises his MACHINE GUN and AIMS IT AT SPIKE. But when he
squeezes the trigger - nothing happens. He realizes that
his GUN HAS RETURNED TO IT'S ORIGINAL PLASTIC FORM.

                    XANDER
               What the - ?

ON SPIKE & BUFFY

As he looks around him to see that his MINIONS are all SCARED
LITTLE TRICK-OR-TREATERS (and two high school students).

The realization sinks in -- and he looks at his hand. It's
still holding Buffy's wig, but her head isn't in it. He
looks back at Buffy. She's smiling.

                    BUFFY
               Hi honey. I'm home.

And she LETS LOOSE on him. All the pent-up rage and
frustration from her last defenseless hours comes pouring
out. A series of BRUTAL KICKS and PUNCHES send him to the
ground. She lifts him back to his feet-

                    BUFFY (cont'd)
               You know what? It's good to be me.

She PUMMELS HIM, until he hits the wall and scampers out of
the building.

BACK ON BUFFY, XANDER, CORDELIA & ANGEL

As they all move together - stunned but alive.

                    XANDER
               Hey, Buff. Welcome back.

                    BUFFY
               Yeah. You too.

                    CORDELIA
               You guys remember what happened?

                    XANDER
               It was way creepy. Like I was
               there - but I couldn't get out.

                    CORDELIA
                    (to Angel)
               I know the feeling. This outfit is
               totally skin-tight-

CONTINUED

54 CONTINUED: (2)   54

But Angel isn't listening. He's focused on Buffy.

                    ANGEL
          You okay?

                    BUFFY
          Yeah.

He takes her by the arm, they move off. CORDELIA and XANDER
watch them. Cordy wears an expression of disbelief.

                    CORDELIA
          Hello? It felt like I was talking.
          My lips were moving-

                    XANDER
          Give it up, Cordy. You're never
          going to get between those two.
          Believe me. I know.

Cordelia turns - looks at all the dazed trick-or-treaters.

                    CORDELIA
          I guess we should get them back to
          their parents.

                    XANDER
          Yeah. It seems like everybody is-
                    (then/realizing)
          Where's Willow?

55 EXT. MRS. PARKER'S YARD - NIGHT   55

Willow's SHEET COVERED corpse stirs. A beat. Then Willow
stands up, ALIVE and in one-piece.

She considers the sheet. Contemplating whether to put it
back on or not. A beat. She tosses it. Walks off, looking
a little bolder than we've seen her before.

56 EXT. STREET - NIGHT   56

OZ'S VAN stops at an intersection, on its way back from a
gig. WILLOW runs in front of it, crossing the street.

57 INT. OZ'S VAN - CONTINUOUS - NIGHT   57

Oz STARES as Willow passes. Totally enchanted.

                                                    CONTINUED

57 CONTINUED: 57

                              OZ
                    Who IS that girl?

58 INT. BUFFY'S ROOM - NIGHT   58

    Angel sits on Buffy's bed, lost in thought. Buffy comes out
    of her bathroom - now in boxers and a big t-shirt. Her face
    is scrubbed clean and her hair hangs loose around her face.

                              BUFFY
                    Taa daa. Just little old 20th
                    century me.

    She sits next to Angel.

                              ANGEL
                    Are you sure you're okay?

                              BUFFY
                    I'll live.

    A beat.

                              ANGEL
                    I don't get it Buffy. Why did you
                    think I'd like you better dressed
                    that way?

                              BUFFY
                    I - I just wanted to be a real girl,
                    for once. The kind of fancy girl you
                    liked when you were my age.

    Angel smiles. Shakes his head.

                              BUFFY (cont'd)
                    What?

                              ANGEL
                    I hated the girls back then.
                    Especially the noblewomen.

                              BUFFY
                    You did?

                              ANGEL
                    They were just incredibly dull.
                    Simpering morons, the lot of them.
                    I always wished I could meet
                    someone... exciting. Interesting.

CONTINUED

58 CONTINUED: 58

                              BUFFY
                Really. Interesting - like how?

Angel smiles. She's baiting him and he knows it.

                              ANGEL
                You know how.

                              BUFFY
                Still, I've had a hard day and you
                should tell me.

They move closer together.

                              ANGEL
                I should.

                              BUFFY
                Oh - definitely...

And he does. Non verbally. Smootchie city

                                             FADE TO:

59 INT. ETHAN'S COSTUME SHOP - DAY   59

    Giles enters. The place is empty -- everything packed and
    gone. He walks around a bit, till he finds a card on the
    counter. Picks it up.

60 ANGLE: THE CARD   60

    On it is written only three words.

    "Be seeing you"

    Giles stares at it, stares ahead. His thoughts unreadable.

                                             BLACK OUT.

                           THE END